MATTHIAS:

WOLVES KILL SHEEP

SHAWN HICKS

First Paperback Edition

Brok'n English Publications, LLC
Linktree: broknenglishpub
Email: broknenglishpub@gmail.com

Library of Congress Control Number: 2025915434

ISBN: 979-8-9995385-0-5

PROLOGUE

Circa 2000's.

New York, NY

In a penthouse on Central Park West, a man code-named Thomas Andreus rises and shakes off his sleep with fifty pushups. After the set, he switches to ab crunches, cranking out a hundred. Then comes ten minutes of shadow boxing—his jabs and crosses crackling with imagined parries and dodges. He finishes his wake-up by walking onto the terrace, where the crisp air of the night counters his body heat like a cold plunge. He takes it in for a moment, inhaling a few breaths, before snapping from its euphoria with stark reality:

Life is bitter. Life is cold. And wolves kill sheep.

Andreus steps back in to get dressed. He puts on a bulletproof vest, followed by a plain white painter's uniform. He checks his watch: 4:27 a.m. Andreus inserts a SIM card into his phone. At 4:30, the phone rings.

"The subject is in place," a woman says on the other end.

"How many guards are with him?"

"I do not know how many. So, make it clean if you can. Simply get in and get out."

"Affirmative," he says.

"Also," she injects, "might I implore, that you shelve those snappy retorts you hurl at the targets. They could be categorized as statements from witnesses during the investigation."

"But how will they remember me when they're burning in Hell?"

"Apart from your interpretation of how Catholicism works, the authenticators prefer if you keep your calling cards to yourself."

"You take the fun out of an assassination, Dak."

"If only I had a bucket to catch my tears," she says dryly. "If there are no other matters, I wish you good luck."

Andreus hangs up and takes out the SIM card from the phone. He then grabs a duffle bag, and steps out to the world.

An hour later, Andreus stands at the edge of Central Park East, eyeing a gated alley used as a freight entrance. After days of reconnaissance, he figures it's his best shot into the building without being spotted. He hops over the short brick wall that borders the park and crosses the street.

Andreus approaches the chain-linked gate, about twelve feet high and topped with barb wire. He grips the gate and climbs, stopping short to the barb wire. He secures his position, leaps, somersaults over the barb wire, and lands lightly.

"Fuck," he grimaces, feeling the sting from a cut on his left arm through the uniform. He inspects the wound—not worth bandaging. He then glances at the barb wire, where his blood darkens the blades.

Well, so much for not leaving calling cards.

Andreus continues to a door leading into the building. He notices a wire running from inside the building to the top hinge. Pulling out a knife from a multi-tool device, he cuts the wire. It won't kill the alarm, but it should disrupt the security trackers enough for someone to investigate.

Ten minutes later, the door opens, and a security officer with a flashlight steps out into the alleyway.

Andreus pounces from the shadows, driving his elbow into the base of the officer's skull. He then slips inside the building as the officer collapses from being knocked out.

Six flights later, he stops at a door leading to the floor's hallway. In his duffle bag, he pulls out a gun, with a suppressor he attaches.

Andreus inches the stairway door open, minding any creaking from the hinges. He scans the corridor. About forty feet ahead, two men stand outside an apartment, with Uzis in their grips.

Andreus aims. *They're at the six-to-ten and six-to-eleven o'clock positions. Clear!*

Thwrt, thwrt—goes the gun with the suppressor.

The men slump to the floor, revealing their blood and brains on the walls left behind them.

Andreus trots to the apartment door, transferring the gun back into the duffle bag, and pulling out a lock-picking kit. Ignoring the bodies on the floor, he scans the door— simple household deadbolts with no alarm. After thirty seconds later of finagling, the deadbolts are clicked open from the lock picks.

Andreus grabs an Uzi from one of the slain, cocks it, and without hesitation kicks the door in.

RATTA RATTA RATTA!!—the sharp staccato fills the air. A guard by the front door barely registers what's going on before his body succumbs to the bullets.

Andreus sweeps the hallway, firing through each door without hesitation. A closet. An empty bathroom. The Uzi then clicks empty as he hears yelling from the back of the apartment.

Andreus retreats to the fallen guard, grabbing the MP5 submachine gun beside him, when from the corner of his eye a figure emerges. Instinct kicks in, and he dives for cover around the hallway bend.

Gunfire erupts, narrowly missing him.

Andreus recovers by the wall and reaches into his bag, pulling out a canister. He pulls the pin and tosses it around the corner of the hallway.

More shooting from the hallway, then—

BOOOM!!—the phosphorous grenade explodes.

After a moment of thermal stillness, Andreus peeks around the bend. The air is thick with smoldering embers, and the walls are scorched. But most importantly, the guard is down.

Andreus moves forward. There's one more door left. He kicks it in.

"*Wie ben je? Schiet me niet neer, alsjeblieft,*" pleads an elderly man with a Dutch accent. He looks for cover but only scrambles to the far corner of the bedroom.

"Please no," the elderly man says in hazy English. "What you want? Who are you?"

"Your consequences are due," Andreus says.

"What?" the elderly man says. "I no…con…seq…"

"*Ihre Folgen sind fällig,*" Andreus repeats in German, since he doesn't speak Dutch. It's close enough for the man to understand, if the MP5 wasn't a hint.

"No, no," says the man. "I am wealthy. I'll give you—"

Andreus squeezes the trigger and empties the MP5.

The elderly man convulses with each layer of bullets, before collapsing on the floor. Andreus drops the MP5 and leaves.

"Perhaps you need to know what the word 'clean' means," Dak says hours later. "Clean means spotless and orderly. It does not mean behaving like a raggamuffin."

"Raggamuffin? Were you born sixty years old?"

"Why did you use grenades? Now the ATF will be involved."

"I like it when things go boom. And no mission goes textbook. Improvisation is sometimes needed." He then aims his words toward her. "Especially when the analysis is insufficient."

"Are you challenging my intelligence gathering?" Dak replies defensively.

"You didn't tell me how many guards he had, and you didn't provide schematics of the building for me to have an exit strategy. I had to run out there like a streaker in a ballgame."

"Well," she says, "since you find my analysis inefficient, you wouldn't want me to deliver to you the evac route. You're capable of getting through the heightened security on your own."

Andreus grimaces at the thought of trying to maneuver around the police checkpoints he's sure are being established now. Plus, with his blood on the barbed wire, it won't be long before forensics place him at the scene. He's going to need her.

"My apologies, Dak. I didn't intend to blame your analysis. You know I get riled after a mission."

"Hubris, hubris," Dak says with a huff. "Andreus with his hubris."

"And how long will it take Dr. Suess to deliver the route?"

"It'll be delivered in ten minutes," she says. "On a side note, did you hear about your old employer? He's about to get a new contract with that State Department."

"Hope he celebrates by drinking bleach. Anything else?"

"No."

Andreus hangs up. He then looks around his latest abode—a placid motel room along the side streets of Harlem. It's no penthouse; but that was merely to be within proximity of the target. This place is for laying low. With that, he turns on the TV and flips to the news, which leads with the assassination of a U.N. delegate who came to speak to the assembly about lifting sanctions on South Africa.

"This is a tragedy for the country and its inclusion into the world stage," an official said.

Andreus scoffs in response. The guy was a part of the CCB—a covert unit that killed anti-apartheid activists throughout Central Africa—so the prick had it coming. No one gets to run from their sins. If they could he wouldn't have a job.

His thoughts are interrupted when an argument builds outside the motel. Andreus just turns up the volume of the TV to drown the noise.

"Get the fuck over here" he hears someone shout from outside.

"Do not do this," goes a woman's plea, her voice thick with an accent. "I have my baby here with me."

"Fuck that kid. Do you want to go to jail? Then you will get on your knees and swallow what I put in your mouth."

"Why do you do this? You are police. You are to protect."

"Get over here...DON'T YOU MOVE!"

Scuffling between them ensues, then—

POW! POW! POW! POW! POW!

For a few seconds, dead silence. Then, the cries of a baby pierce the air.

Andreus goes to the window. He's on the fourth floor, and the action is across the street, giving him a partial view of a woman on the ground. Next to her, a baby in a stroller, wailing.

"Fuck," the officer mutters, his gun still trained on the woman as if she's a threat. He then grabs his radio. "Officer Russo on patrol. Shots fired at 148th and 8th Ave. Suspect is down. Need backup immediately."

"You're doing what?" Dak exclaims over the phone. "Have you gone injured your head? You should have left New York by now."

"I am leaving. After I do this."

"Is this why I haven't heard from you in two days? You are raising the chances of you being apprehended."

"Just do what I ask, Dak. If you don't hear from me in twenty-four hours, assumed the worst and distribute my assets to my next-of-kin."

"You don't have any next-of-kin."

"Oh," Andreus replies. "Well, never mind then."

"You must be experiencing post-traumatic stress," she then says. "I'm advising you to continue with the evacuation route, then come in for a wellness check."

"I do not need a wellness check. I am aware of my surroundings and I'm acting on my own accord."

"What could you gain from doing this, Andreus? That is not your child. Its predicament is not of your concern."

"Like I said, sometimes improvisation is needed to make things right."

Dak is heard sighing over the phone, before relenting. "If your actions lead to the implication of the Merchants of

Pierrepont being the sponsor of the mission, you will be placed in *Ex-Delicto*. Do you know what that means?"

"They'll put me in a bamboo prison and give me a thousand tickles?"

"Hardly," she replies. "The authenticators will be notified of your deviation to the evac route."

Andreus hangs up and then stares across the street at a dock entrance of Harlem Hospital, where the biohazard dumpsters are and where a waste management truck is parked. After thirty minutes of recon, he determines this is the best point of entry. He moves onto the dock, past the dumpsters, and slips through the side door.

After checking the directory for Laundry Services, he heads to the sub-basement. He spots a group of Spanish-speaking workers, folding towels while chatting among themselves.

"*Disculpe,*" he says to them, "*¿tienen algún uniforme médico disponible? Lo necesitan para un residente en la sala de emergencias.*"

"*Ellos están ahi,*" one replies, pointing to a rack of scrubs and surgical masks.

He grabs a set of scrubs and a mask before stepping into the lavatory to change. Once disguised, he slips up the stairwell.

In the Pediatrics Department, Andreus moves stealthily through the corridors, seeing there's no security on the floor, only a few nurses stationed at the front desk. Just as he calculated—as urban hospitals typically don't have money for extra staff. He continues into the nursery, where rows of babies lie in bassinets. He then checks the nametag for the one he's looking for, finding the infant as it sleeps away its horrors. Last name: Noah. First name: Matihu.

For a moment, he just looks at him, as empathy creeps through his armor. He's risking his life for some damn baby. A baby whisked away as his immigrant mother lay cold on the ground, gunned down by a trigger-happy cop. A baby left in the hospital as half-hearted attempts were made to find relatives. A baby slotted to be a statistic, on the path to being forgotten.

He then glances out the nursery window, to a world full of wolves. He knows what needs to be done.

This kid is going to need a new name.

CHAPTER 1

Present day

New York, NY

"I'm here," Matthias Monroe says into his phone.

"Have you picked up your packages?"

"The main ones, yes. In a few days I'll retrieve the rest and then will do some shopping."

"Look for someone who has a federal firearms license," Andreus says on the other end. "They should have the things you need that they may sell under the table. If you can't find one, you can go black market."

"I hate the black market," Matthias says. "They're mostly run by sketchy motherfuckers living off porn and video games."

"Could be. Also, remember this is a project and not a mission. The authenticators will be monitoring your progress to see how prepared you are for the field."

"You say project, I say vendetta. Tomato, *tomato*."

"I say tomato, so to you it's tomato. Keep in mind your actions are to be contained locally. Any event that spreads internationally, any act in dereliction, or if you just smart off as you often do, you could be deemed *Ex-Delicto*."

"Well, we wouldn't want that," Matthias says sarcastically. "Heaven forbid those mopheads feel some kind of way. And this from someone who killed enough heads of states to start another Cold War."

"I don't know what you're talking about," states Andreus. "And you're illustrating what I'm talking about; speaking on phones as if no one else is listening, running off at the mouth."

"Apples don't fall far from the tree," Matthias replies with a smile. "You want some cider?"

Andreus exhales his frustrations slowly. "I want your status in two days." He then hangs up.

Matthias puts down his phone and closes his eyes, lying on his back in the grass of Central Park. It's been years since he's been in the States, and after a long flight before embarking on an endeavor sure to involve blood and bedlam, he's going to soak in the afternoon sun—its warmth rarely found in Central Europe.

"Romania. Zurich. Sudan. Florianópolis. Bangkok," Matthias chants his hypnotic and neurolinguistic phrases, meant to relax him. Gradually, he sinks from the chatter into a noiseless peace, as he basks in the heat, not having a care in the world.

His senses summon a warning; he feels a presence creeping toward him, and his nose catches a foul smell. He opens his eyes to see three vagrant men less than ten feet away from him, drawing closer, radiating malice.

"What do you want?" Matthias barks at them. "Don't you see I'm meditating?"

The men stop, momentarily thrown by his abruptness. One of them pulls out a knife.

"Just run your shit," he says. "And you won't get hurt."

Matthias immediately gauges them. *Three men, all right-handed. Their heights are about five-foot-seven to five-foot-nine. Their posture indicates no true fighting skills—they're just homeless robbers.* His gaze shifts to the duffel bag beside him, containing about $100,000 in cash and items.

"Tell you what," he says to them, "you go on your separate ways, and I won't beat you to a pulp."

"Motherfucker," one of them say as he throws a kick to Matthias' head.

Matthias buffers and catches the foot before it reaches his skull.

In one swift motion, he bends the ankle until—*SNAP!*

"AARRGGHH!!" screams the man, crumbling to the ground.

The other two men looks down at their friend, who is withing in pain. They turn back to Matthias, who has sprung to his feet, revealing his six-foot-two, muscular frame. He settles into a stance, fists raised in guard, legs primed for combat. He then flips them the finger.

"Oh," says the one with the knife. "I got this shank for you for real now."

The two men rush him, the knife-wielder leading the charge.

Matthias sidesteps the attack, catches the man's wrist, and stops the knife cold.

With his free hand, he delivers a sharp palm strike to the nose. The man buckles. His knife falls to the grass.

Matthias turns to the other guy and fires a side kick into his stomach, making him double over. He then delivers a punch to the guy's jaw, making him crash to the ground.

Matthias turns back to the lead man. He delivers two punches to the ribs. He then locks the man into a contorting arm bar.

"Alright, alright," the man groans in pain. "I give up. Let me go."

Matthias lets out a sulfurous growl. *Wolves kill sheep.*

He cocks back his free arm and lands a blow against the man's limb, fracturing the humerus.

"AWWWAAHH!!" wallows the man as he hits the ground. "Awww shit! My arm!"

He looks at his carnage. Three men down, in twenty-four seconds. He's usually done within twenty. He's getting rusty. Matthias picks up his duffle bag and leaves.

"Are you the concierge?" he asks as he approaches a non-descript office building, where a man stands in front. "I'm a new tenant here. Matthias Monroe."

"I am the office manager," the man replies with a British accent. "Ownership informed me you would arrive today. My name is Nigel. It's a pleasure to meet you."

Nigel extends his hand to greet him. As they shake, he glances down, feeling the rough texture of the chemical burns along Matthias' fingers and palms.

"My goodness," he says. "What happened to your hands?"

"Long story," Matthias says. "It involves a hooker and a curling iron. Maybe I'll tell you later. Are all the items arrived in the office?"

"Indeed," replies Nigel as they make their way into the office building toward the elevators. "Everything has been prepared just as you requested—laptop computers, gym equipment, a steel front door with a camera and private access into the building through the service alley. Do you have the key card that was sent to you by post?"

Matthias shows him the white plastic card.

"Simply slide the card into the slot and enter the combination on the keypad. For the moment, it's set to five zeros. You can change it to whatever you prefer."

Moments later, Matthias swipes the key card and presses the buttons for entry, stepping into a loft. He drops his duffle bag and heads first to the workstation desk, where various computer and internet equipment sit. Then, he notices a wooden box next to a white envelope. He opens the box first and finds a black Patek Philippe watch with a card inside:

'So you have no reason not to know when to call. Love, Mum.'

Matthias smiles at the sentiment as he sets down the box, then opens the envelope. Inside, he finds a leaflet flyer for *Fat Pat the Bail Bondsman.* This must be the asset she wants him to use to establish his cover. He sets the leaflet aside and resumes his inspection. At the far end of the office sits a workout bench with a range of iron plates, a 140 lbs. heavy bag, and a wooden makiwara striking post mounted on the wall.

He approaches the makiwara and tests its hardwood with repeated strikes, his fists alternating between the upper and lower panels with precision. Then, he switches to elbow strikes, each one harder than the last, with enough force to rupture a person's temples. A minute into his makiwara drills, a knock comes from the front door.

"No," says a voice from the other side. "No more making noise. You give me headache. You said you finish."

Matthias walks to the office door's camera monitor embedded in the entry wall, and sees a woman in her sixties, her face etched with anguish. He opens the door, and she hesitates upon seeing him, before resuming her expression.

"No more construction," she says with a profound accent. "You men said you would finish by now."

"I'm not with construction. I'm the tenant."

"You new tenant? You who everyone make noise for? I had to go home to Westchester for deadline. Much noise no good for my head."

"Sorry," Matthias says. "They're finished with construction, so there'll be no more noise." Matthias then deciphers the origin of her accent. *"Ty govorish' po-russki?"*

The woman perks up when hearing her native tongue. *"Da,"* she replies. *"Vy tozhe govorite po-russki?"*

"Lish' nekotoryye," Matthias answers.

The woman then proceeds to speak Russian at breakneck speed, accentuating with her hands.

"Whoa, whoa," says Matthias, slowing her down. "I said I only know a little."

"You learn Russian," she says. "It's good to know language."

"I know five languages. Russian is my worst one."

"You should buy my novels to know Russian," she says. "I'm Anna Dereschuk. I write romance novels." She then looks him up and down. "You big like bear. Are you boxer? Or fútbol player? I can write a story about you. They love stories about big black men in Russia."

"No, I'm not a boxer or play fútbol. I'm a bail enforcement agent."

"What is that?"

"I catch people who skip bail. A bounty hunter."

"Oh, you catch bad men? I need stories from you." She then glances at his hands, noticing the scars. *"Batyushki!"* she exclaims. "What wrong with hands?"

"I caught bad men with them. Anyway, I'll try to keep the noises down, Okay? I don't need the Kremlin coming down on me for you to write smut stories."

"No smut," Ms. Dereschuk retorts. "Romance. Making love to Russian soldier is best. Most passion."

"I'll take your word for it. I'm closing the door now."

"Da," she says. "We will talk stories later. Goodbye, big bear." Ms. Dereschuk walks off.

CHAPTER 2

A few hours later, Matthias steps into an empty pawnshop, past the flickering glow from the ceiling lights and glass displays lining the walls, to a counter sealed behind bulletproof glass. On the other side, a man with a double chin barely stirs as he gazes at the TV beside him.

"You're Fat Pat?" Matthias says to him.

"You're paying in full or just putting something down?" says the man, not taking his eyes off the TV. "Either way you better have your ticket."

"I'm Matthias Monroe. I'm a bail enforcement officer looking to work with a bondsman."

Fat Pat perks up. "Then you found the right guy. I need enforcement officers that can beat the shit out of these jumpers and get back my money."

"Well, I just moved from Florida, where I have enforcement credentials, as well as in Georgia and North

Carolina. I'm also a private investigator and have a license to carry—"

"Hold on. Hold on," Fat Pat says. "I just want to see your license. I can check out the other stuff myself."

Matthias slides his bail enforcement agent ID card through the slot in the window. Fat Pat looks at the card.

"Alright then," he says. "Now we can talk. You like making money, right? Of course your long talking ass do. Walk through the door so I can check you out."

Fat Pat points to a door beside the wall and presses a button to buzz it open. Matthias pushes through and walks down a corridor to the other side of the counter—a cramped cubbyhole where the bondsman sits, looking distinctly unhealthy.

"How much do you weigh? I'm guessing 400 pounds."

"I have a glandular problem," snaps Fat Pat. "Now, you passed all background checks and State requirements, and your fingerprints were processed in the NYPD database?"

"I have fingerprints in the system, but they're old."

"What do you mean old? How do fingerprints get old?"

Matthias shows Fat Pat the burns on his fingers and palms. "I was in an accident a long time ago."

"Must be hard to jerk off with no feeling in your hands," snickers Fat Pat. "You probably twist your thing like a pretzel."

Matthias sneers as Fat Pat waddles to a copying machine to make a print of the ID. *Did Mum really suggest this guy to be an asset? She must've been having a senior moment.*

"I'll do a check on your credentials," Fat Pat says as he hands back the card. "If you're good, then we can talk business."

"That's it?"

"What you want, a hug? You don't have to go home but you can get out of here. Unless you want to buy something for your moms or girl. I just copped a gold bracelet from a meth head. I'll sell it to you for $200."

"No thanks."

"$100. $85. That my best offer."

A thought enters his mind, deciding to match the hustle energy. "Rather than that, how about we become friends, and you tell me where I can go for a discreet federal firearms license dealer."

"What do you mean discreet?"

"I need things. I can't be a bounty hunter with zip ties and a pen light. And New York laws only let me register handguns. But if you can point me to an FFL dealer to get certain things, it can go a long way in making sure you get your money back."

Fat Pat studies him for a moment, then leans back into his seat. "I can perhaps help you find someone who knows someone." He then smirks at Matthias. "But before that, let's discuss the bracelet again. I believe the last offer was $400."

"$400?"

"Welcome to New York, friend."

Matthias looks at the military surplus store he's been surveying from across the street. From the look of things, he doubts this place has anything worthwhile. It seems small and nestled between other storefronts, its entrance looking more like a stairwell than an FFL. Well, no harm in checking it out.

He crosses the street and steps inside. As he guessed, the place is small and reeks of mildew, making him crinkle his nose. Mannequins stand dressed in fatigues, as boxes of uniforms are stacked along the walls, behind display cases filled with patches and mementos from infantries gone by. Just being around these relics might give him PTSD.

"Hello," he calls out.

"Just put the mail on the counter, Jim," he hears from the back of the store.

"I'm looking for Lieutenant Jason Hodges," Matthias says. "I was recommended here by Patrick Hennerman."

Seconds later, a scrawny man comes from the background. He looks at Matthias skeptically. "Who are you?"

"Patrick Hennerman said I can come here to get some things for my business. That a Lieutenant Hodges could help me."

"Help for what?"

"I'm a private investigator and a bail enforcement agent." Matthias pulls out his ID card and shows it to him. "Are you Lieutenant Hodges?"

"What obscure things are you talking about?"

"Guns. And other stuff."

"Go to a gun shop," the man then says, rubbing the corner of his eye momentarily. "This place only has an FFL to import. The item is held here until the buyer picks them up. That's it."

Matthias picks up the tell—rubbing the eye to avoid eye contact; the guy's lying. Well, maybe this will open him up.

"Here is $5000," Matthias pulls out an envelope, tossing it to the man's feet. "Well, $4600. All in hundreds and can be traced by their serial numbers to prove they're not counterfeit. If you think they have tracking dye on them, you can throw the money in a bucket of water with an activation solution. Now, I'm not a Fed or a street banger. I just prefer not to deal with background checks and ATF regulations for stuff used in a weekend paintball game. So, if you can't help me, point me to someone who can."

The man picks up the envelope and looks inside. He thumbs over the bills before turning back to Matthias. "What happened to your hands? You got vitiligo or something?"

"Are you Lieutenant Hodges or not?"

The man relents with a chuckle. "Relax, youngster. Pat called me and said you might be coming."

"So you were testing me?"

"Pat said you seem smart, so I wanted to see for myself. To be fair, I've seen worse, but you did fall for the tell of me rubbing my eye. Made you play your hand. Never show the money until the deal is secure, kid."

Hodges smirks as Matthias twists his mouth for falling for the feint.

"Well, now that we got the parlor tricks out of the way," Matthias says as he pulls out a piece of paper, "these are the things I need."

He hands it to Hodges, who looks over the list.

"This is advanced for paintball," Hodges replies. "Who is this for?"

"When did you serve, Lieutenant?" Matthias asks, sidestepping the question.

"From 82-99. I was Pat's commanding officer during *Desert Storm*."

"He was in the Gulf War? Did they had a pie eating contest there?"

"He was 250 pounds lighter then. Dickhead got court martial for looting antiques from the Iraqi museums and was discharged." Hodges look back down at the list. "Some of the things here I'll have to make some calls. But some…come with me to the back."

CHAPTER 3

Washington, DC

Robert Bridges checks his watch as he sits alone in a boardroom within the Defense Contract Management Agency. *Thirty minutes already wasted*, he concludes, fuming. *These pencil pushers can't even show up to their own damn meeting.* His mind drifts into recall; to a time when his name would move mountains and change the landscape of world politics. Now it can't move him faster than someone in line at the DMV. He then smirks darkly as his mind turns toward retribution. *Maybe I should send a few soldiers to these fucks homes and tidy them with some pipe bombs and Molotov's. Maybe then they'd start respecting my time.*

His thoughts are interrupted when his phone rings, the caller ID displaying a number from Tallahassee.

"Mr. Bridges," says a voice on the other end, "this is the first officer at the recon center. An old account you once administered has been reactivated. We have protocols to contact you when such events occur."

"It's probably the CIA using the money for one of their informants," he says. "How much was moved?"

"$200,000 was transferred from Zurich to New York two days ago."

"What's the name on the account?"

"Johnathan Monroe, sir."

The name makes Bridges roll his eyes. *That motherfucker.* He then looks up to see a silhouette appear through the frosted window of the boardroom.

"Send the details to my email," Bridges says. He then hangs up as a man enters.

"Mr. Bridges," he says. "I'm Jonas Adams, Chief Coordinator for the DCMA. I'm sorry for the delay. My briefing was longer than usual."

"Not a problem. I understand everyone is busy."

"Then let us begin," Adams says, sitting down across from Bridges. "As you may know, the GAO is partnering with the DoD to audit contracts that contribute to budget inefficiencies. And as you're aware, your contract is up for review."

"Are you trying to lowball me again?" Bridges snaps at Adams. "We took a 20% cut on the last renewal."

"Mr. Bridges, there are new requirements—"

"You can't keep expecting us to give discounts. We provide a vital service to both agency operations and territories abroad—"

"Mr. Bridges, the decision has been made that the DoD will not renew the contract."

Bridges is frozen for a moment, looking at Adams as if he's insane.

"Again," Adams reiterates, "agencies have new procurement requirements to ensure contract are cost-efficient, and your company has been viewed as a sunk cost. Now, this doesn't exclude the company from future agreements, but certain conditions must be met to comply with the submission process."

Bridges continues to peer at Adams. A pipe bomb through this guy's window would look really good right now.

"What conditions do you suggest?" he ask instead, tepidly.

"Well, the personnel on each contract would have to be cut down significantly—only a handful of your employees per deployment."

"Sure. Let's penny pinch going to hostile territories to protect diplomats and U.S. embassies. We can pocket the saving to take the insurgents out to brunch."

"You add 30% for auxiliary, forensics, and reconnaissance units, yet those expenses are never included in your budget expenditures. Meanwhile, other companies practice proper accounting measures and operate at a third of the cost."

"Quality costs," says Bridges, "and you can't protect the track by replacing a thoroughbred with a donkey." He then pauses, folding his arms across his chest. "This isn't about the budget. You can cut to the bone, and you still won't make a dent in what this country spends on defense. So why don't you tell me the real reason why you're terminating the agreement."

At first, Adams' face cringes, then he smirks, like a kid who's always wanted to tell the bully a thing or two.

"Since you ask, Mr. Bridges, numerous reports have been made over the years about your employees' conduct—"

"They are not employees," affirms Bridges. "That's the second time you said that. They are soldiers."

"—And how their actions led to the destabilization of sovereign agreements. Just last year, one of your soldiers killed a member of a drug cartel in Pakistan. He was later found in Jeddah with a kilo of heroin, distributing it to one of the princes of the Saudi royal family."

"For one, that guy was an outlier. Two, that case is still under investigation. And three, how come no one is asking if the Saudis are a drug cartel? That's the more important question."

"Are you trying to accuse the Saudis of being a cartel to deflect from one of your soldiers' selling drugs to that very cartel?"

Bridges shifts his eyes for a moment. "So what's your point?"

"The point is your company has a habit of breaking international laws and using the United States government for cover." Adams leans in toward Bridges. "And then there's the issue of your decorum."

"What about my decorum?"

"Your abrupt personality, quite frankly, has grown tiresome. The way you talk to heads of state, the way you address Cabinet members, the way you approach diplomats—I'm surprised you're not in prison by now."

Oh, fuck this guy. "Who cares about my personality. This is defending a nation. If you want to get some bullshit company because they know how to use a spreadsheet, go ahead. But for real Americans, we want someone who will find an imminent threat and blast them in the fucking head."

"If you ever needed proof of your lack of decorum," Adams says with certainty, leaning back in his chair. "There's really nothing left to discuss, Mr. Bridges. The Defense Secretary has already spoken with your CEO. The DoD will honor the contract until its term, then all dealings will be dissolved."

CHAPTER 4

Bridges steps off the elevator onto the executive floor, and storms through the corridors, weaving past the employees in the halls toward a pair of office doors.

"Is he in there?" Bridges stops at the secretary's desk.

"Yes sir," she says anxiously.

"MCBRIDE!" Bridges bellows as he storms towards the office.

"Mr. Bridges," says the secretary. "Wait."

"It's okay, Lillian," comes a voice through the walls from the office. "He can come in."

The doors fly open as Bridges pushes through, revealing the avant-garde décor of a corner office. A man in his early forties, holding a putter and focusing on a shot on a putting mat, remains unfazed by the interruption.

"What took you so long?" says Quentin McBride. "I figured you'd get here quicker if you flew on your broom."

"What the hell are you doing, agreeing to not renew with the DoD? Are you not going take a stance when there's a full conspiracy to bogart the company from business?"

"As treacherous as you make it sound," says McBride, before tapping the golf ball and watching it roll across the putting mat. "The company can survive losing one contract. We're in line for more lucrative contracts in the pipeline."

"Such as what? What is there in the pipeline that I don't know about, that can replace $55 million?"

"Well, I have a tentative agreement to license our decryption software to the Bureau of Industry and Security, and our counterintelligence training will be integrated into the DCSA to secure classified information."

"Those are minor acquisitions. Any tech firm that wants to play peek-a-boo with hackers can handle those bids."

"We're also about to form a partnership with the Millennium Challenge Program."

"What the fuck is that?" Bridges says.

"It's an initiative focused on assisting developing countries. We're subletting our satellite lease for corruption control."

Bridges peers at McBride. "While we're at it, why don't we just hand out candy during parades?"

McBride huffs. "When I came on as CEO, the primary objective was to encourage new ways of thinking about international risk management."

"Which is the press release we fed to the agencies while we keep on course as the premier paramilitary company for the government. Not to turn into mall cops."

"What you're not understanding is the U.S. government is no longer writing checks to let anyone play spy games. Based on how spending is being scrutinized by the interest groups—"

"Fuck the interest groups! Let them pick up a rifle if they're so concerned. What about our personnel? Those resources we lost were for their operations."

"I bet if I look at your bank account I could find where some of the contract money went."

"You mean to the founder of this company?" Bridges replies. "The one who was protecting this country since you were shitting in diapers? I earned every cent and put it back into the company when warranted. Including your salary."

"Yeah, thanks for that," McBride quips. "And for the company shares. I'm thinking of selling them to buy a boat."

Bridges folds his arms across his chest. "You're supposed to be good for business, not hinder it. You're supposed to be our connection to military contracts, not whipping it out to work with the Do-Gooder Fund. And since you can't seem to do anything but choke on a Par 4, I'm recommending your resignation at the next board meeting."

"On what grounds?"

"Fiduciary and executive malfeasance," Bridges says. "We can always find another nepo baby to kiss the taint."

McBride taps his putter in his hands, resisting the urge to swing it at Bridges. "Since we're being so candid, none of the agencies want to deal with you. For years they see you bully your way through Capitol Hill and the Pentagon. They're tired of it, so they want you gone—like a fart in the wind."

"Who told you that? Your father?"

"People that like me more than they like you. But the fact that you worked with the government for so long is a problem. You know too much. But rather than put a bullet in your head—as some suggested—they decided to put you in the gilded cage."

"What does that mean?"

"That means the company will land contracts to be—what you called—mall cops, so you don't disturb the big boy table. And as long as I'm here you'll at least get that. Maybe they won't have the flair you're used to, but you'll accept it because it'll at least give you some illusion of importance. Or you cannot accept it and do everyone a favor and jump off the roof. Either way, I don't care." McBride then motions for Bridges to leave. "Now, if you're done throwing tantrums, get out. I'm working on reading the greens."

Bridges watches as McBride turns back to the putting mat to continue his play, making him more incensed. Then, withdrawing from the impulse to have the last word, he leaves the office.

He storms through the corridors, terrifying the workers and making them veer away from his path. He enters his office and slams the door behind him, proceeding to drop into his chair behind his desk. There, he broods: *all the secrets he knows and where the bodies are buried—and they do this to him? Well, he'll teach these politicians and directors he's not the one to fuck with.*

Then, after a few moments, his thirst for the blame game subsides and reflection creeps in:

He should've seen this coming.

Maybe he's grown comfortable, or assumed he was too in to be outed, but he should've seen this coming. It would be against their nature not to eat their young—even when they're old. *Maybe calling it a career wouldn't be so bad. Retirement. Sunsets on beaches. Icecap vistas on winter cruises. That's what they do, right?*

Bridges then sits up in his chair, rejecting the notion before it takes root. *Fuck that. They're just assholes. If they want to play, he'll match their asshole with more asshole. He just doesn't know how to—yet.*

Bridges logs on to his desk computer to clear his mind, and sees the email delivered from the recon center. $200,000 in bearer cheques were shipped from the Suisse Assurance and Securities Financial Company in Zurich to a parcel's facility in New York.

Interesting. But from whom? CIA? Special Ops? Either that or the one operative that crossed him found a bank to withdraw from. Doubtful, but he must follow up, in case the Feds starts inquiring. Bridges picks up his office phone and dials an extension.

"Records Department," says a voice on the other end. "How may I help you, Mr. Bridges?"

"Get me a file archived. *The El Sharif File.*

CHAPTER 5

Back in his office, after inspecting the flashbangs and smoke grenades he purchased from Hodges, Matthias cracks open the box with his real toys: three Glock 19s. One is for registration; the other two don't have serial numbers, so those stay off the books. As he assembles the ghost guns with new slides, triggers, and grips, one of his burner phones rings.

"Hello, Pat."

"Wassup, Burnt Hands? Good news. Your background checked out. You're almost good to be making this money."

"What do you mean, almost?"

"I'll give you a trial run. There's this guy who bought a bond from me; some gang member who was supposed to be in court two weeks ago. You bring him back in five days—"

"Five days? That's no time. I have to skip-trace phone records and cross check last known addresses—"

"You bring him back in five days and I'll pay you two grand. If not, then you can go kiss my ass after I eat a pound of bologna."

Matthias winces from the thought. Well, this is all for his cover anyway. "Fine. Email me his file."

Hours later, as Matthias reads the file from Fat Pat, another one of his phones rings. It's an international number, from Switzerland.

"*Hallo Mum*," says Matthias with a German inflection.

"*Du klingst müde,*" says the woman on the other end.

"How would you know if I'm tired over the phone? And why are you not asleep? It's after 4 a.m. there."

"Old people do not sleep. We wander in the night with ghosts made from decades of decisions."

"At least you're getting exercise."

"Ha ha," she responds. "Did you get the watch I sent to you?"

"Yes. It's very nice. Along with the tip."

"What tip?"

"The leaflet for the bondsman. It was in the office."

"I have not passed on any leaflet," she says. "Andreus must've given it for you. In any case, I have the software you've asked for. It's on your cloud server."

"Hopefully this auto-generates. My tech savviness is minimal."

"Well, if you'd studied network security like I've suggested, instead of spinning on your head with those karate moves—"

"You mean the Hapkido and the Krav Maga?"

"—you could have done this remotely. But since that's not the case, you'll have to put it in manually."

"Did you test it to see if it works?"

"We check all collateral before doing business with a client."

"Do that client knows your crew of mopheads will then take their collateral and reengineer it for the black market?"

"I have no idea what you are talking about," she says. "But if the client does file a claim, there are five lawsuits pending from previous clients. So they will stand in queue."

"Since we're speaking legalese," Matthias says, shifting the topic, "what are the boundaries for a bail enforcement agent operating outside his domicile?"

"Why are you so concerned with your alias? It's just so you can carry a gun if the authorities stop you."

"Can't have an alias if you don't know what the alias does."

"Perhaps you should reconsider having a logistics analyst to assist you, so you would not have any ambiguity with your cover? A project cannot run with only one individual."

"I don't want outsiders involved. Besides, I have you. Why get a nobody when I have you for the nobody?"

"Well," she then replies dryly, "it's always nice when your child thinks so little of you and everything you've provided."

"I'm being sarcastic, mum. I mean nothing by it."

"Of course not, Matthias. You're always sarcastic. You never mean anything you say."

He twists his mouth in response. *Well, this conversation took an unexpected turn.*

"I must go now, mum. I'll keep you posted."

"Very well. In the meantime, I'll pace around with my ghosts. *Hab dich lieb.*"

"*Ich liebe dich auch.*" Matthias hangs up, then checks for the software, seeing the .exe file of a black-market program capable of hacking encrypted sites—like the one he needs to break into.

As he downloads the file, he reflects on Mum's behavior. She's been snippy lately. Maybe the empty nest is getting to her. She did, after all, raise him as her own, stepping in when the training pushed him past the brink. When he was drilled into him guerrilla tactics, she took him to India to decompress. When the trainers tried to throw him into an underground boxing ring, she brought him to the Sudan to help build schools. Then there was the time they wanted him to wrestle a bear.

"You do something like that to him again," she said to the trainers as he laid in the hospital with three broken ribs and a pierced lung, *"I will kill all of you!"*

Reactively, Matthias places a hand on the left side of his torso, feeling the concave scars from the surgery. That was the only time they eased up—and he spent that year with her in Brazil to recover. When the project is over, he should take a trip to see her. They can stroll through Zurich's Old Town as she chatters about the evils of the world. Maybe then she'll finally sleep.

CHAPTER 6

Bridges sits in a booth in The District Diner, a hole-in-the-wall where truckers go when they pull off the Beltway. He measures the crowd as they drone on about their families or favorite sports team, feeling disgusted by their banality. Nothing about the upcoming sanctions against Iran? Or the intelligence report on North Korea? Or anything to force them to keep their heads on a swivel? *No*, he reckons. *Why would they? They're just lemmings—too stupid to know they're over the edge with their double chins and muffin tops.*

His attention shifts as a black sedan pulls up outside. A man steps from his car, walks in, scans the diner, then heads to him.

"I see you still like to be in the outskirts," says Aaron Chambers, Deputy Secretary of the Department of Homeland Security. "We could've met at my office."

"The best deals are done in places like these," he replies. "Besides, I've been to the Hill already this month. Any more than that and I'll need a tetanus shot."

Chambers sits down across from Bridges. "We're making a deal? Maybe I should get that tetanus shot. Any chance they have smoked swordfish with wasabi sorbet here?"

"I think they have a tuna melt."

"No thanks," says Chambers. "So let me get to the point. I cannot help you land contracts with DHS."

"I wasn't going to ask you for a contract."

"Because I figured you'd backdoor your way past the agency directors with favors and IOUs."

"What makes you think that? I have plenty of contracts."

Chambers smirks. "Like the Millennium Challenge Program?"

Bridges sneers. "Shut up."

"What did you call me for?"

"I need you to remove my CEO."

Chambers looks around for anyone within earshot, before returning to Bridges. "What do you mean, remove?"

"He's turning the company into the Green Party. He's one step away from having us sponsor a telethon. He needs to go."

"You want a three-tour veteran, and the son of a Deputy Secretary of the State Department killed, because he's forcing you to play nice with others?"

"I don't want him killed. I just need something for him to resign from. Drugs. Gambling debts. Him attending a glory hole. Something scandalous."

"DHS does not exist to execute a citizen's grudge," Chambers says. "Especially when that citizen has a record like yours."

"What record?"

"Oh, off the top of my head: in 2012, your men strip-searched three guards working for the Iraqi Ministry. And in 2015, one of your men got drunk and drove his SUV into an Army Humvee in Fallujah."

Bridges scoffs. "Those claims were thrown out of court."

"Those are just a few of the transgressions your company has committed. Furthermore, there are actions that warrant course correction, but removing CEOs without just cause is not one of them. We're not here for you to get back at a neighbor who didn't recycle the trash."

Bridges sneers again, then grins. First, he asks. Then, he orders.

"I was brushing up on an old file yesterday. *The El Sharif File*. That's when we dissuaded a presidential candidate from winning the election in Egypt."

"Dissuade is a generous way to put it," says Chambers.

"That led to the next mission: *Operation Aziz-Islamia*. We were tasked with recon on the Egyptian president's opposition party. At one point, he claimed there was a facility in North Sinai producing chemical weapons. So, your Army battalion flew in two Apache helicopters and fired four Hydra 70 rockets to destroy it. You were one of the pilots on that mission."

"I remember. What is your point?"

"That wasn't a weapons base. That was a small hospital. Forty people were killed and twenty-eight were wounded."

For a moment, Chambers starts to turn pale, then lets out a scoff of his own. "That's bullshit. You're trying to play your mind tricks. We had ISR confirmation. Thermal scans showed armed personnel. The intel was authenticated and approved by the commanding officers."

"And who provided the confirmation? We did. The Egyptian president wanted to attack the extremist group, so he told us to fabricate an incident so he could blame it on them."

"I was debriefed after every mission," Chambers pushes back further. "There was no mention of a false target."

"The government isn't going to admit a covert op, even to its own soldiers. Besides, we took the blame. It's harder to charge contractors with war crimes. That's why the government uses us: for our tactical enforcement, intel gathering, and our ever popular Get Out of Jail Free cards. So, when you list our record, make sure you include that one."

"You also have a record of being a lying sack of shit. I only take information from the commanders I served under, not from some sociopath resorting to ambulance chasing."

Bridges pauses at the slight. He then pulls a folder from beside him, handing it to Chambers.

"Here's our file for *Operation Aziz-Islamia*. You'll see the planning, the staging, and the execution of the target.."

"I'm supposed to believe this?" Chambers holds up the file. "A bunch of notes?"

"Then you won't find in the post-op section who signed off on the target: Members of the Joint Chiefs of Staff, the DoS director, and your own Brigadier General."

Chambers squints at Bridges, still in disbelief, then opens the file. As he flips through the pages, his face falls—his unknown sins surfacing before him.

He turns to Bridges, his voice slightly quivering. "Why are you showing me this?"

"Because the human rights lobbyist been handing out subpoenas to the company for us to release files. They're ravenous about finding anyone who operated outside the rules of combat. Based on the file, that would be you."

"I've done what I was told," Chambers remarks. "You're not roping me into some war crime."

"Don't worry, Aaron. The Secretary of State knows how to handle things like this. A Sergeant First Class tortured a prisoner in GITMO and only got reassigned to a reserve unit in Louisville. He wasn't the Deputy Secretary for Homeland Security, but I'm sure he'd welcome the company."

Bridges then sits back into his seat. "Or, like I suggested earlier Aaron; remove my CEO."

CHAPTER 7

Satisfied with Chambers' compliance of his demands, Bridges returns to his office and checks the time. Europe is still within business hours. He picks up his phone and dials an international number.

"God dag," goes a Norwegian receptionist. *"Suisse Assurance and Securities. Hvordan kan jeg hjelpe deg?"*

"Do you speak English?"

"Yes sir," she replies.

"This is Robert Bridges, with the U.S. Defense Department. I have information regarding possible fraud against your institution. I need to speak Delores Gruber."

"Hold please." Bridges waits a few moments before another woman picks up the line. "Ms. Gruber speaking. Mr. Bridges?"

"Yes. I'm with the Department of—"

"I know who you are. You were verified through our screening process as a contractor with the U.S. Defense Department."

"Let me get to the point, then. Your bank reactivated a frozen CIA account and transferred $200,000 to a location within the U.S. I need to know who authorized that transaction."

"Do you have the account number?"

Bridges gives her the number and then waits on hold once more, only for her to return and say, "I'm sorry, but I cannot relay that information."

"What do you mean? This is a situation that needs your cooperation."

"This information is classified. That is all I'm required to say."

"I'm not asking to tell me what the money is for, just who authorized the transfer."

"I cannot relay that information. Not without clearance from the U.S. Department of State and a Swiss court order."

First, he asks. Then, he orders. "I know very well who you are, Ms. Delores Gruber. Along with running that bank, you're on the board for the IMF, which is against their rules, so you know how to twist around legalities."

"Are you implying my position was garnered unethically?"

"I'm saying that at my urging, the Swiss Financial Market Authority might be interested in how a bank executive is also has a seat with the IMF. If it smells like collusion to me, I'm sure it would to them, and have the institution audited for any dubious practices you have going on there. Or, like I suggested earlier; you can tell me who authorized opening the account."

There's a pause on her end, then:

"The IMF permits me to hold both positions as I oversee the institution's monetary policy, not its private banking. If you have evidence to the contrary, please forward your claim to whatever party you're comfortable with. I'm sure the international agencies with accounts here—and their legal teams at our disposal—would be interested in the inquiry."

"Look, Ms. Gruber—"

"Furthermore, I maintain that I cannot disclose details about the account without clearance from U.S. and Swiss authorities." She then changes to a more pleasing tone. "Now, is there anything else I can assist you with? We offer an excellent tax-free annuity underwritten by the

Pierrepont Insurance Company. Would you care for some literature on it?"

Bridges angrily hangs up on her. *Fucking bitch.*

He stews for a moment before he pulls a cigar from the stash in his desk, clipping and lighting it. He puffs as he thinks of a solution. He then dials the number again.

"God dag. Suisse Assurance and Securities. Hvordan kan jeg hjelpe deg?"

"I want to speak to someone in Parcel Services."

"Is there anyone in particular that—"

"I want to speak to someone in Parcel Services."

"Sir, Parcel Services does not accept external calls. Perhaps if you inform me—"

"Aren't they listed as part of your operations?"

"Yes sir."

"Do they handle your international mail?"

"They are directed to send and deliver—"

"Then I want to speak to someone in Parcel Services. I can do this all day, lady."

Silence, then: "Please hold."

After a few moments, another person picks up the line. *"Hallo?"*

"Is this Parcel Services?"

"Yes. This is Liam. How may I help you?"

"You've done enough, Liam. I was supposed to get a package delivered and you fucked that up."

"Sir," says Liam. "I don't know what you mean. Please clarify so I can understand—"

"I closed an account. Its contents in the deposit box were supposed to be sent to Monaco. I went to the airport, but the package never arrived. Now, either you put me through to your manager so I can collect the $1,000,000 insurance on it, or you get on your hindquarters and tell me where my package is."

"I am not familiar with the term 'hindquarters'," says Liam, "but I can help locate your package. Can you give me your name and account number?"

"Johnathan Monroe," says Bridges, and after giving the account number he smokes his cigar as he waits for an answer.

"Sir," Liam says. "The package was delivered to a parcel facility in Manhattan. It was signed for and collected a few days ago."

"It wasn't supposed to be routed there. Who picked up my package?"

"Matthias Monroe. Verified as your son."

Bridges blinks and hangs up on Liam. A son?
Johnathan has a son? He's going to need more intel. He
picks up his smartphone and begins texting:

'Madison, come to headquarters. I need you to go to New York.'

Bridges sends the message and takes a toke of his cigar.
Then, his phone buzzes with a reply:

'Can I shoot someone this time?'

'Get here first,' Bridges responds. *'Then we'll talk.'*

CHAPTER 8

Camden, NJ

"Bridges called the bank."

"How do you know?"

"Your mother told me," Andreus says over the phone. "He called the bank about the transfer. His inquiry got diverted for now, but if he's thorough, he'll start retracing your steps—starting with you picking up the bearer checks. Then he'll put together a composite and send someone after you."

"I went to the packaging facility, then to multiple banks to cash the checks. My trail is too cluttered to be retraced."

"Every trail can be retraced," Andreus replies. "Where was the packaging facility located? That'll be his first stop."

"Chinatown."

"Where in Chinatown?"

"I can't recall," says Matthias.

"You can't recall where a location was after you went there?"

"I went by the geohash coordinates Mum gave me, not by the address. I could point it out if I was in the vicinity."

"Says a lot about your ability to know your surroundings. Maybe you need to be put back in the oven to cook more."

Matthias frowns from the remark. "And your old boss is tracking me to find you. Says a lot about your people skills. Maybe you need to sign up for a Dale Carnegie class."

Silence—then, "Don't you have recon to do?"

"I was in the middle of it when you called."

"I'll monitor Bridges on my end. Just keep doing what you're doing." Andreus hangs up.

Parked in a rental car, Matthias resumes his surveillance. It's not the recon he should be doing, but it's the one he's on nonetheless, as Fat Pat's deadline has forced him to put boots on the ground earlier than he'd like. He peers at a house among a stretch of row homes, watching three men out front, doing what they do out in the open, exposing themselves to arrests. *Idiots. Leave it to criminals to tell how stupid they are.*

As he surveys, he catches a shadow within his peripheral vision. Someone is nearby. He slowly reaches for the Glock 19 beside him. He grips the handle and looks out the window.

A kid, maybe ten, stands at the window, staring at him.

"Can I help you?" Matthias asks, releasing his hand off the gun.

"You're a cop?" the kid says.

Matthias blinks. "What makes you think I'm a cop?"

"You been parked here for a while looking at AB's house. That's what cops do. My grandma's house is right here so I've seen you since you got here. Plus, your car got New York plates, so you're not from here."

It doesn't say a lot about him if a kid can make him out doing recon. Andreus would be laughing at this. "Shouldn't you be in school?"

"I'm home schooled," the kid replies. "I'm on break before my online science class starts." The kid then points at Matthias hands. "Why do your hands look like that?"

"I smoked cigarettes while pumping gas. You should go back inside to your schoolwork."

"Jeremy!" Matthias hears from the house closest to them, as a woman storms out the front door, snatching the kid from the curb. "What did I tell you about wandering from the house?"

Sorry, grandma," Jeremy says. "But I saw this guy outside and I thought he was here to see about AB. He's a cop."

"I'm not a cop," Matthias restates.

"Well, who the hell are you then?" she snarls. "You like talking to kids like some pervert?"

"I'm with New York Bail Enforcement. I'm here to do surveillance on a suspect and I parked here to be inconspicuous."

"I knew you were a cop," says Jeremy.

"Boy, get inside and start your lesson," she says. She peers at Jeremy who trots in the house, then once he's inside turns back to Matthias. "Let me see some identification if you are who you say you are."

Matthias hands her his ID. "He's a precocious kid. You should tell him to curb it down before it gets his ass whipped."

After looking over the ID, she relaxes as she hands it back to Matthias. "I tell him not to wander around because these kids here are on some other shit."

"You homeschool him in this neighborhood?"

"The schools near my daughter aren't safe, so she brings him to me. I used to be a teacher, so I handle his curriculum while she works." She then turns and looks down the street, toward his target. "You're going to do something about those assholes? Because the police won't."

"Does Armani Becton live there?"

"Yeah. Everyone here knows AB. He leaves in the morning with his crew. When my daughter drops off Jeremy, she sometimes runs into them, and they try to talk to her. They even follow her when she drives off sometimes. I called the police about it, but they just give the run-around."

"You say he leaves in the morning. When does he get back?"

"Not until late."

"What kind of car he usually drives?"

"He's usually in a Benz. It's one of those truck types."

"How many guys are usually with him?"

"At least two are with him, and three are usually in the house."

Matthias looks again toward AB's house. With kids and civilians living in the neighborhood, his best bet is to strike at night. Six-to-one at best, and they're all sure to be armed. He might need some backup.

"Alright," he says. "I'm not making any promises, just know the situation will be handled. And tell the kid to take up martial arts. It's better than science."

Matthias arrives at the Camden police precinct, introducing himself to the desk sergeant and sharing his details about the target. He then waits another twenty minutes before an officer approaches him.

"Mr. Monroe, I'm the Camden City police liaison. I'm told you want to notify us about a possible bail fugitive?"

"Yes. I have information that he is residing in Camden, and I'm notifying the police of his apprehension."

"Well, let's talk at my desk," the officer says before leading Matthias past the front of the precinct into the back offices.

"Your credentials check out," the officer continues as he takes a seat at his desk, "and there is a warrant in New York for an Armani Becton's arrest. Now, if you don't know, a new law recently passed requiring all police officers in New Jersey to accompany enforcement agents during an apprehension. The issue is that we are understaffed and do not have the manpower available."

"And when will you have officers available?"

"We may be able to update and prep staff for the arrest at the end of the month."

"That's in three weeks," Matthias says. "He could be long gone by then, especially if he hears bail enforcement is on him."

"The only other way to expedite the matter is to hand the warrant to the State's Fugitive Unit so they can put the case on their docket."

"If I hand over the warrant, then I don't get paid. The state gets the reward."

"That's the situation," the officer says. "It's either through the Fugitive Unit, or you'll have to come back in three weeks. Operating otherwise could trigger your surety bond being revoked. You currently have a $250,000 policy with the Pierrepont Insurance Co., correct? Be a shame to have that tied up."

Matthias sneers as the officer smirks. Are they trying to shake him down for his company's bond? He guesses the grandmother's assessment was spot on; these cops don't want to do anything, unless they're on the take.

"Never mind," Matthias says, rising from the desk. "I'll try again in three weeks. Or maybe he'll come to New York to watch the ball drop on New Year's Eve—seeing as you don't have any balls here." He then walks from the desk and out the precinct.

CHAPTER 9

Around the same time, two men walk through Manhattan's Chinatown, stopping at a storefront.

"What do you see?" says one of them, Madison.

"A store," replies the other, Burroughs.

"I mean, do you see any threats that catch your eye? Any onlookers watching from the windows? Any signalers tipping people off to our arrival?"

"I just see a lot of Chinese people."

"So you didn't notice the police cameras across the street, mounted on the street posts?"

Burroughs turns and looks to the cameras. "Oh," he says. "Those."

Madison huffs as he steps inside the storefront. He hates New York. And he hates training newbies. And between the two, the last four hours since leaving D.C. have been hell.

"May I help you?" asks the clerk at the counter.

"I'm Special Agent Madison, with the United States Defense Department," he says, showing his ID. "Is your manager here?"

The clerk is taken aback before calling toward the back office. "Jimmy, you should come out here."

Another man approaches the counter. "Is there a problem?"

"We need to see your security footage from a few days ago," says Burroughs. "And your pickup logs. Now."

"What my partner means to say," Madison interjects, showing his ID to the man, "is that we're agents from the U.S. Defense Department, and we have reason to believe your company received and delivered a package containing sensitive materials related to national security. Not your fault. You're not in trouble. But we need to look at your records to track this package."

"Uhm," Jimmy says, scratching his head. "I need to a search warrant for what you're talking about. I can't just let—"

"We just told you you're not in trouble," Burroughs cuts in. "So let us see the video logs."

Jimmy frowns. "I have the right to withhold information without a warrant, and I don't have to give you anything that might incriminate me."

"My, my," says Madison derisively. "Don't we read the law books."

"For your information, I go to John Jay College for International Law."

"Is that a small school? I went to Annapolis. I don't know of any small schools."

"Perhaps you should speak to my lawyer," Jimmy says. "I'm not required to hand you anything without a court subpoena or search warrant."

"Are you sure you want to do that?" says Madison. "I don't want to make this messy."

"Are you threatening me? You can't come in—"

Before he can finish, Burroughs vaults over the counter.

A sharp right to Jimmy's head sends him stumbling. Without wasted motion, Burroughs pivots, driving an elbow into the other clerk's temple.

He turns back to Jimmy—an uppercut snaps his head back, knocking him out.

Back to the clerk—a haymaker to the jaw, and he's off like a light switch, collapsing to the floor like dead weight.

"I prefer messy," says Burroughs.

"And I prefer you don't get blood on my suit," Madison says, wiping the splatters off his jacket. "Tie them up and dose them with a shot of Haloperidol. I'll check the video logs."

"What's the damage?" Bridges says on the phone, an hour later.

"Only two," says Madison. "They've been sedated."

"Are there police cameras nearby?"

"Yes sir."

"Clean up your tracks, then you and Burroughs book a hotel. I'll handle the cameras."

Bridges hangs up his smartphone and picks up the office phone on his desk. He dials a series of numbers and waits. There's no ringing—only a series of clicks—before a woman answers.

"This is the NYPD Federal Dispatch. This call is under surveillance for security and training purposes. Who am I speaking to?"

"This is Robert Bridges, with the Department of Defense."

"Please wait for verification," she says. A few minutes later, "What can I do for you, Mr. Bridges?"

"I need a video scrub on a camera footprint between 4:30 to 4:38 p.m., and at 5:27 to 5:40 p.m. Pell Street, from the Bowery to Mott Street."

"Purpose?"

"Standard training operation."

"There's currently no training operations approved by the Commissioner's office," she says.

"Did I say standard?" Bridges readjusts. "I meant covert training operation."

Silence on her end for a moment, then, "Approval?"

"Aaron Chambers, Deputy Secretary of the Department of Homeland Security." Chambers won't mind the name drop.

"Your request will be sent to the Commissioner's office for approval," she says. "In the meantime, any footage will be withheld from investigations until the request is approved or denied. You will be notified once a decision is made."

Bridges hangs up and moves to his desk computer, pulling up the info Madison retrieved and sent to his email. He watches the video footage of the suspect picking up his package.

So, this is Johnathan's son. Bridges then leans in, focusing on the suspect's hands—scarred, just like Johnathan's were.

Did he scorch his son's hands to burn off the fingerprints? Seems like his old tricks rubbed off on the ingrate. But what does he want after all these years? What could be his motivation?

He grabs a file from his desk which he had pulled from Archives, opening it to the top page. Johnathan Monroe: high school Tae Kwon Do champion. Also practiced Judo and Brazilian Jujitsu. Attended Missouri State before enlisting at Fort Wood. Served as First Sergeant during *Operation Golden Pheasant* and *Operation Just Cause,* racking up numerous commendations, including a Silver Star recommendation.

Bridges reclines in his chair, reminiscing about the young recruit. It would take a lot to reel in a skill set like his.

"When your Army contract is up, I'll pay you a $300,000 a year to kill some bad guys," Bridges said to the recruit.

A year later, the recruit signed the contract, and from there the disrupter was in motion. From Haiti to Yemen to Burkina Faso, he set up coup d'états with kills or prevented them with kills. All to Bridges' delight as he was rewarded with more contracts. Until somewhere along the way the disrupter grew a conscience.

"Why do you only want me in countries that aren't white ethnic? Is it a race thing?"

"No, it's a strategic thing," Bridges replied. "You being black, you wouldn't exactly blend along the Eastern Bloc. Besides, I can't be racist. I've killed more white people than Nat Turner."

"Well, I'm not cool with destabilizing countries with people that are just trying to exercise their human rights. All so your cronies can have their resources for the cheap."

Dammit. A thinking soldier is a turncoat in waiting. Better to move him to security detail for a while.

"Fine. We just got a contract to shadow the new Egyptian prime minister. The first woman to hold that position. I'll make you the head of her security detail."

From there, the disrupter was assigned to guard her as she began her campaign to run against the president, uncovering his embezzlement of funds into secret bank accounts—

Bridges stops mid-thought, as his recollection shifts to a solution for the present. *Secret bank. The Bank Secrecy Act. That could work.* He picks up the phone once more and dials.

"Yes sir," Madison answers. "We're almost finished here."

"Good. Now tomorrow go to the U.S. Treasury building. Ask for a printout of checks deposited from Switzerland to Manhattan over the past few days. If they balk, tell them The Bank Secrecy Act allows us to monitor possible activity to money laundering and sponsored terrorism. And tell them the order came from the Deputy Secretary of DHS. That should tell us what banks the suspect went to and where he went from there."

"Yes, sir," Madison replies.

Bridges hangs up and stews in the silence of his smoke-filled office. He may not yet know what Johnathan or his son wants, but they're a loose thread. And since he didn't get to where he is by waiting, he'll stay preemptive on their asses with the heat of a thousand suns.

CHAPTER 10

As the Camden sky transitions to nighttime, Matthias watches the target's house from blocks away. He checks the body armor he has on, tapping the plates of his vest. Next, he inspects his Glock 19 and a launcher for the flashbangs. Finally, he looks over his latest rental from behind the wheel—a specialized black GMC Savanna 3500. *This thing better live up to its reputation, given what he intends to do with it.*

With everything else checked off, only one thing remains. From the driver's seat, he triggers his neurolinguistic phrases. "Romania. Zurich. Sudan. Florianópolis. Bangkok."

Matthias feels himself sinking—past the night hum and his clanging heartbeat—into the noiseless peace. From there, he launches into a separate phrase:

"Leiden die Kinder, denn ihnen gehört das Himmelreich."

His mind clicks like an unlocked tumbler, flashing back to a younger self—adolescent and tortured—where the trainers planted their poison.

"It is well to kill," they told him between zaps from cattle prods.

"The wolf sees sheep; the wolf kills sheep," as they confined him to a sweatbox.

"Pain is subjective," as they cranked the levers on the stretch rack, forcing his bones past their limits to make him taller.

"Your hesitation is why you are here," as they prepped him for surgery after the bear attack, while he choked on his own blood. *"Hesitation is death. Wolves do not wait to kill."*

Matthias opens his eyes and peers past the windshield: the world is now stark and eerie, as if the night is made of endless specters and demons. He lets out a sulfurous growl.

Minutes later, or hours—in this state he wouldn't know—a blue G-Wagon pulls up and parks across from the target's house.

Matthias starts the van, fastening his seatbelt as the men exit their vehicle. He drives toward them, then jerks the wheel hard and floors the gas, veering straight to the G-Wagon.

CRASH!!

Matthias bounces violently within the seatbelt from the collision. The bulletproof windshield fractures as the front end of the van crumples. His vision is blurred, and his limbs are cut from the protruding shrapnel of the crushed dashboard.

From there, moments of stillness, before he snaps through the disarray.

Move. Move! MOVE!

Matthias grabs both his gun and the grenade launcher, rushing from the van. One man is down. The remaining two stand frozen, staring at the wrecked G-Wagon.

"What the…," one of them says, as Matthias emerges, raising the launcher towards them.

"It's a hit," says the other. "Move out!"

PA-toot PA-toot—goes the launcher, propelling two canisters towards them. Matthias then crouches behind the van for cover.

The flashbangs detonate when they land with an explosion, turning the night into a blinding light. Car alarms wail in response to the boom, overwhelming the streets with sirens.

Matthias reemerges with his gun. *Six-to-two o'clock-shot. Clear!*

He fires two shots at the closest target.

The man buckles with each shot into his shoulder and hip. He crumples in a heap.

Gunfire erupts in Matthias' direction. He darts for cover as bullets pummel the van, chiming the air as its bulletproof façade holds.

Matthias darts to the other side of the G-Wagon. He takes position as three men sprint toward the van. Not finding him there, they scan the area.

One of them glances toward the G-Wagon, his left side exposed.

A shot rings. The man hollers as he collapses to the ground, blood gushing from his left leg.

"There he goes!" exclaims one of the others before letting off several shots towards the G-Wagon.

They run to the other side of the wreckage. No one is there. Instead, two active grenades lie in his place.

BOOM!—goes the flashbangs. The men stagger back from the heat and light.

One is then met with a punch to the jaw, followed by a kick to the groin, and an elbow strike to the top of the spine. He falls.

The other man blinks, trying to clear his vision. He raises his gun toward the figure moving toward him. He fires two shots.

"Uugh," he hears. Matthias falls.

The man still in a daze stumbles off. He turns to find the guy he shot, still on the ground. No, wait. He's still moving.

Six-to-eleven shot! Clear!

A shot rings. The man falls; a bullet piercing his torso.

Matthias lowers his gun and gets up. He checks his body armor, eyeing the two bullet holes along his sternum. He quickly checks for any punctures beyond the metal plates, then runs a hand over his chest for blood. *Negative on both. Keep going.*

RATTA RATTA RATTA RATTA!—automatic gunfire erupts towards him.

Matthias dives to the ground, rolling back to the G-Wagon.

More shots ring from another man, wielding a custom .50 Desert Eagle with an extended magazine.

"YOUR ASS IS DEAD, BITCH!" the man bellows. He rushes to the G-Wagon—no one is there.

He then spots movement from the van, as if someone is inside.

The Desert Eagle roars, its rounds shattering the van's bulletproof windshield as it finally gives way.

The man rushes to the driver's side and, without hesitation, empties his magazine into the van's interior. No one is there. He looks around.

"WHERE ARE YOU MOTHFUCKER?" he yells, above the car alarms. "POKE YOUR HEAD OUT SO I CAN SEND YOU TO HELL WITH YOUR MOTHER!"

"Fire in the hole," he hears, before a canister falls onto his feet.

BOOM!—the man falters back, blinded from the flashbang.

Matthias hops off the top of the van, where he was perched, and approaches with one thought:

Wolves kill sheep.

Matthias delivers a palm strike to the head, then a blow to the forearm to make the man drop the Desert Eagle.

He then unleashes a flurry of blows, driving his fists into the man's vital organs as if striking the makiwara. The man convulses with blood pouring from his mouth and nose, before falling face-first onto the ground.

"And don't talk about my mother again," Matthias says, before he kicks his target in the head. He then stews within the war zone around him. He feels like howling.

CHAPTER 11

Hours later, back in Manhattan, Matthias strides through the lobby of One Police Plaza and stops at the bench desk. "I'm a bail enforcement officer requesting extradition of a violator for arraignment."

"Why don't you say hello first, pal?" replies the desk sergeant. "You come in here all huffy ain't gonna get you any favors, *capeesh?*"

Matthias shoots a look at the sergeant before easing to a more agreeable expression. For now, he'll play nice. He needs access to their computer.

"How you're doing?" Matthias asks, showing his bail enforcement ID. "Having a good day? Hope so. Sgt. Giordano, right? That's what your nameplate says. I'm putting in a request to extradite a bail violator in a holding cell in Camden, New Jersey. Here's the paperwork and the arrest warrant."

"You couldn't bring the guy back yourself?"

"My van had a flat tire," Matthias says. *More like a smashed engine and bullet holes.* "Besides, he has other warrants there. Once they arraign him, they'll hold him to be picked up."

Sgt. Giordano looks over the paperwork. "Why don't you join the force if you want to catch criminals? We could use big guys like you."

"You guys don't pay well. I can make more selling pics of my feet on the internet."

Sgt. Giordano frowns at Matthias. "Well, it's better than dressing up in riot gear for bail jumpers."

"Sgt. Giordano, I just want my paperwork processed and to use a computer to electronically deliver the warrant. I've been up for twenty-eight hours and traveled two hundred miles for this, so I'm a little tired. If you don't want to do it, can you bring me someone who can?"

"Twenty-eight hours?" Sgt. Giordano says. "That's it? I once spent four days straight bagging gang members in the Brooklyn, in between arresting a drug mule charged with a drive-by. Cry me a river, kid."

Matthias begins to twitch. *Drag this portly bitch through the bench desk's window and snap his neck. Wolves kill sheep.*

Sgt. Giordno then chuckles. "Relax, tough guy. I'm just busting your chops a little." He turns to the computer on the desk. "What's your name?"

"Matthias Monroe."

"Matthias Monroe," Giordano repeats slowly, typing on the keyboard. "I don't think with a name like that you came outta the projects."

"I grew up in Switzerland, if you must know."

"Switzerland? So you're an international man. No wonder you don't get New York humor." A few moments later, he pulls from his computer. "Okay, you're registered with the State. Go down this hall to the computer terminals and do what you gotta do."

Matthias follows Sgt. Giordano's directions to a computer room, where officers from various agencies are stationed at cubicles. He sits at a workstation and navigates through the NYPD intranet until he locates the secure site for Internal Affairs, requiring a username and password to proceed.

Matthias pulls out his phone, launching the password-hacking app downloaded from his cloud server, and plugs it into the computer tower. He opens the app, enters the Internal Affairs URL, and starts the process.

The monitor flickers, displaying a series of dialog boxes that flash lines of code, cycling permutations on screen. After a few minutes, the app on the phone generates a dummy login and password.

Matthias enters the password on the site and scrolls through the access granted. He navigates to the Investigative Review database and types in his birth mother's name: Olufemi Noah. One file appears. He begins reading the summary.

‘*Officer Frank Russo responded to a report of a woman with an infant behaving erratically at West 148th Street and 8th Avenue. Upon approach, the suspect, later identified as Olufemi Noah, attempted to assault Officer Russo with a pocketknife. In response, Officer Russo discharged three rounds from his service weapon. Noah was pronounced DOA at Harlem Hospital at 11:41 a.m. The infant was transferred to the Administration for Children's Services for evaluation. The case was referred to Internal Affairs, which exonerated Officer Russo, citing the event a justifiable and defensible shooting.*’

Matthias' temper rises and his jaw tightens. He rereads the words on the screen, hoping if not willing them to make sense. They don't. He lets out another growl, as he feels his breath going shallow. He then looks at the officers in the room, as they sip coffee and exchange details about their cases, feeling the need to rip their hearts from their chests.

"Romania. Zurich. Sudan. Florianópolis. Bangkok," he mutters under his breath, grasping for the familiar descent into calm. Nothing—no sinking, no stillness, as the phrases are programmed to do. Only continued rage.

"*Leiden die Kinder,*" he then says without him knowing.

Matthias exhales sharply, dragging his fury under control, redirecting his attention toward Russo. He searches for information—addresses, family members, social media—but most of the details are greyed out and blurred, redacted from view.

That's odd, he concludes, before scanning Russo's credentials: a 31-year NYPD veteran who climbed the ranks from patrol officer to sergeant, then captain of the Bronx Crime Squad—and then Assistant Chief of the Detective Bureau.

Fuck! He's high up on the food chain. All of his personal records would be classified. He'll have to find another way to find this bastard.

"Hey, buddy," Sgt. Giordano calls from the bench desk as Matthias heads toward the exit. "We called the police in Camden. You caused a shit-ton of trouble there? You're not supposed to use pyro canisters to make an arrest."

"You can't use pyros," says Matthias. "I can. Bail enforcement don't have to play the same rules you do."

"You can argue with them about that. Meanwhile, it's gonna be a fee to extradite the guy from there to here. About $1200. You gotta pay us so we can pay them, so add 30% on that."

"$1560? That'll eat into my profits. I would have gone out there and risk my life for nothing."

"Welcome to the NYPD, international man," smirks Sgt. Giordano, handing him an invoice. "Pay the clerk before you leave."

CHAPTER 12

"I see you're one of those action-movie types," says Fat Pat in the back room of his pawn shop. "Someone who wants to blow shit up and walk away with flames behind them in slow motion."

"Things were a little turbulent," Matthias says, "but the target is in custody. That's all that matters."

"Turbulent? You killed two guys, and one of them is in critical. Not to mention you played psycho video game all up on their streets. I'm surprised you're not in a cell next to him."

"Because, beyond the fireworks, the cops know it was a legit apprehension. No laws were broken, just a few city ordinances. And none of them were good guys to begin with. The police just didn't bring them in."

"Good thing they didn't. If they did, I wouldn't have got my money back. But don't be surprised if the police come right around and arrest you." Fat Pat then lets out a smirk. "If they do, I'll post your bail. You'll just need fifteen percent of the bond in cash, sign over your property deeds, and hand me a kidney. Or a liver. They fetch well on the black market."

Matthias lets out an exhausted huff. He's been up for thirty hours straight. He's petering out.

"Oh, did scabby hands have a rough night?" Fat Pat then says. "Well, once again I have come to deliver for the lost souls. I went to my favorite gentleman's club last night and a girl that works there needs some help, so I thought of you."

"What kind of help?"

"She wants you to tail a guy. Some private investigating stuff. You do that too, right? Plus, she's got that hourglass shape that always make you want to check the time, so if you play your cards right you might be drooling on her like a baby during a lullaby."

Back in his office, after some much-needed rest, Matthias sits on the floor in the lotus position, attempting to meditate into the noiseless peace. His hypnotic phrases are not getting him there, and since triggering the German axiom, he's been beset with those specters and demons, making him think dark. *So what if he killed some drug dealers? Big fucking deal. Their consequences were due. Fuck them—let their corpses burn. Leiden die Kinder.*

Matthias tries once more to grasp the transcendental, pulling up memories of good times—hanging with friends in Zurich, rounds of Kabaddi in the Sudan, ATV racing in Florianópolis, playing poker with burlesque dancers in Bangkok.

The dark thoughts intervene; *now he's a killer, all started by that cop who ripped his mother from him. So how about showing that fuck what he'd made? How about foot roasting him with a soldering iron? Or waterboard him with vinegar? Or tying him down and flaying him strip by strip, peeling his skin off until his flesh is red as a stewed tomato? Leiden die Kinder.*

Matthias exhales futilely. His thoughts are on some shit today.

His focus is then shifted when there's a faint knock on the door. He gets up to check the door monitor and sees a woman standing outside.

"Are you Mr. Monroe?" she asks with a Spanish accent when he opens the door. "My name is Ms. Navarro. Pat told me to contact you about a problem I have."

From her almond skin and champagne eyes to her ample chest and the jeans hugging her hips, she stands at the doorway with an allure—pouty yet contrived—as if knowing she can strike a match to any man's libido.

Well, he muses, as his dark thoughts simmer. *Okay, then.*

"Yes," he recovers with a burrowed focus. "He said you need an investigator. What is the situation?"

"There is this guy. He has been harassing me at work, and I need help in making him go away."

Matthias steps aside, inviting her in. *"Tome asiento,"* he says to her as he closes the door. *"¿De dónde es, por cierto?"*

She smirks as she sits in a chair. *"Soy de San Ignacio, en Belice. ¿Sabe bien español, Señor Monroe? ¿O solo lo suficiente para impresionar a las latinas?"*

"Lo suficiente para seguir el ritmo de mis telenovelas. Y puedes llamarme Matthias."

"Matthias? Pardon me if I'm impolite, but is Matthias a popular name for a black man?"

"As popular as a white guy named Farooq," he replies as he sits in a chair beside her. "Now what do you mean when you said you want this guy to go away? Because I'm not a hitman."

"No. I meant for him to stop coming to the club I work in."

"Pat did mention that you work in a strip club," Matthias says, slightly dismissive.

"Angelfish is more than a strip club. It is a venue for the accomplished man." She then grows defensive. "And why do you say it that way?"

"Because guys getting in a tizzy is an occupational hazard for a stripper. Maybe this will go away once he rubs one out and takes a cold shower."

"I no longer dance," she says. "I'm a waitress. And should I be threatened because he cannot control himself?"

"What is he doing exactly?"

"He comes in very intimidating, always asking me out. I say no but he doesn't take that for an answer. He starts fight with other patrons that talk to me, telling them I'm his woman when I am not. And his crew bothers the other girls there too, so they think we're all for them to harass."

"This crew with him, is it a gang?"

"They call themselves the Mott Haven Pirus. He also runs some record label. He makes some of the trap music that is out now." She then leans in toward him. "The last time he was there, he told me what he wants to do to me, and said he knows where I live and that he'll come over soon to do it."

"Well, he seems to fit the gangster stalker vibe. Why don't you tell the owners you don't feel safe with him around? Or go to the cops with a complaint?"

"He spends a lot of money there, so they let him stay and tell me not to make a fuss. And the police do not take us girls seriously. There has to be a lot of proof for them to do something. That is why I am here."

"Why don't you just leave altogether?"

"He said he knows where I live, so that wouldn't matter." She then goes into her handbag and pulls out a folder. "His name is Laquan Jackson. Here is the information I could find on him. His arrests records and court documents. I also have pictures of his license plate." She then leans towards him again, touching his arm, striking the match. "Maybe there is something here you can find on him so I can go to the police."

Matthias looks at her as she once again pouts a little. He shouldn't partake in this, playing detective when he has his own project to conduct. And the event in Camden has to settle before he can be a menace on these streets.

Then again, what the hell? She is fine.

"I could start with the arrest records," he says as he takes the folder from her. "And if he's with the Bloods and runs a music company, perhaps there's some illegalities there that can be fished out." Matthias then remembers the amount he paid to the police earlier. He wants some of his money back. "For a few days of surveillance, that'll be $750."

She doesn't flinch as she reaches into her handbag again, pulling out a bankroll and counting through the large bills. "Do you have change for a hundred?"

Matthias goes to his desk and opens the petty cash lockbox, thumbing through the stack of bills inside. "Afraid not. Just give me seven and owe me a lap dance later."

She puts her hand on her hip, playfully. "I told you I don't dance anymore. And when I did mine weren't $50."

"With how you're built I don't doubt it. Leave me your number so I can contact you."

She reaches into her handbag once more and pulls out a business card, handing it to him along with the cash. He flips it over, finding only a picture of an angelfish.

"What is this?" Matthias asks.

"This is how you can reach me," she says. "The card has one of those QR codes where you scan the picture, and the number pops up on your phone."

"I should contact you in a few days, Ms. Navarro."

She smiles as she stands to leave, "Please, call me Amora. I look forward to hearing from you."

Matthias watches Amora as she turns and leaves the office, her apple bottom swaying out the door.

Look at that ass, slithers into his mind as the dark thoughts reappear.

Matthias lets out a huff. His thoughts are on some shit today.

CHAPTER 13

Jacksonville, NC

Bridges lies in a military base' hospital bed—one arm strapped to an IV delivering a chelation concoction, while a nurse preps the other with a syringe filled with Sermorelin, giving him the vigor of a man twenty years younger. As he's injected, his phone rings. It's Chambers.

"Yeah."

"Where are you? Your office said you left town."

"I'm getting some of your guys' happy juice. I'll be back tomorrow."

"Well, you need to come back to D.C."

"My charter is refueling for the evening. What is this about?"

"Robert," a man's voice sharply interjects, revealing a three-way call. "This is Secretary Bellinger. I'm going to contact the base commander to have MPs escort you to the airport. Be at the Pentagon in three hours."

A taxi rolls up to the Pentagon entrance and slows to a stop. Bridges steps out, making his way up the portico, where he's met by Chambers.

"Follow me," says Chambers, who brusquely turns into the building.

"Hello, Robert," mocks Bridges to the frostiness as he follows. "How was your trip? What movie did you see on the plane? Did the kid who sat behind you kick your seat during the flight? Yes, he did. Thank you for asking, Aaron."

Chambers turns to Bridges while continuing through the Pentagon halls. "What are you doing using my name to sign off on video scrubs and bank data searches in New York?"

"It's for a training op. Is that what this is about?"

"No. But it's a dick move."

"I didn't mean to upset you," Bridges says insincerely. "Do you want a hug?"

"Save your hugs for them," Chambers replies before they enter a nondescript boardroom.

Three people are inside, sitting on one side of the table. Bridges is only familiar with one of them: Kevin Bellinger, Secretary of the Department of Homeland Security.

"Mister Secretary," greets Bridges.

"Sit down, Robert," Bellinger says without preamble. "And for your information, The International Criminal Court won't charge war crimes without a resolution from a UN tribunal and a majority vote from both the House and the Senate. Threatening Aaron wouldn't have gone anywhere."

"I know," says Bridges as he takes a seat. "You should ask why he didn't know that."

"Because he has more pressing matters than to counterpoint someone who takes meetings in diners." Bellinger then motions to the other two beside him. "This is Nathan Kennedy, Deputy Commander of U.S. Cyber Command, and Jessica Bright, Deputy Commissioner for the Department of Energy."

"Hello to you both," says Bridges.

"Robert," says Bellinger, "a few days ago, you asked Aaron to investigate Quentin McBride. While tracing a private citizen is generally frowned upon—especially for personal reasons—Aaron discovered something that warrants further investigation. Aaron, please relay the findings of your inquiry."

"There was no unusual chatter with his phone," says Chambers, "but when checking his cloud server, the team found a file from a SIM card to a network flagged for criminal activity. From there I contacted Cyber Command for analysis. Here the Deputy Commander will proceed with the details."

"Our surveillance worked around the cloud server's security to access the metadata of the file." Kennedy pulls out his phone. "We extracted text exchanges between McBride and an unknown person. Here's their interaction." Kennedy then reads from his phone:

"Unknown – *'We will secure cargo when near Jebel Ali.'*
McBride – *'Who to deliver to at port?'*
Unknown – *'Yom al-Kabash at Oman Radiology Centre.'*"

"And here's another set of messages," Kennedy says:

"Unknown – *'Blueprints are not understood.'*
McBride – *'What is not understood?'*
Unknown – *'We use C4.'*
McBride – *'Your chemist should use Octogen.'*"

"Octogen is an explosive resourced from Syria," says Bellinger. "They're used to detonate a radiological dispersal device—a dirty bomb."

"Mr. Bridges," then says Deputy Bright, "six months ago, Mr. McBride reached an agreement with a company called RNTI Energy in South Africa. They export radiochemical products to medical supply companies for cancer treatment. McBride is to employ your privateers—"

"Soldiers, Deputy Bright," Bridges interrupts. "They are soldiers."

"—to provide security and logistics as RNTI ships their products abroad."

"And how would you know this?"

"The DoE has been monitoring rogue entities in their ability to obtain radioactive materials. Last month, one of RNTI's clients ordered Strontium-90 for a radiology center in Oman. Only there is no listing for this clinic, yet two shipments were already made to this Yom al-Kabash person. A full search was made, and the only thing pulled up was the interpretation of his name. Yom al-Kabash in Arabic means Day of the Ram."

"Robert," says Bellinger, "we believe your company could be trafficking nuclear materials to a criminal network, with McBride being a point of contact."

Bridges looks at each one, then smirks. "Kevin, I left my day spa for this shit?"

"Mr. Bridges," Kennedy says, "these allegations are serious."

"So is chlamydia. Rub ointment on it, and it'll go away."

"Jesus, Robert," exclaims Chambers.

"That's alright, Aaron," Kennedy replies. "I've been informed of his brand of speaking. It's just assumed he's taken a mortar shell to the head."

"You're saying my company is making dirty bombs, and I'm the one off in the head? You've been monitoring this company for months with no leads or suspects, but suddenly you have enough intel for a secret meeting?"

"We had no support beyond speculation," says Bright, "until you gave Aaron your CEO's information, and then we discovered the thread."

"You guys fucked up your intel and are trying to frame the company to cover up." Bridges turns to Bellinger. "What's next Kevin, search warrants for Bigfoot?"

"While there are some gaps in the analysis," Bellinger replies, "that doesn't make it a red herring. Your guy is a participant in the illegal possession of radioactive material, and we need to know the extent of his involvement. Now, all three of us agree that this is imperative to national security. However, we need more evidence before bringing this to The Cabinet, which is why we need your cooperation in providing us with knowledge on this matter."

"Cooperation? Or coercion?"

"Whichever makes you comfortable."

"In return," says Bright, "we are willing to offer you immunity from prosecution."

"You're offering me whistleblower protection? You want me to go to Quentin and ask him if he's been making dirty bombs for terrorists, and after he stop rolling on the floor from laughter, is he supposed to show me the blueprints?"

"We are confident that you will gather the information in an appropriate manner."

"Are you now?" Bridges leans back in his chair. "And if I refuse?"

"Then we'll report this without your cooperation," Bellinger replies, "who amid The Cabinet's inquiry, will freeze your assets and charge your entire board with providing materials to terrorists. However, cooperating can give you an umbrella from any seizures or prosecutions."

Bridges from his seat assess his options: turn on one of his soldiers or watch as the company get bombarded with federal indictments. Sure, he wanted dirt on McBride, but only to fire him—not for espionage and treason. On the other hand, if McBride is indeed being nefarious at the helm, it'll be a death blow for the company. He'll need time to think this over.

"I'll need time to think this over."

"There isn't a play you can maneuver from, Robert," Bellinger says. "You'll either accept this now, or its no deal."

Bridges twists his mouth in response. He's already doing circus acts for shit contracts. He can't afford the company to be branded as duplicitous on the government's dime. He has no choice but to play along—for now.

"I guess I'm your man then," he says. "Perhaps Bigfoot will be with Amelia Ehrhardt riding shotgun."

CHAPTER 14

As Matthias sits in his office, peering into his computer for anything he can find on Russo, one of his phone's rings—from Unknown.

"Hello, Andreus."

"Are you out of your mind?" Andreus seethes on the other end.

"Please leave a message after the beep," Matthias replies dryly. "I'll get to you at my earliest convenience."

"Your mother and I heard about your ruckus in New Jersey. What are you doing getting involved in domestic affairs? And why are you using munitions that will attract an investigation from federal agencies?"

"I think you're blowing this out of proportion. There were a few scraped knees. That's all."

"And where did you get a bulletproof van?"

"I rented it from a traveling dominatrix," Matthias says with a smirk. "She'll throw in a free month if I find someone to be her sub. Want her number?"

"I am not in the mood, little boy," Andreus scolds.

Matthias squints from the slight. "I'm not a little boy, Johnathan."

Andreus mumbles from being called his government name, before returning to Matthias. "Your alias as a bail enforcement officer is just that—an alias. It is not for you to swing around like some comic book hero."

"Those guys were terrorizing the neighborhood, and the cops there did nothing about it."

"So you diverged from your project for a couple of gangbangers. Going forward, you'll be assigned a logistics analyst to monitor your activities, with authority to overrule your actions when they don't comply with the directives of your project."

"I do not need an analyst. I can run my own project without someone shadowing me."

"I'm not suggesting. I'm telling you that you will have one."

"And if I say no?" Matthias asks defiantly.

"Then I'll come to America and shoot you in the head."

Matthias simmers at the threat—not that Andreus made it, but that the old man could carry it out. "What's next? You want me to ask for permission to go to the bathroom?"

"You know how to shit on yourself without one, that's for sure. You call me with your analyst tomorrow."

He hangs up abruptly, leaving Matthias to stew in the silence. He then reaches for one of his other phones and dials the number for Zurich. He'll cut this decision off at the root.

"Matthias," she says when she picks up. "How is life in America treating you?"

"Mum, did you assign an analyst to me?"

"Are you well? I heard your recent adventure was rather distressing."

"I do not need—"

"Judging by your recent activities," she interrupts, "the authenticators have concluded otherwise. From your mayhem—with the bond call from the Camden police, and the insurance claim from the facility you acquired the armored vehicle from—your expenses have ranged above your budget."

"They can afford it," Matthias erupts. "If those mopheads can force countries to be their constituents for the World Bank, they can pay a surety bond."

"I do not know what you're talking about," she says coolly. "Apparently, you tell tales when you have free rein. This only illustrates the need for an analyst, to prevent you from going off the reservation. This is what the authenticators will accept in lieu of deeming you *Ex-Delicto*. Since neither you nor I would want that, this addendum will be accepted by you. Tomorrow at 9 a.m. your time, I will expect a status report with your analyst present."

"Andreus already scheduled me for a status report."

"Then you will give two," she says. "*Verstanden?*"

He's silent at first, then reluctantly complies. "*Verstanden.*"

"Now if there are no other matters, I must attend a conference call. *Ich hab' dich lieb.*"

"Hmmph," Matthias grunts, before he hangs up the phone. He then feels the specters and demons within him claw to the surface—goading him. *Fuck them. Fuck the authenticators. This is his project. He will not be told who to work with.* Matthias glances at his workout area, at the heavy bag hanging from the ceiling. He walks to it, picking it as the prey to unleash on.

Thump, thump-thump, thump, he hammers and kicks at the weight. Ten minutes in, sweaty and panting from his assault, the morbid thoughts continue. *This undermining is fucking unacceptable. Now if something happened to their dipshit analyst, it would be their fault. A mishap of some kind. Poisoned food. Severed brake lines. Or maybe just a fucking broken neck from a guillotine headlock. Leiden die Kinder.*

A knock comes from the front door. Matthias pauses his violent fantasy and checks the door monitor, to see Nigel standing on the other side, holding a manila folder. What does he want?

"Hello, Mr. Monroe," says Nigel. "I think this is a good time to introduce myself to you."

"Nigel, we've met."

"Yes, but not as your logistics analyst."

Matthias' eyes grow wide. "What's that now?"

"I'm here to be your logistics analyst for your project."

Mathias looks at him, stilled in the moment. Is this a trick? "I don't know what you're talking about. What is a logic assessor?"

"Logistics analyst," Nigel corrects. "I believe you know what it is."

"Nigel, you're probably thinking of another tenant in the building. I don't know anything about being a logging advisor."

"I understand you wanting to maintain anonymity," Nigel says, "but I am the one who set up your office, to your specifications and at Ms. Gruber's request. So I would have to have some knowledge of your project for you to operate."

"What project are you talking about?" Matthias asks. "I'm a bail enforcement agent. My projects are catching jumpers."

"I guess we can keep up this charade," Nigel says as he looks around the office floor's hallway, "but can we do it inside? I prefer not to discuss this in the open hall. Ms. Dereschuk has an affinity for eavesdropping."

There are no tells in his mannerisms that Matthias picks up: no lying ticks or spasms, no feet shuffling or uneven vocal inflections. And his denials didn't make Nigel waver, instead saying enough to perk interest. Squinting suspiciously, Matthias moves aside to let him in.

"It's rather drab in here," Nigel says, looking around the office. "You should get a throw rug. You'd be surprised how it adds to the decor."

"Since when did the authenticators start using concierges for logistic analysts?" Matthias asks as he closes the door, ending his rebuff. "They need to upgrade their hiring pool."

"I'm the building manager. Ms. Gruber arranged for me to oversee things here while I work on my master's, with the condition that I'm to be unassuming until the time for assistance. Now seems to be that time."

"So you're here to spy on me."

"You should think of it as Ms. Gruber anticipating your eventual need. And I do tangible work here in the building. I arrange for building repairs and maintain its appearance."

"Because you're the concierge."

"Again, I'm the building manager."

"Then go change some lightbulbs," rages Matthias, the effects of his dark thoughts reigniting. "I don't need a chaperone, tattling to the headmaster about my business."

"She mentioned you might be resistant, perhaps distrust stemming from training for survival since a toddler."

He scoffs. "You don't know about my background."

"I've seen your dossier before you arrived, so I have some gathering of your account."

"You seen my dossier?" Matthias asks.

"Parts of it. Is it true you were attacked by a bear? That must've been traumatizing."

"Hey Sigmund, save the therapy for your next client. I run my project my way. And that doesn't include you."

Nigel shows the folder in his hand. "Perhaps this will change your perspective on whether you need my services."

"And what is that?"

"The details you were looking for on Frank Russo. Ms. Gruber told me to look him up, as my knowledge of computer science and data retrieval grants me access you'd wouldn't be privy to."

Matthias eyes Nigel skeptically as he takes the folder, where he sees a divorce decree, filings for a restraining order, and a real estate listing for a house on sale.

"While police officers' personal details are kept off internet searches," Nigel resumes, "their families aren't. His wife filed for divorce last year and issued a restraining order against him, and is selling the house they used to live in."

As Matthias scans the folder, he unlocks the ruse. *The downloaded software, the dead end at the police precinct—it was all meant to compel him toward the need for an analyst. Then one appears and all along it's the guy taking out the garbage. That tricky broad.*

"I could've paid a hacker for this," Matthias then says.

"With the computer lab at Columbia University at my disposal, my analysis would be more in-depth than someone mucking about on a TOR browser." Nigel heads for the door. "I'll leave you to have a proper look through the material, and tomorrow we can discuss a plan of action." Nigel opens the door and turns to Matthias. "You should get some plants as well. A few ferns would spruce up the place." He leaves.

Matthias tosses the folder onto his desk. *He's been duped by his mother, threatened with being shot by his trainer, and is getting punked now by some twerp who was laying down rat pellets a minute ago.* Matthias looks at the heavy bag once more. He needs to beat the hell out of something.

CHAPTER 15

"The target has relocated since his divorce," says Nigel the next morning in the office, speaking into Matthias' phone. "However, the property he lived in is still on the market. Miranda Ortiz is the estate agent handling the sale, so I could infiltrate her computer to find his current location. In the meantime, Matthias will go to the house and see if there's information that might give a clue to his whereabouts—junk mail, council notices, rubbish bins."

Matthias turns to Nigel. "You want me to go through garbage?"

"You will swim through sewer pipes if you need to," Andreus answers from the other end of the phone. "Also, talk to this estate agent. Act as though you're interested in buying the house to see if she would disclose his whereabouts."

"Both the house and the realtor are in Tarrytown. That's a ninety-minute drive from here."

"You should get along then," Andreus says.

Minutes later, Matthias sits behind the wheel of his rental car, staring blankly at the city roads. *Being ordered around by this twerp must be an abomination. No sheep should ever bleat at a wolf.*

Determined to put some distance between him and the orders forced on him, he drives toward lower Manhattan. He needs to collect the rest of his stuff from Hodges anyway.

Nearly ten miles in, as Matthias parks across from the military surplus store, his phone rings. It's Nigel.

"Didn't I just see you half an hour ago?"

"And apparently, you've already meandered off to somewhere. Why are you in lower Manhattan?"

"What makes you think that?"

After a moment of silence, Nigel returns, "You're on Delancy Street between Allen and Orchard."

"Are you tracking me?"

"I could be tracking your car. Or your mobile. Or perhaps I have a drone tailing you. I might even be using satellite imagery and sending the snapshots to Ms. Gruber. Or maybe all in combination."

Matthias stares out the car window. *He can't maneuver if he's being snitched on. A little misdirection should get this fuck off his back.*

"If you must know, I'm in Chinatown for some Kung Pao Chicken."

"Pardon?"

"The ride to Tarrytown's ninety minutes, and I'm hungry, so I'm getting food before I go dumpster diving. What's the point of me having an analyst if I'm still doing the legwork—I would ask. Not that I'm complaining."

"I'm compiling the estate agent's background as we speak," Nigel says defensively. "I'm doing my part. I'll assume you'll be off doing yours shortly."

"Yeah. Right on it." Matthias hangs up and tosses the phone into the back seat. He then looks across to the surplus store. Maybe Hodges has something that could assist in his freedom.

"Hey, numbskull," he hears as he walks into the store. "That stunt you did in New Jersey could get my FFL revoked. The State Police traced the model number of the flashbangs to my store."

"Hello to you too," Matthias replies. "And what do you expect when selling military-grade weapons, that they don't get used? Besides, the police have to trace any explosive device used as a formality."

"They can still make an inquiry to the Feds. The ATF could raid the place and confiscate my inventory."

"I wouldn't want them trampling through Shangri-La," Matthias says, waving his arms to showcase the grime of the store, "so if they do show up, tell them the flashbangs were never picked up by the buyer, which made them yours to sell. And you did—to a professional bondsman in pursuit of a fugitive. You haven't broken any laws."

"You must've been one of those kids that played a lot of shooter video games. Those guys always screwed up in actual campaigns."

"How about we discuss my readiness for combat later. I'm here to get the rest of my stuff. And I also need a radio frequency signal detector."

Hodges huffs off the argument. "Wait here," he says before he goes into his back office. Moments later, he returns with a duffle bag and a small box. He hands Matthias the bag.

"You've got two unlocked phones, three boxes of hollow-point 9mm rounds for your Glocks, more plates for your vests, and a police radio scanner." He then hands him the box. "This RF detector can pinpoint Bluetooth, Wi-Fi, and GPS signals within fifty feet. That about clears your credit."

"And what's the status on the special order I asked you about?"

"I know a guy that can build it," Hodges says. "For $7000."

"What? I can build my own for a thousand."

"If you can build an AR-15 with a carbine upper, a high-end trigger, an ambidextrous lower receiver, a .30-caliber suppressor, and a collapsible buttstock, go for it. But you know you won't find an FFL dealer willing to accept the parts banned in the city. That's why you asked for someone out of state to build it. So, if you want them to do it and bring it into New York, it's going to cost you $7000."

Matthias rolls his eyes. *He's sure he's being price gouged. And to get the money, he'd have to go to the office and then come back, letting Nigel pin his locations with the trackers and develop a pattern to follow. Never mind. It isn't essential for the project.*

"What kind of watch is that?" Hodges then asks, suddenly distracted, pointing to Matthias' wrist. "Is that a Patek Philippe?"

"Yeah."

"I had one of those once," he says, slightly reflective. "When I joined the Army, my father gave it to me as a gift. White gold with a blue dial, and a clear back so you can see the mechanisms. That was the best gift I ever got. I lost it when I was deployed in Lebanon." He's silent for a moment, then says, "Tell you what, if you give me the watch, I'll get you the rifle with a $10,000 credit to the store."

"Forget it. This watch is worth much more."

"You're going to need supplies at some point," Hodges says, now with a salesman's tone. "More bullets. More plates for your vest. Surveillance equipment. Hell, I'll get you enough flashbangs and grenades to look like fireworks on the Fourth of July. People in your line of work need a plug."

"Weren't you just worried about your FFL being taken away? Now you want to run arms like the cartels?"

"I can have it shipped to Pat. He has a pawnbroker's FFL."

Matthias twists his mouth and strokes his face in thought. *Maybe he's being worked over by Hodges again. And he's not keen on giving away gifts from Mum. But one gets things to get more things. Besides, assets have to be maintained. Their turnaround's a bitch to deal with.*

"Fine," he says, removing the watch and handing it to Hodges. "But the line of credit is twenty grand. And I want the rifle ASAP."

"Yeah. Sure," Hodges says, already tuning him out as he admires the watch in the light.

After loading the items inside the car, Matthias pulls out the RF detector to sweep the vehicle for any devices Nigel might have planted. Finding nothing suspicious, he figures it must be the phone. He swaps the SIM into a new phone and drops the old one down a sewer grate.

Matthias then gets in the car and settles behind the wheel, reflecting on the directives given to him. *Travel ninety minutes to comb through trash, or...he could go somewhere else. He would just need to swing by the office for cash. Good thing there's an alternate route inside.*

Within the hour, Matthias parks behind his office building, where a steel gate topped with barbed wire guards the service alley. He goes to the gate, punches in the code on its keypad and walks into the alley, heading straight for the service elevator to take to his floor.

Once in his office, he goes to his wall safe. He pulls out $10,000, slips the cash into an envelope, and tucks it into the inside of his jacket. Then he turns right around and exit the office.

Where he's met by Nigel in front of the doorway, peering inquisitively at him like a bloodhound.

"Hey," says Matthias, closing the door behind him. "How are you? How's the family?"

"You're here," Nigel says. "But you shouldn't be."

"Then it must be magic. Hocus pocus. Abracadabra. Poof. Now I'm gone." He then proceeds to the passenger elevators.

"Why are you back?" Nigel asks as he trails behind him. "You should be on the way to Tarrytown."

"I'm heading there now."

"Why didn't you come in through the front entrance?"

"How do you know I didn't?"

"The service alley is monitored with security cameras and motion detectors."

"You must have a lot of videos of cats humping in the alley," Mathias says as he presses the elevator button.

Nigel walks up to him and folds his arms across his chest. "You still haven't explained why you came back."

"I had to use the bathroom," Matthias says as the elevator arrives. "Kung Pao Chicken from a street vendor runs right through you."

CHAPTER 16

An hour later, Matthias is parked in the Bronx, looking at a bar within a mix of storefronts along its strip. A crumbling-looking dive—not for those with a taste for merlot. More for a gang-affiliated music man loving to dwell in the muck. He watches as henchmen enter the bar in numbers, configuring a way to approach. *There's no way to reach the crux without getting stung. Better to stir the hive with smoke to get to its queen.*

Matthias crosses the street and enters the bar, the stench of liquor and depression hitting him, as a few soulless patrons drink at their tables. He spots a bartender behind the counter and walks to him.

"How you're doing? May I have your best light IPA?"

The bartender scowls. "You want what?"

"A light IPA. An import from Belgium would be fantastic."

"I don't got no IPA," the bartender blurts. "Go to some other bar for that import shit."

"Do you sell Heineken?"

"Yeah."

"They're from Holland. Belgium's next door. If you can get one, you could get the other."

"I don't have it, so maybe you should leave. This is a private bar anyway."

"Oh," says Matthias. "How much for membership? I've been looking for an exclusive club to join."

"Listen, motherfucker. There ain't nothing here for you but an ass kicking if you don't get out."

"Or, you can take this for yourself," Matthias pulls out the envelope and counts off $200, placing it on the counter, "and tell Laquan someone's here to talk business."

The bartender glances at the money, then at Matthias. "Who the fuck are you, and why the fuck you wanna talk to Laquan?"

"You should refrain from cursing. It doesn't make you intimidating. Just tell Laquan someone's here to speak to him."

The bartender takes a moment before scooping the money into his pocket. "You know what? You want to see him? You can walk there yourself. He's in the back, wearing a red suit."

Matthias slides the envelope back into his jacket, then looks at the bartender again. "Gimme a beer."

The bartender returns his scorn, then grabs a bottle and hands it over to him.

Matthias takes the bottle and walks down a corridor to the back of the bar. The space opens into a room filled with people talking, their smoke and liquor pulsing the air.

Wearing a red suit, huh? he muses. *They all have on red, like an army for the Kool Aid Man.* He scans through the crowd until he spots a man sitting alone towards the back, surrounded by a few henchmen at adjoined tables. *He looks important. That must be him.*

Matthias slips into a chair and sips his beer as he continues his recon. He picks up a few looks from the crew toward him, as his clothes makes him stand out to their red vibe. A few start to murmur. A few guns are gripped in their hands.

"Yo, motherfucker," he hears, a deep voice cutting through the room. He looks up to see a large guy beside him. About six-foot-four and 300 lbs., with a bug-eyed look. "You in my seat. Get the fuck up!"

The chatter halts, as all eyes shift to Matthias and the brute. Matthias looks the guy over. He scoffs and takes another sip of beer.

"You hear me, bitch?" the brute snarls as he steps closer, towering over Matthias. "Get up, or I'll make you crawl for life."

Matthias looks back up at the man. *Time for smoke.*

In a flash—a kick the knee, then a brutal heel stomp to the foot.

The brute hops and buckles from the attack, off balance.

Matthias leaps from his chair. He grabs the beer bottle and smashes it across the guy's face.

The henchman reels back further, beer and blood trickling off his forehead.

Matthias pivots around him and kicks out the back of the injured knee. He falls back, right into Matthias' arms, who locks him into a full nelson grappling hold.

The brute thrashes wildly, his unbalance leading them both to slam into the nearest wall with a thud.

Then, several *clicks* echo throughout the room. Matthias looks up to spot the other henchmen aiming their guns at him.

"Careful, boys," Matthias says, keeping his captive shielded in front of him. "You might miss and hit me."

"Bitch," one of them growls. "You touching my crew like you bulletproof?"

"I just need a few minutes with the main man," he nods to Laquan. He tightens his grip, hearing pings and crackles from the ligaments under the vice. "Make it quick, because his neck is going to snap."

"I'm the one that's gonna snap you," snarls another crew member, as the group begins shifting for a clear shot. *He's got maybe ten seconds before they make him fit for an urn. Sell the bluff.*

"You want to build a pipeline for distribution?" Matthias aims his words to Laquan. "Be number one on the charts and on the streets? Then tell them to back off and hear me out. Killing me would just be the start of a very bad day. And keep you from making more money. With the right connect you can be Pablo Escobar and Suge Knight at the same time."

As the room squawk like vultures, Laquan looks at Matthias with a cold squint. He then lifts a hand.

"Stop y'all," he says. "I want to hear what he has to say to save his life."

His men stop, lowering their guns and stalling their malice. Matthias releases the hold, and the brute crumples to the floor. Matthias then walks past the men and their steely gazes to take a seat across from Laquan at his table.

"You're either crazy or stupid," Laquan says, "thinking busting a bottle over one of my men's head is healthy for you."

"I wanted to talk. Couldn't get your attention any other way."

"You got my attention," he says. "You also got two minutes to say why you shouldn't have a bullet in your head."

"You got your music on the East Coast and the South, but the Midwest don't know who you are. You need a channel to get into that lane."

"And you are who? Thinking you know what I need."

"My name is J Ruck. I'm with the All Guttah Bloods in Detroit. Just got out of Sing Sing. 'Bout to head home but wanted to make friends before I do."

"You make friends like that?" Laquan motions to his injured henchman, helped up onto a chair by the other men.

"You do in Gen-Pop," says Matthias.

"Kill that bitch, Quan," the brute says, his voice shaky with pain. "I think he broke my foot and fucked up my knee."

"I could've also broken your neck." He turns back to Laquan and reaches into his pocket, tossing his envelope onto the table. "I need a liter of Ice Cream."

"The supermarket is down the block."

"You know what I mean. I need to bring home a liter of liquid methamphetamine."

Laquan lowers his eyes to the envelope. He opens it, sees the money, and starts counting. "There's only $9800 here."

"I took out $200 to buy gum."

"I'd think that amount would run at least fifteen grand. So you're a little short. Besides, what makes you think I'm into drugs? We just rap about the lifestyle. Doesn't mean we live it."

"You ran corners in Mott Haven, got your weight up transporting to upstate, and now you're telling me you left that to do music?" Matthias leans back in the chair. "My set does check ins for the music artists entering our city, so we have a handle on what venues they get to use and what radio stations they promote in. Your artists would be the only East Coast acts able to perform without paying the streets and gyp club owners."

"If it's that easy for you, give your deal to someone else. Why you here if you got a winning ticket?"

"You can't run this with music people liking that limelight shit, or some plug thinking doing twenty for birds is the wave. They'll fuck it up. I'm a wolf, and I know when another wolf who gets it."

"What you sound like is a Fed grabbing at straws," Laquan says, tossing the money back toward Matthias.

"A Fed just fucked up your boy to make a case? That's a mistrial if I was. Besides, this can't be a bust if we don't make it hand-to-hand." Matthias stands. "The drop's directions are in the envelope. The rest of the money will be there. You bring the product there, and you have a connect for both games. If you don't see it, the deal's off and you can keep the money."

"Maybe I'll just keep the money and have you crushed in a car compactor in a junkyard," Laquan replies, a few of his men chuckling in agreement.

"Wild thoughts from someone who just makes music. If you're that thirsty for $9800, you need another job. Or you can give me what I need, and I get you what you need. You've got two days to decide."

Matthias turns to leave, seeing the henchmen close behind him, blocking his path.

"Let him walk out," Laquan says. "He paid for a meet and greet. He must be a groupie."

The worker bees chuckle again as they let Matthias through, watching him make his way out of the back room.

"Bitch ass motherfucker," the injured brute snipes, his foot swelling. "Don't let me see you around here no more."

"At least you have your seat back." Matthias then winks at him.

He resumes into the main area, where the remaining patrons look at him in fear, and the bartender behind the counter throws him his steely gaze. While holding a shotgun in his hands.

"You tearing up my bar, boy?" he goes, pumping a shell into the barrel.

"Blame the guy back there," Matthias says as he walks out of the bar. "He didn't know what an IPA was either."

CHAPTER 17

"He went to three separate banks across the city," Madison says on the phone to Bridges. "One in Chinatown, another on East 39th, and one more on East 68th. I couldn't follow him from that point. He was alone as far as I know."

"Okay," Bridges says. "You and Burroughs stand by while I figure out our next move."

"Yes, sir." Madison hangs up.

Bridges sits in his office, pondering what Johnathan could be up to. *On a mission? Tying up loose ends? Or maybe some broad compelled him to poke his head out for a cause. Wouldn't be the first time.*

He then opens the *El Sharif File* to refamiliarize himself with the target: a prime minister who campaigned for a more egalitarian state. She admonished the Egyptian president for lining his pockets with the country's coffers. She scrutinized his enforcement of Sharia law while delving into his extramarital affairs. She even called him a *dumya—*

a lackey for the West. Typical mudslinging, until she broadcast that the U.S. had secret bases in Cairo, which caused one of them to be attacked. That was a no-no. Plus—more importantly for him—she was fucking his killing machine, who he had sent to watch over her. She had to go.

"You did what?" Johnathan had said to Bridges when he was debriefed.

"The State Department told us to stand pat and let the Egyptian president handle her on his own."

"A guy with a suicide vest had blown himself up at her rally. She and five people were killed."

"Elections can be savage," Bridges replied.

"Is that why you left me off her detail that day?"

"Yes. Otherwise, you would've been killed too. And let this be a lesson to you: don't get attached to clients. They are just things. Maybe you'll think twice about who you have bent over."

Then, Johnathan went AWOL, and a year later a .300 Winchester Magnum found its way into the Egyptian president. Authorities found the sniper rifle, still perched on its mount a hundred meters away, with an old picture of Latifa El Sharif. There also was a note:

'Don't get attached. Presidents are just things.'

Tensions swelled in the region, and the Joint Chiefs had a field day with Bridges.

"This could put a strain on U.S. operations in the Middle East."

"Put this Monroe guy on the No-Fly list as a contributor to a foreign campaign."

"We want a list of all your employees and their operations. We don't need any more of your cowboys undermine the government."

Bridges twists his mouth in resolve. The company lost contracts and reputation from that shot, taking him years to recover. He doesn't intend to get caught in such a quagmire again. Not for Johnathan, or Quentin, or anyone.

Bridges turns to his computer, searching through the company's files. No contracts rendered to RNTI Energy. No status reports. Not even a consultation meeting.

He leans back in his chair and stares at the screen, zoning out into space—to see spatially for an answer. After a moment, he picks up the phone and dials an extension.

"Human Resources," says a woman. "Hello, Mr. Bridges."

"How many inactive personnel do we have on payroll?"

"We have sixty-three on file."

"What's the breakdown?"

"Seven are on vacation, twelve are on medical leave, nineteen are suspended pending criminal charges, and twenty-five are incarcerated."

Cowboys are frisky. "Cross-reference the inactives with anyone using their service passports in the last six months."

"Seven used their service passports within that window. All of them made to continuing trips to Dubai and to Johannesburg, South Africa."

Atlanta, GA

Bridges waits in a palliative care unit at a veteran's hospital, having flown in to meet the only available thread to his search. As he watches wounded soldiers struggle to recover from decisions made by men like him, a nurse approaches.

"He will see you now," she says.

Bridges follows her down the corridor to a private room, where a man lies in bed, coughing lightly.

"Mr. John Maynard. I'm Robert Bridges."

"I know who you are," Maynard replies. "You're the one who fired me."

"You weren't fired. You're on leave, pending an investigation into the incident with one of the family members of the Serbian ambassador."

"On leave for over a year?" Maynard snaps, sitting up abruptly in his bed. "You didn't want your diplomat embarrassed by the press over his affair, so you made me the scapegoat."

"Mr. Maynard, you shoved his child, with his assistant as the eyewitness."

"You mean the assistant he's sleeping with? And that kid was a brat. I only pushed her a little. But all you suits are going to cover yourselves, aren't you?"

"Perhaps we can dig into the details later. I'm here about your travels to South Africa and Dubai."

"Don't you have the mission reports? You didn't talk to your guy McBride?"

"Yes," Bridges lies, "but we're conducting exit reviews to improve safety protocols."

"You should've had them in place beforehand. Me and three guys I was with got radiation sickness because of you fucks."

Bridges resists the urge to make Maynard change his tone, letting himself be the source of the guy's frustrations. "I'm willing to compensate you for your troubles."

"Compensate me for my troubles? Well, lay-dee-fucking-da. My medical bill is in the six-figures, because your guy kept me off the books and I don't have insurance. I'm now behind on my mortgage, and my ex-wife is bitching about child support. So if you want me quiet about how you suits are dealing with bad actors, you're going to compensate me, alright."

Enough of this. "Mr. Maynard. I have a number in mind to write on a check. Every time you don't answer me fully; I'm taking $20,000 off. And I don't respond to blackmail unless I'm the one doing it. So, it's best if you answer my questions."

Maynard glares at Bridges, before his face shows compliance. "What you want to know?"

"Why were you in South Africa?"

"You don't know? It's your company's account."

"I'm deducting $20,000," says Bridges. "Why were you in South Africa?"

Maynard huffs. "McBride contacted me with a job. Security work for a cargo ship traveling from Johannesburg to Dubai. Two weeks per trip, with $25,000 in cash at the end of each one. I did three trips before I got sick."

"What was in the cargo?"

"McBride said it was medical supplies, but it must've been some radioactive shit."

"How do you know?"

"Because I'm in here, jackass."

"I'm deducting another $20,000. How do you know the cargo contained radioactive materials?"

"We were told not to go near one container. Just guard the route and stay on post. The first two trips were fine. But during the third, we started feeling sick. We thought it was the flu, but then our teeth started hurting. A few guys' hair started falling out. By the time we got to Dubai, one of the guys was throwing up blood. At the hospital, we found out we had radiation poisoning. Every day they gave us a pill and an IV with some stuff I can't pronounce."

"Most likely the pill is potassium iodide," says Bridges, "and the IV would be diethylenetriamine pentaacetate."

Maynard stares at hm. "You must've read my medical records. You don't know that on your own."

"I know everything. That's why I get to wear the suit. Did you tell the doctors there about the ship?"

"No. McBride said he'd handle it with the hospital and told us to go home when we were released. I tried calling him when I got here, to get him to cover my bills, but he didn't answer."

"You mentioned bad actors. How are you certain?"

"Each time we docked in Dubai, we saw the people unloading the container off the ship. A bunch of sketchy motherfuckers, shouting something in Arabic. One of the guys with me speaks the language said they were saying

'Day of the Ram.' Do those sound like medical professionals to you?"

Bridges stands there, processing the words said to him. He has more questions but doubts this guy has more to offer. Then with a calculating expression, Bridges pulls out his checkbook and writes out $460,000. He hands it to Maynard. "Tell the hospital to mail me the bill for your treatment when it's complete."

Maynard looks at the check, his expression sour. "This is it? I'd probably would make more telling this story to the news."

"You signed a non-disclosure agreement when you worked with us," Bridges replies. "If you reveal anything without a subpoena, you'll face litigation. So unless you want to blow that check hiring a lawyer, cash out and shut up."

Maynard looks at Bridges. "You really are a piece of work."

"That's what my ex-wife said after I made her honor the prenup. She now works at a hardware store." Bridges walks out of the hospital room.

CHAPTER 18

Matthias exits the office building and heads to his car when he sees Nigel leaning against the vehicle.

"Why are you at my car?"

"I'm coming along with you to Tarrytown," Nigel says.

"Why?"

"Because yesterday, you didn't come back until nighttime. Your gross delay has left me no choice but to monitor you directly."

"There was no gross delay. I overshot the highway exit, and it took a while to reroute into town."

"For six hours?"

"American roads can be a bitch," he says. "Look, I've already scheduled an appointment with the estate agent today about the house for sale. I'll get information on Russo from her and will be back shortly."

"Indeed," says Nigel. "And I'm coming along to make sure you get there without veering off into Canada." He then folds his arms across his chest, clearly vexed. "And before you trot out any more arguments, know that I've informed Ms. Gruber and she is the one who ordered this, in lieu of trusting you on your own. So you can call her if you want to continue with any objections."

Matthias squints at Nigel. "Fine. Just know I'm singing *'99 Bottles'* all the way. Off-key. Right in your ear."

Tarrytown, NY

"Amazing," says Nigel as he looks onto his wristwatch. "It took you seventy-eight minutes to arrive here. Yet yesterday it took you all day."

"It must be the company," Matthias says as he parks across the road from a house with a 'For Sale' sign on its lawn. "For now on I'll hang you off the dashboard like a GPS reader."

"At least you will not wander from what was instructed to you to do."

"Why are you so pissy? And not just British pissy. All world pissy."

"I'm pissy—as you say—because your hostility toward my proposal has been evident from the start, and I'm left to think you disappeared yesterday out of sheer rebelliousness."

"I didn't disappear. It just took time to find the place. I checked the house once I got here. No leaflets or notices on the door. No mail with a forwarding address, and no scraps left in the trash with the nuclear launch codes you wanted."

Nigel turns towards the house. "This place isn't well secured. You could've broken in and rummage through it."

"Do I look like a TV detective? What next, you want me to car chase a drug lord?"

"Perhaps something involving that woman who visit your office the other day may have something to do with why you were delayed."

He's referring to Amora. *Nigel must be monitoring who's coming in the building to see him. Better to get him off his scent, as well as needle him on his insecurities.*

"Or, perhaps you're mad you couldn't track me with these." Matthias goes into his pocket and pulls out two small microchip devices. "I found these while scanning my clothes and office for bugs, planted in my shoes and jacket button. And I swapped out my phones and SIM cards in case you're tailing me that way. And I will sweep the car when we get back to the office in case you planted any more devices on the sly."

Nigel fidgets before taking the microchips. "You found them because I told you that you were traced. If I haven't you would be none the wiser."

"But you did tell me. If this was a real op, and you reveal to your target your tracking devices, you would be killed. Not by the target, but by your own organization. Because when things are compromised, the analyst is the first to be removed."

"Duly noted," says Nigel. "Going forward I will not tell you how I survey you."

"Or maybe you should take this as a notion that you are not ready for this world. If you want to work as an analyst, go apply for a government job."

"I'm where I want to be. And Ms. Gruber assures me I'm competent for the position."

"You think you know Mum? She tossed more bodies in mass graves than a dictator with a bulldozer." Then, unknowing, he says, *"leiden die Kinder."*

With that Nigel looks at him wildly. "What did you say?"

"I'm saying to find another line of work before they make you swim in a lava pit for not hacking into a cloud server."

"No. That phrase," Nigel says, now with an imploring tone. "Where did you learn it from?"

"I didn't say anything." Matthias then sees a car pull up into the house driveway. "The agent's here. Stay in the car."

Matthias exits and walks to the house, approaching the driveway as a woman step from her vehicle.

Miranda Ortiz?" he says, extending a hand. "I'm Sergeant Jack Reaves. It's a pleasure to meet you."

Miranda's eyes widen at the sight of his athletic frame, and she grins broadly. "Hello, Sergeant. I hope I haven't kept you waiting long." Then as they shake hands, she feels the scars on his hand. "My lord," she says. "Your hands. What happened?"

"I played Pat-A-Cake with an electric fence. Won two out of three." He pauses from Miranda's laughter from the quip. "In truth I was handling a flash grenade during a training exercise, and it ignited prematurely. Been on desk duty since. Hopefully this transfer to the Army Reserve in town will let me keep active in some way."

"Well, you sure look active to me, Sergeant," she exclaims with a whiff of lure.

Matthias turns to Russo's house. "So this is the place. Sort of a fixer-upper, isn't it?"

"Well, it could use a little upkeeping," Miranda says as she motions him toward the entrance. "But the essentials are solid. The owners also upgraded the HVAC." She then opens the front door, ushering him past the foyer into a bare living room.

"Will the owners be joining us?"

"No," she says. "Sellers don't accompany the walkthroughs with prospects."

"Hmmph," he grunts, his gaze sweeping the room as he tunes out Miranda's sales pitch. No pictures or personal items. No paperwork to Russo's location. Not even junk mail to scavenge for a clue. He'll have to pry the info out of her.

"Also," Miranda continues, "the school system is ranked in the top ten by the State's education department. Do you have any children?"

"No kids, and I'm not married. Are you volunteering?"

"Oh," she laughs nervously, brushing a strand of hair behind her ear. "Well, I am single."

"Good to know," he says. "Perhaps we should focus on the house before we take this conversation to the wedding chapel."

Miranda laughs and playfully nudges him, her hand lingering on his arm. "Yes, we should."

"I'd like to speak with the owners," Matthias says. "It would be good to know about any liens or taxes attached to the property, or any HOA fees required."

"Well, I can provide details about homeowner costs at the office, and any real estate lawyer you hire should be able to find public records on liens."

"Still, it's always better to meet the sellers in person. Perhaps you can give me their phone number?"

"I'm afraid I can't disclose information outside of what's listed with the property," she says.

He smiles again. She gave too many tells from her behavior to not try.

"Well, I wouldn't want you to break their anonymity," he steps closer to her. "It's that I'm good at reading people. Like now I can read that you want me to ask you out tonight."

Miranda shows a mixture of emotions, from flattery to discomfort. "Well, Sergeant Reaves, while I appreciate—"

"Call me Jack. And maybe it's me buying this house and not having anyone to put in it, or that intoxicating scent of perfume you have on, but I think the best decision was to move here to meet you."

"Well…while I'm flattered—"

"How about I pick you up for dinner at whatever restaurant you choose, so that we can get to know each other? Maybe this could be the start of a story we tell."

Miranda blushes faintly. "You are a smooth talker, Jack."

"Give me your phone so I can type in my private number?"

Miranda gives one more bit of hesitation before she retrieves her phone and hands it over. Matthias types in his number and then presses to call it. His phone rings.

"Excuse me for a moment," Matthias says, stepping back to answer the call. "Sergeant Reaves…Yes Commander…The progress files are in the shared drive, sir…You need my password? One moment, sir." Matthias pulls from his phone and to Miranda. "I have to take this. I'll just step into the kitchen." Matthias immediately turns and strides away before she objects.

"Yes sir," he says into his phone, continuing his ruse around the bend into the kitchen and out of her line of sight. There he starts scrolling through her phone until he finds her address book. He looks for Frank Russo's number. Got it.

"I'm sorry, Miranda," he says apologetically as he returns. "My base needs me to locate some files. I'll have to postpone our tour. Oh, I still have your phone."

Miranda takes back her phone from him, her brow furrowed. "And what about our date tonight?"

"We will have to push it to tomorrow. But it will give me a whole day to imagine how you'd look in a red dress."

"I don't think I have a red dress."

Matthias pulls out cash from his pocket, peeling off $500. "You think you can find one for tomorrow?"

Miranda is flustered as she takes the money. "I think I can put something together."

"I'll call you tomorrow, then." Matthias heads back outside. *At least the money will suffice when she's left in the lurch. Can't run a project with a jilted woman on his phone.*

CHAPTER 19

"I got something to go on," Matthias says as he returns to the car. "I hope those computer skills of yours are good enough to find a phone through its number."

Nigel doesn't answer. In fact, his expression is crestfallen as he sits in silence on the ride back.

"Why are you so quiet now?" Matthias asks.

Nigel turns to Matthias. "You call Ms. Gruber 'mum'. Why?"

"No, I didn't."

"Earlier you called her 'mum'. Before, I thought you were just an operative in training, but you have a bond with her no one else has."

"How do you know what I have, or what she has with any of her employees?"

"Everyone who works under her calls her Ms. Gruber. Except you. Is she your mother?"

"She's nothing more than an authenticator," lies Matthias. "She's someone who gives directives. That's it."

"You mean directives like this?" Nigel then speaks in German: "*Leiden die Kinder, denn ihnen gehört das Himmelreich.*"

Matthias' eyes soften as the axiom is triggered, his mind flooding with recall. The cattle prods, the sweatbox, the stretch rack. Rubber bullets to the chest during martial arts training. Being forced into a bed with four-point restraints. Having chemical water poured over his hands to mutilate his fingerprints. All as the trainers yell into his psyche:

"*The fear of death; is death.*"

"*To be conquered is for the normal. To conquer is for the immortal.*"

"*The only thing that can stop war, is more war.*"

Matthias snaps out of his trance enough to pull the car to the nearest curb, the wheels screeching from the sudden stop. He turns to Nigel with his eyes filling with rage.

"How do you know that verse?"

"Again, you muttered parts of it earlier," says Nigel. "What does that do to you?"

Matthias lets out a sulfurous growl. *He has been infiltrated. Kill him. Kill him now. Leiden die Kinder.*

Nigel, sensing the shift to something grim, slowly raises his hands in surrender. "I do not mean to upset you. It was something my sister—"

Matthias' hearing dims, as a taste of metal forms in his mouth; the iron in his blood starting to boil. His muscles twitch as his specters and demons resurface, screaming murder. *Wring his neck with your hands. We wish to dance on his entrails. Wolves kill sheep.*

Matthias instead fights against the screams and collapses his head into his hands.

"Romania. Zurich. Sudan. Florianópolis. Bangkok," he then mutters his neurolinguistic phrases, repeatedly, hoping to cancel the lust of the axiom.

Minutes later—few or several, in this state he wouldn't know— his heart rate slows and the twitching retreats. He turns to Nigel.

"Motherfucker, don't ever say that to me again, you hear me?"

"Understood," says a wide-eyed Nigel. "I only brought it up because it's something you and my sister have in common. She learned it at a boarding school in the Swiss Alps. A school sponsored by the Merchants of Pierrepont."

Level-headedness slowly trickles back into Matthias. Still; "So the fuck what?"

Nigel gathers the courage to disclose to the predator in front of him. "My mother worked for the IMF, when she and my dad were killed in a car crash. I was five at the time, and my sister, Keila, was ten. We moved to London to stay with my uncle, but when she was fourteen, she was sent to the boarding school. At first, she loved it there. But over time, her behavior began to shift. Every time I called her, she'd say that phrase to me in German: Suffer the children—"

"For theirs is the kingdom of Heaven," Matthias interrupts. "And don't say it to me in English either."

Nigel takes a gulp before continuing. "After Keila graduated, I lost contact with her. Then, in my last year in college, Ms. Gruber showed up. She said she knew my mum, and that she arranged my sister to attend the boarding school. She then said I could go to uni for Ethical Hacking while I work at an insurance office, feeding the adjusters with coordinates for sites to go to. But the locations we provided weren't ordinary. Like Kosovo, North Korea, and Myanmar."

"Those aren't insurance adjusters," says Matthias. "Those are operatives. And those weren't places an accident happened. They're targets. I still don't see a connection to your sister."

"About a few years in, I received a package of bullet casings. Each casing had numbers written on it. The gaffer there analyzed them, and they came from artillery used in the assassination of a Hezbollah general. I realized then that the numbers were her birthday. About a month later, Ms. Gruber offered me this position here so I could go for my master's degree."

"To get you out of the way," Matthias says. "I'm surprised they didn't have you killed."

"I suppose that's some comfort," Nigel replies, his tone shifting to almost a whimper. "I haven't seen Keila in eight years. I'm afraid she's caught up in this wickedness. So, I was thinking, you might be able to help me find her."

"And how do you think that?"

"Perhaps you could ask Ms. Gruber where she is and what she is doing. Or retrieve some file of Keila's whereabouts. She wouldn't tell me, but she would tell you."

Matthias looks at Nigel, reading no tells from him suggesting this is a set-up. And though his fervor has cooled, he still feels the specters and demons chide him for his restraint. *If you're not going to kill him, at least make him squeal.*

"How did you install the trackers in my clothes?"

"Ms. Gruber told me to set up an override for your office door in case I needed access. That's how I managed to plant the chips on your clothes. And to the watch she gave you."

"The Patek Philippe?"

"It has a GPS transmitter inside," says Nigel. "It gave me a ten-mile radius where I can locate your position."

Matthias looks out the car window. *That tricky broad. Fine, then. Maybe he can turn the tables on her.*

"I'll look for the info you want. But this means you work for me now, so I want some things in return."

"Such as?" Nigel's voice wavers.

Matthias smiles, his breath still fuming with iron.

CHAPTER 20

As Bridges is at his desk, when there's a knock at the door. "Come in," he says. Two women in business suits enter the office and approach.

"Mr. Bridges," one of them says, "I'm Angela Rizzoli, and this is Renee Clarke. We were sent from the training center at your request."

"I requested male recruits," Bridges says. "It's hard to trust anyone with more mood changes than the weather." He then watches as the women shift uncomfortably, murmuring under their breaths at the comment.

"I'm only razzing you, ladies," he says. "I knew you were coming. Besides, I've killed too many men to be a misogynist. Do you have something for me?"

Clarke reaches into her pocket and pulls out a small envelope. She hands it to Bridges, who opens it and removes a blank key card.

"The security head at the center said you can use this while you have your lost card replaced. But he wondered why you didn't ask security here to do it."

"We're at odds over me smoking in the office," he replies. "If they catch me one more time, they'll report me to the fire marshal. Anyway, I read your files beforehand. Angela Rizzoli. Eight years at Fort Sam, then three deployed in Afghanistan. How did you wind up with us?"

"If you have my file, then you read the report," she says.

"Humor me. I love a good round-up story."

"My platoon encountered a weapons dealer in Jalalabad, and during the interrogation, things were handled inappropriately. Or so the U.S. Attorney's Office described it."

"You tied him to the back of a motorcycle and dragged him until he disclosed his hideout."

"Those details were overblown." Rizzoli then lets out a scandalous smirk. "And he said he needed a ride home."

"Hey. I respect the process." He then turns to Clarke. "And you? What's your deal?"

"I worked for seven years at Quantico. There was an incident during a traffic stop. A carjacker tried to strong-arm a woman out of her vehicle. I intervened, and he was shot in the leg."

"Did you identify yourself as an FBI agent?"

"There was no time. Apparently, that violated his rights, and I was forced to resign."

"Ain't being woke a bitch?" Bridges says. "So let me get to why you're here. Do you two know what our False Flag Division is?"

"We've heard rumblings about it at the center," Rizzoli says, "but the trainers didn't acknowledge it."

"Because we can't legally say we're contracted to break shit for the government. But the FFD acts as agent provocateurs at their behest. Sabotaging fringe groups. Disguising as opposition to be disorderly during a protest. Maybe even cause a few riots with arson and vandalism. Anyway, two slots opened, and I have a task that needs doing. Do it right, and I'll push you two through. Unless you'd prefer to head back to the training center and keep getting leered at in the gym when you're doing squats."

They exchange looks of disapproval at the alternative. "What's the task, sir?" Clarke asks.

◇◇◇

"How's the damage?" Bridges asks later, into his phone, as he stands on the building's rooftop.

"As you wanted, sir," Clarke says on the other end. "Deconstructive. I think Rizzoli liked it a little too much. She broke the water heater to flood the basement."

"Where's the target now?"

"She's heading back. About half a mile away."

"You two wait until she goes in the house, then come back to the office."

Bridges hangs up and looks over the D.C. skyline. There he calculates. After sending them to place a tracker on the wife's car and waiting for her to leave so they could break in, he figures it'll take five minutes after she returns before she calls her husband.

Slowpoke, he reckons, as twelve minutes later he watches from the roof a man dart from the building's entrance below. The man rushes to his car and pulls out of the parking lot toward the Beltway.

Bridges heads into the building, minutes later approaching McBride's secretary.

"Mr. Bridges," she says. "Mr. McBride just left moments ago."

"Where did he go?"

"He stepped out abruptly. He didn't say where."

"Well, we have a meeting. Let me into his office, and I'll wait for him there."

"I don't have the authority to allow anyone in his office," she says. "I can page him to let him know you're here."

Bridges smiles and sits on the edge of her desk. Nothing scatters deer like pheromone and fear.

"You know, I'm not really concerned about him right now. I'm more interested in your blouse."

She blinks. "What's wrong with my blouse? It's within the company dress code."

"Maybe so, but it's a disservice to what's underneath. Don't you know gifts are meant to be unwrapped?"

"Uh…Mr. Bridges—"

"Lillian, right? How about you come into my office, and I'll tell you the story of Robert and his Magic Beans."

"Mr. Bridges, this is highly improper for you—"

"Do you want to see Robert's magic beans?"

"I…I have to go." Lillian grabs her purse and hurries to the nearest stairwell.

Well, no story time for her. Bridges approaches the office and pulls out the key card—a visitor pass, programmed for single-day entry. But unbeknown to most, the scanners don't differentiate visitor passes; they can open any office for that day. How else would he know what his employees are doing? If he can't snoop on them, what else are they here for? He can type his own letters.

He swipes the card over the scanner, and the door clicks open. He steps into McBride's office, and his eyes land on the accent piece on the wall. *Is that a Warhol? Even he doesn't have a Warhol. Bastard.*

He strides to the desk, hoping McBride's computer is unlocked in his rush to leave. No. The desk drawers are locked as well. He scans the desk for a cue to a password. Nothing.

Bridges exhales, unsure what to search for next. He then zones out into space—to see spatially for an answer. After a few minutes, he turns back to the Warhol: a retro piece clashing with the décor of the office.

"That shouldn't be here," Bridges mutters, walking over to inspect the painting. It's a reprint, and the artist's signature is in Arabic. This isn't an accent piece—it's a marker, a reminder of something.

Bridges goes to the computer, switches the language settings from English to Arabic, and types in the painting's signature. He hits Enter. Jackpot.

Bridges sits down to investigate the computer's desktop. This isn't the company's network—it's a separate file partition. None of the icons are familiar, their script also in Arabic. Except one folder, labeled: ARIES.

"What the hell are you into?" Bridges mutters, as he begins to dive in.

CHAPTER 21

Matthias steps from his office building and glances around the street, looking for his ride, before a car horn blares for his attention. At the corner, he spots his rental car. He walks to it and opens the passenger-side door to see Nigel behind the wheel.

"Did you get the device?" Matthias asks as he hops in.

"It's in the glove compartment," Nigel says before driving off down the street.

Matthias opens the lid and retrieves a small box, pulling from it a polished onyx stone, carved into a dog tag and attached to a simple neck chain.

"My mates from my software class designed it for a surveillance competition," he says as he drives. "It has a camera with a microSD card hidden in the quartz to record. There's also an app you can download to sync it with your phone."

"It doesn't record sound?"

"There wasn't room to add a microphone without distortion."

"Maybe that's why they didn't win the competition," Matthias remarks as he pulls out his phone to activate the device.

"I'll let them know of your analysis," Nigel replies dryly. "I believe I'd upheld my end of your demands. May I ask my questions now?"

"We're not at the destination yet."

"We're heading there now," he says as he turns onto the Triborough Bridge.

"Did you reset the lock to my office so that only I can get in?"

Nigel reaches into his shirt pocket to hand Matthias a new key card. "The scanner will only respond to it once you input any eight-digit code you prefer."

"Did you find Russo's location from the number I gave you?"

"I haven't yet. He must have VPN software on his mobile. I'd have to ping the number off the phone masts, which isn't exactly legal."

"Well, your incarceration is a chance I'm willing to take."

"How benevolent of you," Nigel says. "It's a miracle—basking in your altruism—that I don't drive on the left side of the road as I do in London, and have you sideswiped."

"No one likes a sassy chauffeur," Matthias quips. "What do you want to know?"

"I understand that your project is for revenge for what happened to you as an infant, but there are times when Ms. Gruber uses the term mission as an operation different from a project. What's the difference?"

"A mission is orchestrated by the authenticators," he says, continuing to sync his phone to the camera. "A project, on the other hand, is personal. It could be an operative robbing a bank to secure funds, arranging a prison escape for someone, or even an exercise to determine if they're ready for a mission."

"So your project is to see if you can become a full operative?"

"I'm not interested in being an operative," Matthias says. "I'm just doing this to settle a score. These mophead have already taken more from me than what I allowed."

"Why do you call them mopheads?" Nigel asks.

"Merchants of Pierrepont. M.O.P. Mopheads. Just my way of saying they stink."

"How are these—as you call them—mopheads so involved in global affairs? On the surface they're a banking and insurance company."

"They are, but for governments. If a country needs a loan, they act as a middleman to the IMF and World Bank, and they insure their collateral. For a fee."

"What would be their fee?"

"I've heard of deals where the lender pays 400% in interest."

"Goodness," says Nigel, shaking his head slightly.

"Precisely. The mopheads are loan sharks that wear ascots."

"What if the country cannot make their premiums?"

"If they want to keep it light, they might sabotage the country's imports or poison the water supply."

"And if they want to make it heavy?"

"Then they'll kill the president," Matthias says. "And prop up some disgruntled soldiers to start a coup."

As Nigel drives into Queens, Matthias finishes the sync and holds the pendant up to his face, watching the camera relay his image to the phone. He slips the pendant around his neck.

"Tell me about their boarding schools," Nigel resumes. "Such as the one Keila attended. What are they like?"

"They create orphanages and boarding schools under the guise of humanitarianism," Matthias replies, "then sift through the rosters for outliers. I had more intricate training, so I was never pulled from a roster, but that's how they recruit."

"And say they find one that they like, what do they do then?"

"They install them into their apostolate program."

Nigel glares at Matthias. "A what?"

"That's what they call their training. They find an orphan, convert them, and send them out on a mission. For their fee."

"So they lure children like my sister into their shadow games, and everyone is fine with this?" Nigel grows emphatic from behind the wheel. "They're using children as pawns."

"You're thinking of children as kids," Matthias says. "They think of them as malleable soldiers. By the time training is over, they'll be adults with the acumen of a platoon general. They'd know several languages, master styles of combat, and operate in environments ranging from -40° to 43° Celsius." He then turns to Nigel. "If your sister knew the German axiom, she would've had to be in training to become an apostle. And those shells she sent you is probably a sign she indoctrinated in the fold."

"No," Nigel says, shaking his head. "I refuse to believe that. She's not capable of doing anything nefarious."

"You haven't seen her in eight years. People can change a lot in that time."

"Maybe she's been brainwashed," he says, still clinging to something plausible. "Like how you are when you hear the axiom. Maybe she's doing things out of her control and sent me those casings as a cry for help." He turns to Matthias again. "You must help me find her. I need to pull her out of this."

"I'll talk to Mum," Matthias replies. "But we never speak about her affairs as an authenticator. The moment I bring it up it'll kindle her suspicions."

"See what you can do," Nigel implores. "She's the only family I have left."

Matthias picks up on his tells as Nigel drives jittery with trepidation. He's like a parent to a missing child: trapped with frozen memories, too hopeful to see the hand dealt. Matthias sympathizes, but he knows better. She's either dead, she was a killer and is now dead, or she's a killer making the world dead. In any case, she's gone; for no apostle comes out saved.

CHAPTER 22

"Park there," Matthias says, nodding to a space down the block from a warehouse-turned-club, its walls barely holding in the music.

"So this is where the stripper who visited you works," Nigel says.

"She said she's a waitress, not a stripper."

"She's unlike any waitress I've ever seen."

"That's because you only go to places where the waitress works a drive-thru window," Matthias says as he looks over the warehouse: brick façade, darkened windows. Two bouncers stand out front. There are no signs to state the name or purpose—only a signboard bolted to the front, depicting an angelfish.

"Okay," Matthias says after a few more minutes of recon. "I'm going in. Wait here."

"Without me?" Nigel asks. "Why?"

"I'm only going to be there for a few minutes."

"In the meantime, I can take in the environment. In truth, I'm sort of a voyeur."

"A what?"

Nigel then says in candor, "I take pleasure in watching people. Perhaps that is why Ms. Gruber thought I would perform well as an analyst."

"Now you tell me? She made you an analyst because you're a peeping tom?"

"I do not invade anyone's personal space," he says defensively. "I just prefer to be a fly on the wall, if you will.

Matthias hands Nigel his phone. "Then be a fly and stick to this phone. Make sure the camera is working."

"But what if you need me to back you up?"

"I'd rather have a porcupine for a catheter. Stay in the car."

Matthias heads to the club, and after the formalities of getting searched by the bouncers and paying the cover charge—he enters a space thick with lust and gluttony.

He slips into a corner to survey the room. On one side: a bar lined with patrons. The other: couches of old men and young women trading attention for currency. Along the inner rung are tables, where waitresses attend with food and drinks. He looks up to the upper tier, where groups of men gallivant. And at the center: a stage where strippers perform, showered in money from the masses along its edges.

"Hola, guapo," he hears, as a Latina beauty approaches, dressed in a florescent two-piece swimsuit, matching the glowing LED bracelet on her wrist. "No need to stand by the wall. Let Domencia take care of you. What do you need, handsome?"

Matthias looks at her in a moment of weakness, before he collects himself. "I'm looking for Amora Navarro. Is she here?"

Domencia stiffens at the name, her smile fading. "What do you want to see her for?"

"She gave me her card," he says, showing her the business card Amora previous gave him. "I'm someone she has business with."

Domencia rolls her eyes. *"Puta de mierda,"* she mutters, before pointing to the upper tier. "By VIP."

There she is, wearing a business suit, among those gallivanting. He then spots a familiar face. He's here too? Interesting.

Matthias pulls out a hundred-dollar bill and hands it to Domencia. "Give her this and tell her someone is here to see her." He then pulls out another hundred. "This is for you."

Domencia's face lights up as she takes the money. "Right on it." She then strokes his face with her hand. "*Guapo.*"

She bolts to the VIP section until she reaches Amora. Matthias watches as Domencia points in his direction while speaking to her. Amora then locks eyes with him before she makes her way down from the upper tier to him.

"What are you doing here?"

"I'm here to give you a status report on your case with Laquan."

"You could've called. I would've come to your office."

"I wanted to see you in your habitat. I didn't know waitresses wore business suits."

"I'm promoted to shift manager," she says, holding the jacket by its front edges to reveal the white blouse underneath. "So I wanted to dress the part. You like? It's hard to find a suit that fits the curves well."

"Very nice," he says. "I'm sure Laquan's men in the VIP section are popping a stitch from the sight of you."

Amora releases the jacket ends. "Management still lets them in, as long as they spend money. But so far they haven't been any trouble."

"I would introduce myself, but we've already met. Especially the fat guy with the cast on his foot when I broke it."

"You did that to Ox?"

"Ox is his name?" Matthias quips. "He's as dumb as one. Anyway. We should talk somewhere private."

"Come with me." Amora grabs Matthias' hand to lead him, stopping when feeling his skin. "How did your hands get so scarred?"

"I gave a hand job to a beehive."

She glances at him with an incredulous look, before they continue to a stairway guarded by a bouncer, who steps aside as she approaches, almost in reverence, allowing them to pass.

Matthias grunts in response as they ascend the stairs, noting the silent exchange. *That's a lot of respect for a bottle waitress.*

They reach the third floor, and his eyes adjust to both the bright florescent lighting, and the bullpen filled with women. Some change outfits as they gossip. Others count stacks of money. And a few coo softly into their phones.

And all of them wear glowing LED bracelets on their wrists.

"What's with the bracelets?" Matthias asks, as they pass by the bullpen and through another hallway. "A fashion statement?"

"Those are trackers," says Amora. "In case a girl gets harassed, she can send a signal to one of the bouncers for help."

They continue to the end of the hallway, where two more bouncers stand post over a row of doors. From behind them, moans filter through the thresholds. Amora leads Matthias past one of the doors and into a room the size of a walk-in closet, with a futon inside.

"This is where we can talk," she says, closing the door behind them. "Away from the crowd and music."

"And into hearing johns fuck next door," Matthias says. "So you're more than a waitress, then?"

"Shift manager," she corrects. "And when I was a stripper, I stayed a stripper. In fact, I'm sure word is getting around I'm even in here. They'll think you're important to pull me."

"I guess that's flattering."

"It should be," Amora replies with certainty. "So, what do you have so far?"

"I contacted Laquan and arranged for him to sell me some liquid meth. He sent it to a drop-off locker I set up, so now there's at least evidence he knows about the arrangement."

"That should be enough, then?"

"Perhaps. Because this isn't a law enforcement investigation, it might not be enough to compel a prosecutor to move forward. For the case to have bite and for it to stick, they'd want the supplier too. That's where you come in."

"How?"

"You know the strippers they cozy up to. Ask those girls about what they've heard from their pillow talk."

"*¡Qué va!*" says Amora, shaking her head. "They won't do it. Once they start talking, it could be dangerous for them. Besides, they're not about to mess up their money by telling their men's business."

"Then you need to do it."

"Why? You're the investigator. Not me."

"You're already in places I'm not. Just act as a decoy to get them to give up information on who their supplier is and how he distributes."

"I've turned down their advances all this time, then suddenly I'm seducing them for information. They will not fall for that."

"I have a hard time believing you can't get them to talk about their operation." Matthias then smirks, attempting to stoke her vanity. "Unless you're not as fine as you think you are."

Amora puts her hands on her hips. "I once had a regular offer me a Ferrari from his car collection. *No trates de desafiarme, chico.*"

"The new shift manager?" Matthias says. "Never. And now that you're making the big bucks, let's discuss your payment for services rendered,"

"I already paid you."

"That was for surveillance, not for undercover work. Between setting up the points of exchange, acquiring the meth, and the risk of dealing with people of ill repute—"

"Ill what?" Amora asks.

"Ill repute. The cost has gone up. $500 a day for two days of footwork."

"You have proof of this footwork? So far, all you've shown is talk."

"I can go to VIP and let Laquan's men vouch for the deal, but that will get back to him, and he'll start wondering. And that means he'll start questioning you. Do you want that?"

Amora frowns at Matthias, before conceding. "Fine. I'll get you the information you need."

"And the money?"

Amora pauses for a moment, before her body shifts from vexed to alluring, as she wraps her arms around his waist.

"How about you let me work that off," she purrs, pulling him to her and kissing him passionately.

Electricity runs through him as he reciprocates, his instincts overriding his usual caution. He grabs one of her breasts, peeling it free from her white blouse, exposing it fully to his touch. Amora grips his member through his pants while he caresses her mound. She kisses his neck and guides her breast to his mouth. He suckles. She moans.

Amora leads him to sit on the futon, straddling his lap, grinding him. He's a closed zipper away from releasing his—

Ox—his warnings blares through the haze like trumpets. *The enemy is near. Do not be compromised.*

With all his strength, Matthias pushes her off his lap, making her stand back from him.

"What are you doing?" Amora asks in amazement.

He closes his eyes for a moment, steadying his breath. "I'm sure it's nice, but I don't work for free. That'll be a thousand."

He opens his eyes to see Amora glare at him, before she fixes herself into her clothes.

"I dried up when you said 'ill repute' anyway," she says.

"And give me my hundred back. That was to get your attention."

"What hundred?"

"The hundred I told the stripper to give you to come over."

"All she did was point that you were here. You never give a stripper money for someone else. That money is gone, *chico*." Amora finishes redressing and steps back to him, her expression cold. "You'll get paid when I see evidence of this footwork you claim you've done. And I'll let you know when I have information about Laquan's supplier. Now if you don't have anything else, I need to get back to work."

Amora turns and swings the door open abruptly as she leaves. From the hallway, she calls out, "Escort him out of the club."

Matthias, still on the futon, his breath icy from her kiss, sees the two bouncers approach the room, motioning for him to leave. He gathers his composure as they escort him out of the room, then down a stairway, and out of the club.

He returns to his car, greeted with a mischievous smirk from Nigel.

"Why are you looking at me like that?"

"Because, based on the footage," Nigel replies, holding up the phone, "you had an eventful time with your friends. I suppose being an operative has its perks."

"And apparently, the camera works," he says. "Now that you had your peeping fix, drive me to the office."

CHAPTER 23

Bridges twirls his cigar within his booth at The District Diner—minding none of the glares from those irritated by the smoke. He's too busy prepping for the upcoming conversation to care about air quality right now. He mentally checks his arguments for flaws to refine his strategy, as he glances at his smartwatch. Back in the day it took teams of technicians to wiretap a room. Now, he can record from his wrist. He may need to allocate funds toward emerging tech to stay ahead, for the moment a missile can be launched from an app is when he's out of business.

"Hey, buddy," Bridges hears from across the diner. He looks up to see a truck driver scowling at him. "There's no smoking in here. Put that out!"

In response, Bridges defiantly takes a drag from his cigar, as Rizzoli rises from her covert position in the booth behind him, with a SIG Sauer M17 in hand.

"You know," Bridges says, "I could get your body tossed in the river for the alligators. Go back to your soup."

The trucker looks at Bridges, then at Rizzoli and her gun. He grumbles and retreats out of the diner.

"I'll stand outside in case he comes back with problems," Rizzoli says before exiting to stand guard.

Bridges looks at his cigar, then at the remaining diners—most of them avoiding eye contact. Checkmate. It's good to be the winning king.

About ten minutes later, McBride enters, his face etched with worry. Spotting Bridges, he strides over to him.

"Good to see you, Quentin," Bridges says. "I know you've notified the board about your family leave, but I wanted to see if there's anything I can do for you in your time of need."

McBride slides into the booth across from Bridges. "How about you cut the crap? I'm here because of the message you sent, about knowing who broke into my home and having details about the Day of the Ram. Where did you hear that phrase? And put out the cigar."

Bridges squints before obligingly snuffing it out. "Quentin, before we go further, I need to know if you and your family is Okay."

"What do you care?"

"Because it's crucial to know whether you're being coerced. Is anyone sick? Are there debts? Has anything been forced on you that might push you toward a desperate decision?"

"I am fine, and my family is fine," McBride seethes. "My son's goldfish is fine. Are you done playing the good cop?"

"Quentin, there are people around. Can we keep this quiet?"

"Fuck you telling me what to do," McBride snaps. "Between those ARIES pricks, my father's bullshit, and now your ornery ass, I've had enough of all of you playing games at my expense." He suddenly stops, his expression darkening as if a thought has just hit him. "You work for them, don't you? That's how you know."

"What are you talking about?"

"You know about ARIES because you're one of them." McBride's gaze narrows. "That's how you know about The Day of the Ram. Yeah, that's it."

He's jumpy—like a dog with rabies. It's earlier than Bridges would prefer...but give him the stick.

"Quentin, the Justice Department is running an investigation that could implicate you in harboring nuclear materials to fund a foreign campaign."

McBride snaps from his scattered thoughts. "What? Who told you this?"

"I have a mole who told me there's evidence of isotopes being transported from South Africa to the Middle East, and the company, mainly you, has been linked as the catalyst."

Color drains from McBride's face. "Fuck," he mutters.

"I was told this so the company can wash its hands of you, but that won't stop the Feds from parading you around in handcuffs." Bridges leans in. "Look, Quentin, I can help you. But you have to level with me. You need to tell me how deep this goes, so we can work out a solution that protects you and the company."

"That's all you care about," McBride says. "The company."

"Yes," he replies. "And since you're a part of this company, your problems are my problems. And in case you haven't noticed, I solve a lot of problems."

Bridges notices McBride starting to sweat, whether from the heat in the diner or the mounting pressure on him. "Suzy," he calls out to the waitress. "A glass of water, please."

She approaches with the water, and McBride grabs it, taking several quick gulps. For a moment, silence settles over the booth as the two men lock eyes.

"My mole mentioned this ARIES group, but they don't know the full story. Who are they?"

"Are you sure you're not with them?"

"Quentin, I don't join clandestine groups. I make them."

McBride finishes his water, then begins. "I think they started on fringe message boards, posting a lot of anti-capitalist stuff. They always ended their posts with *Fáte tous ploúsious*—that's 'Eat the rich' in Greek."

"So they're Greek?"

"The ones I met were Middle Eastern."

"Why ARIES? They're into astrology?"

"It stands for Anarchists, Revolutionists, Insurrectionists for an Equal Society. They think the world would be better if everyone was set back to zero."

"How did you meet them?"

"That goes back to when I was in the Corps," McBride says. "Some soldiers got involved in things outside their missions to pass the time. In one instance, a group of businessmen approached us asking for services—namely demolition."

"Why?"

"If a business is in a war zone, the owners might want their building taken out to claim the insurance. But it has to look like an accident and not *force majeure*, which is what war zone is. So they'd ask us to make it look like something else. A gas leak. Electrical fire. Roof collapse. That kind of thing."

"Quentin, were any soldiers paid for these services?"

"There's no reason to do it if there wasn't a financial incentive," McBride replies. "So after a few of those jobs, the businessmen started asking for bigger things, some required sign-off from officials. One run involved a gold mine in Kabul; handling logistics through the war zone to a harbor in Pakistan."

Bridges leans back in his seat. "How much gold are we talking about?"

"One convoy carried about a metric ton. That's roughly thirty million dollars. Thing is, once they loaded the gold onto a ship, they sailed it out into the ocean and dumped it overboard. Right where no one could ever recover it."

"Who would throw away that much gold?"

"People who want the world set back to zero," McBride says. "Anyway, we did about five convoys of that, then it ended. I was told the runs were no longer in play, and that we were to return to our objectives."

"So then, you left the Corps and resumed civilian life. Why did these people contact you after all these years?"

"They wanted me to draw blueprints for something."

"Quentin, my mole says there's evidence you drew blueprints for some kind of radioactive bomb. Is that true?"

"Any chemical engineering student in college can draw plans to build a bomb."

"Maybe. But you have the expertise to build one."

"I only made designs for one," McBride says earnestly. "Bad designs at that, so it wouldn't work the way they intended. Besides, the isotopes they had aren't stable enough to be weaponized." He then lets out a sigh. "I didn't think it would go this far, and I don't want to be responsible for helping them carry out their stupid plot."

"That's what the Day of the Ram is?"

"Yeah. They want to blow something up and contaminate the area with radiation to make it uninhabitable. I don't know what or where."

Bridges peers at McBride, studying him for any tells his story is false. He sees none, but he's certain some things are left out. Time for the carrot.

"Quentin, let me bring you in so we can talk to some guys at the Pentagon. With your father's pull, we can spin this as a military operation and get the allegations nullified."

"You keep my father out of this," McBride snaps, pointing at him. "I don't want him involved."

"I'd think he'd want to help you with this situation."

"He's too wrapped up in his political cache to care about his own son." McBride sinks back into the booth with a scowl.

"Well then, you can turn yourself in. Give them some names from the gold mine jobs to pique their interest."

"I'm not turning on my Corps brothers," dismisses McBride. "Many of them are still rank and file with the Army. No. Forget it."

He's getting jumpy again. Well, he tried the stick and carrot. Now he will use dynamite.

"I know who vandalized your home," Bridges declares. "I did. I arranged it."

"What are you talking about?"

"I had someone break in and tear it up a little. I needed to get into your office and into your computer, so I created a distraction. Oh, and your secretary Lillian quit because I sexually harassed her."

McBride lets out a laugh. "You're trying to do one of those reverse psychology tricks on me. You didn't get into my computer."

"There's a separate partition on your desktop, with notes about people in this ARIES group. There's also invoices from RNTI Energy for a shipment of Strontium-90, with the names of the soldiers you used on the convoy. My guess is they'll get subpoenas soon." Bridges then leans in. "Most importantly, there are scanned diagrams of an RDD you designed."

McBride is at first silent, staring at Bridges. Then, his face hardens. "How did you get into my computer?"

"Your Warhol told me. Listen, Quentin—the authorities are coming. And your father has enemies across the aisle. They'd love to tarnish his image by giving his son conspiracy and sedition charges. I'm trying to create a way out for both of you. If we get ahead of this—"

"Do you know what you've done? What you've made me do?" McBride then buries his head into his hands. "Aw, fuck! They'll know it was me who tipped them off."

"Tipped off who?"

"I contacted the Oman police about a shipment of Octogen coming through Jebel Ali. They got it from another source. Now the port is under surveillance, and it made them revert their plans."

"Anyone could've called the police. They won't know it was you."

"Yes, they will," McBride says. "When I thought they'd broken into my home, I told them I'd make them pay for what they'd done."

"You can contact them? How?"

"None of your business." McBride seethes again, his body tightening. "You miserable old man. Go to hell!"

McBride storms out of the diner, leaving Bridges to watch from the window him getting in his car and peeling away. He then turns and notices the other patrons in the diner glaring at him, scowling from the commotion. And for the duplicity. He lets out a resigned huff, taps his smartwatch to end the recording, then gets up from the booth and walks out of the diner.

Outside, Bridges heads to a sedan where Rizzoli is waiting. She opens the back door, and he steps in, before she takes her place in the front seat, beside Clarke who's behind the wheel.

"Heard enough?" Bridges asks as he settles into his seat.

"Yeah, I heard enough," Chambers says beside him in the backseat, hanging up his own phone from the live eavesdropping. "I'll take this to Bellinger and see what he says. If it checks out, we'll bring him in. Your girl Clarke already placed a tracer on his car, so we'll have his location. I'm also sending agents to your office to retrieve his computer."

"Offer him relocation for his family. And no prison time."

"I doubt the directors will go for that," Chambers replies. "That's a wild card too big for them not to play."

"And how much of a wild card do you think I am?" Bridges counters. "No prison time. And relocation. Somewhere with a beach."

"Why do you care so much about him now? Weren't you trying to get him removed?"

Bridges looks out the car window. "He's just a pawn. The king knows them well."

CHAPTER 24

Matthias, from his office, peers at his computer, reviewing internet maps of a suburban location, when his phone rings. It's a call from Zurich.

"*Guten Morgen, Matthias,*" she says. "It's been a few days since your last update. What is your progress?"

"Nigel was able to triangulate the phone using the number we retrieved. The target is staying with his mother in Mineola, Long Island, while he settles his divorce. I'm reviewing aerial and street coverage of the area and will have a plan shortly."

"Now you see how valuable it is to have an analyst?" she asks. "Projects run smoother when you've got eyes in the back of your head."

"Yeah. He's one big ball of vision." Matthias then prompts her, baiting her need to contest any challenge to her directives: "He also told me how you knew his mother, helped him through university, and enrolled his sister in boarding school. I didn't know there was a school in the Swiss Alps. When did you start recruiting so close to home?"

There's a brief silence on the other end of the line before she answers coldly. "I do not discuss our affairs. You know this, Matthias. And when did Nigel become so enamored with you to share his life story?"

"We're bonding. Didn't you want us to bond?" Matthias leans into the provocation. "I asked questions, he answered. It's not like I had a dossier on his life. Like he had on mine."

"All analysts are given dossiers of who they support."

"Experienced analysts. Not someone pulled from dispatch after a few years. You brought someone in without approval. Then, when he asked about his sister's role, you had him transferred. Presumably to keep him from floating in the Thames."

"Need I remind you that my phone lines are not always secure? And his time at the office is none of your concern."

"Still, when did it become protocol to relay an unvetted analyst's intel about an operative?"

"Firstly," she says, "you are no operative. You are still in training. And he was vetted—by me. Do you question my competence, Matthias?"

"No, mother. I just needed your attention to ask a few sensitive questions and maybe help me forget the breach your mophead friends would surely frown upon."

Again, silence, before she speaks. "There is an old German saying: children love their mothers, then despise them for the milk she gave them."

"I believe Oscar Wilde said it better."

"Nonetheless," she replies, "if it satisfies your curiosity—as well as your impudence, which has always been my shame—I will allow a handful of questions about authenticator business. But if I choose not to answer, then I simply will not. *Verstanden?*"

"*Verstanden,*" Matthias says. "Is Nigel's sister an apostle?"

Silence—neither confirming nor denying.

"Was she ever trained to be one?"

"I did not oversee any schooling she may have received."

"Would Andreus know? You know, the guy who kidnapped me as a baby and who conspired with you to raise me to be a covert hitman? Sounds similar to Keila's story, would you agree?"

"*Du schwörst darauf, meine Geduld zu testen, Matthias!*" she explodes. "This line of questioning is finished—and in truth, your insolence is tiring me. For your sake, I hope your curiosity has been satisfied. Do you have anything else pertaining to your project?"

"*Nein*," he says.

With that she abruptly hangs up.

Matthias tosses the phone aside, disliking how he had to goad her. Then again, she did place trackers on him and sprung Nigel onto his project without his consent; so, fair play. He turns back to his computer, thinking of a way to lure Russo from his lair, when a call rings from one of his other phones. It's Fat Pat.

"Hello, Patrick."

"No one calls me Patrick but my mama," he replies with a slight slur. "So unless you washed my sack as a baby, call me Mister-Your-Holiness-Bondsman-Potentate."

"Have you been drinking?"

"How else do you make it through the day? Anyway, the city returned the bond for the jumper you wrangled, so I've got a nice $2,000 check for you. Unless you want me to blow it on a triple-jointed acrobat who's in town for the circus, be here at my office."

◇◇◇

"This place smells rancid," says Matthias an hour later, as he enters the back room of the pawnshop. "I think you have a dead mouse in here somewhere."

"Never mind how it smells," says Fat Pat, maneuvering to his desk.

"Why didn't you tell me you have an FFL license?"

"You said you wanted a discreet FFL holder," he replies. "Do I look discreet? And I already got motherfuckers coming in here for bail money. I don't want them knowing I can get guns too." Fat Pat then picks up an envelope. "Anyway, here's your check."

Matthias walks to him, and as he stretches to take the envelope, Fat Pat pulls his hand back, holding the check out of reach.

"Y'know," he says, "if you really want to make some serious money, you need to work on federal cases. With me, I can line up some work to grab those guys off the federal warrant list before they're made public. Some of those losers have a five-figure reward on their heads."

"U.S. Marshals handle the federal warrants," Matthias says. "Local bondsmen don't have that kind of access when they're issued."

"Well, I do. I can look up any warrant through the National Crime Information Center database."

"You have access to the NCIC? That's restricted to federal officers. How did you get the credentials?"

"With my effervescent and adoring personality," Fat Pat says stoically. "You want the work or not?"

Matthias' thoughts begin to whirl. *The NCIC is more comprehensive than the police databases, with ties to Interpol for tracking international criminals. He would need that.*

"Tell you what. I'll do it if you can do something for me. I need intel on two people from your federal database. The first is Keila Laine. She resides in Europe. The other is Laquan Jackson, here in New York."

Fat Pat grins. "I see that pretty *ba-dunk-a-dunk* got you running errands so she can scratch your tummy."

He's referring to Amora. "Why do you say she has me running errands?"

"Because she asked for the same thing you're asking for, but she's a civilian, so I couldn't give her that kind of info."

"Amora asked for information on Laquan?"

"Not him," Fat Pat says. "He had a brother Damian. He was killed in Miami."

CHAPTER 25

"Let me see if I have this correctly," Nigel says from the driver's seat of the rental car, across the street from the bar in the Bronx. "You're planning to walk in there and get someone—who's both a gang leader and a music executive—to admit details of his drug operation. On camera."

"Pretty much," Matthias says, looking through an open folder in front of him. "Haven't you heard of a sting?"

"And didn't you say you're not a TV detective?" Nigel remarks. "When Ms. Gruber brought me on to keep you clear of extracurricular activities, I'd say this is a prime example."

"You drove me to Angelfish. That was an extracurricular activity. And looking for information on your sister is an extracurricular activity." Matthias looks up from the folder and to Nigel. "If you're going to be my logistics analyst, you need to be involved in the things I'm involved in. And keep your mouth shut about it."

"That wasn't the agreement we initially made."

"It's an addendum. I can make them up as I go along."

"How manipulative of you," Nigel says wryly.

"I was raised by authenticators. What can I tell ya'?"

"Well," Nigel says, "I reckon Ms. Gruber is getting suspicious. Ever since your confrontation with her about Keila yesterday, she has been rather curt with me. Almost as if she knows I'm holding something back."

"She probably does," Matthias says strategically. "To throw her off the trail, use sleight of hand. Tell her I tossed your trackers so you can't trace me. Say I've been slipping out the service alley and disabled the motion detectors to avoid being caught leaving the building. Then, a day or two later, tell her you discovered I've been going to Angellish and partaking in strippers. She'll focus less on you and more on me being insubordinate to the project."

"And she won't suspect a dupe out of that?"

"That's the point. I want her spinning in doubt— questioning what I'm doing. You don't beat your opponent by countering their move. You beat them by disorienting them, so they don't know what move to make."

"Where did you learn that bit of wisdom?" Nigel then asks.

"It's from *The Art of War*. Just one of the things they drilled in my head." He then unknowing mutters, *"leiden die Kinder."*

"You said it again."

"I said what?"

"That phrase you told me not to repeat. I think you don't realize you're saying it. It could be some unconscious reveal—unresolved tension, maybe."

"Well, if there's anything I've got, it's unresolved tension." Matthias takes the papers from the folder, folds them into quarters, and slips them into his jacket pocket. "I'll work on my mumbling later. Is the camera working?"

Nigel holds up the phone, monitoring the live feed from the camera pendant around Matthias' neck.

"Okay. I'm going in." Matthias steps out of the car and enters the bar. With the same soulless vibes, and with the same man behind the counter.

"You!" the bartender barks. "You came back to start more shit? Laquan got on my ass because of you."

"Just want to talk to the man about business, friend," Matthias says.

"He's not here," the bartender replies, slowly reaching under the bar.

"I guess I'll hang with you until he shows. By any chance, do you have a summer ale?"

The bartender pulls his hands back, holding the shotgun again. "I told you he's not here. Now you can walk out or be carried on a gurney."

"So, what you're saying is, you don't have a summer ale?"

"Joe," a voice call from behind them. One of the henchmen stand by the corridor leading to the back room. "Laquan knows he's coming," he then nods to Matthias. "He's in the back."

"Bye, Joe," Matthias says with a grin to the bartender, before walking to the henchman. The two head down the corridor into the back room, where Laquan sits at a table with two other men.

"I'm taking it you want another meet and greet," Laquan says.

"For real doe," says Matthias, "fam loved that Ice Cream and how it mixes with their own work. Practically got the set out of inventory."

"And what's the name of the set again? Your crew in Detroit?"

"All Guttah Bloods. Sewed up the streets from Southfield to Grandriver."

"Hmmph," Laquan grunts. "And which block you said you were on in Sing Sing?"

"I was in minimum security in Block B." Matthias then pulls out an envelope from his jacket and place it onto the table. "But I'm not here for that 'guess-my-weight' shit. I need more of that mash but don't got time for the lockbox. I need for you to supply that ASAP. Whatever you got here to take now."

Laquan eyes the envelope, stuffed with cash. He looks back at Matthias, draws a gun from his side, and aims it straight at him.

"Search this bird for a wire," Laquan tells his men.

"What the fuck?" Matthias says as the three other men pull out their guns. "What is this for?"

"For one," says Laquan, "Sing Sing doesn't have a minimum-security block—it's all max. And that wasn't meth that got dropped off; it was N-Iso, used to cut it. And you don't talk like you're from Detroit. You talk like some proper-speaking hoe. Or an undercover cop."

"I ain't no cop, cuz," gripes Matthias, as the henchmen yank off his jacket and pat him down. "We already did business. Now you don't trust me after I put money in your hand?"

"What's this?" says one of them, snatching the pendant from his neck. "I like this. What'd it run you?"

"I ran your mother," snarls Matthias. "She worked the track for it."

The henchman reactively throws a hard right toward his chin.

Matthias instinctively parries, slips to the side, and counters with his own right.

The punch snaps the man's jaw and drops him to the ground.

Matthias pivots toward the other henchman. Too late—a punch cracks against his skull, making him buckle.

A kick into his stomach folds him. Then they descend on him like vultures, beating Matthias down to the ground.

"When you fall, it is because of your own error," he recalls from his trainers—as a barrage of kicks makes his skull rattle.

"It is glorious to die, child," flashes back as feet slam down on his chest. *"For yours is the kingdom of Heaven."*

"Fucking numbskull," he imagines Andreus sneering— right as a brutal kick crushes his groin.

In what seems like forever, they bludgeon him with savagery, leaving him sprawled on the floor.

"Pick him up," Laquan finally says to them.

The henchmen stop their assault, panting in glee, before dragging Matthias off the floor and tossing him onto a chair.

"You made a mistake coming in here like it's golden," Laquan says. "No one puts hands on the set like they not gonna bleed."

"There's no wire," one of them reports. "Just some papers in his jacket."

"Gimme," says Laquan, extending a hand. "I want to see if it says he's a big enough of a cop to kill or not."

As the henchman hands over the papers, Matthias wheezes like a train whistle as his head pounds manically. Blood seeps from his mouth. His chest feels broken.

"What is this?" Laquan mutters, flipping through the papers. He turns to Matthias. "Where'd you get these?"

"What's up, Quan?" one of them asks.

"They're about Damian. It says here he was working with the Miami County Vice Unit on some sex trafficking shit."

"What do you mean, working with them?"

Laquan keeps reading. "Looks like he was trying to dig up something on…" He stops, grimacing, head tilting back. "That motherfucker."

"Who?"

"Miguel Espinoza. I knew he was in on it." Laquan walks over to Matthias. "You with the motherfuckers who killed my brother?"

"You think Espinoza wouldn't know?" Matthias grits past the pain to keep his cover. "Your brother was a plant for the Feds."

"My brother wasn't no informant. He didn't even run with the set. He was square from the jump."

"You see the paperwork. He was trying to get info on Espinoza for the Feds to wipe out anything on you."

"That's bullshit," exclaims Laquan.

"Espinoza sent me to get leverage when the Feds come at him, just like your brother tried. Only I'm not working with the Feds like that fucking snitch!"

Laquan, teeth clenched, slams a downward jab. Matthias' head snaps back like he'd been hit with a baton.

"Get the car," Laquan growls to his men. "That bitch been lying to my face this whole time. And throw him in the trunk. I'm burying both these hoes tonight."

CHAPTER 26

Matthias bounces in the tight space of the sedan's trunk, his injuries aggravated with each pothole the car hits. He breathes shallowly to conserve air, trying to make out the voices funneled from the car seats, where Laquan vents to his henchmen.

"Why don't we just kill him first?"

"I want her to verify who he is," Laquan replies. "Then I want her to call Espinoza, so he can hear them beg for their lives."

Matthias contorts within the cramped space, searching for anything he could use to break the trunk lock. Nothing. He's left with his only tool: himself.

Matthias mutters repeatedly, "*leiden die Kinder, denn ihnen gehört das Himmelreich.*"

The dark space seems to expand with light, as phosphene illusions dance along his darkened vision. The specters and demons within him crawl from their lair, shrouding his pain with an insatiable thirst for war:

Kill them. Kill them all.

Look for the underbelly of the armor.

Remove the head, and the body falls.

And at worst, it's glorious to die.

The car slows to a stop, and Matthias hears the men exit. Moments later, the trunk pops open, showing Laquan and his men, aiming their guns at him.

"Get out," Laquan says. "And don't try no funny shit. I will kill you out in the open."

Matthias crawls out of the trunk. He takes in the signs around him—West 85th St. and Columbus, in Manhattan—before being shoved by his men to cross the street. As they move through the intersection, two men step out of a car parked on the other side. One he doesn't recognize, but the other he knows quite well.

"What's he doing here?" Ox huffs to Laquan, limping from the soft cast on his foot. "He's the ops."

"Keep your voice down," Laquan growls. "He's here because I say so. Now follow us."

Ox falls silent as the group moves forward. They stop at a metal door with a keypad. Laquan punches in the combination, and the door clicks open, revealing the service area of the corner building, with a doorway to a flight of stairs. The henchmen shove Matthias forward, urging him to climb.

"Quan," bellows Ox, "I can't walk up the stairs. My foot."

"You motherfucker," Laquan hisses. "You and JoJo wait by the car and keep watch."

Matthias and his captors ascend the stairs. They reach the third floor and step into its hallway, radiating elegance. Persian carpet lines the floor, and abstract art adorns the walls. Even the elevator doors are painted with Baroque designs. Only two apartments are on the floor—one to the east and one to the west. Laquan strides to the western door and rings the doorbell frantically.

"Open up, bitch," Laquan snarls. "I know you're in there. Don't make me break this door down."

The door creaks open, and Laquan forces his way inside, two of his henchmen trailing behind. Shouting erupts from the apartment.

"Move it," says the remaining man, the one who took the pendant. He shoves Matthias toward the door.

The underbelly.

Matthias takes two steps before planting one foot firmly. He pivots his hips, whipping his torso and head around—

And delivers a high kick straight to the henchman's chin.

The man's body jerks upright from the impact, his eyes rolling back as he begins to collapse.

Without hesitation, Matthias drops to one knee and drives a low punch into the man's gut.

The man folds, gasping for air.

He wraps the crumpling man into a front chokehold. Tightening his grip, he drags him down the hallway.

The man flails, struggling to regain his footing. He gropes for the gun in his holster.

Matthias drives his free elbow into the back of the man's neck. Repeatedly.

The man whimpers with each blow. The final strike severs his strength entirely, leaving his body limp like a fresh corpse.

Matthias lowers the man to the floor and grabs the gun from his holster. He moves to the western apartment and opens the door, as the intruders continue arguing.

POW! POW! POW! he fires, dropping the henchmen in a lifeless heap.

Laquan freezes in a moment of shock. Then he turns toward Matthias, raising his gun to shoot.

Then, two shots are fired from the back of the apartment—crashing into Laquan's shoulder and upper chest, knocking him to the floor.

Matthias recoils into his shooting stance and locks on the figure with the gun. *Six-to-ten o'clock shot! Clear!*

"No," he hears with a Spanish accent. "Don't shoot. It's me."

Matthias stalls his reflexes and lowers the weapon, recognizing the figure in the background.

Amora emerges with her hands up in surrender, still clutching her gun.

"Uhnngh," Laquan groans, writhing on the floor. He reaches for the gun beside him. "You shot me, you fucking—"

"Your consequences are due," Matthias says before silencing him with a shot to the head.

CHAPTER 27

"You've got about ten minutes," Matthias says to Amora. "Grab some things and put them in a bag."

Amora lowers her hands, her gaze shifting from the dead bodies on the floor. "What? No. I'm not going. I need to stay. I can tell the police—"

"You're not staying for the police. You need to come with me so I can assess what's going on. Some of Laquan's men are still outside. I don't know if they heard the shots."

"How did you know I stay here?"

"I was with him to get info for your case against him. I didn't know he was coming here to confront you about his brother's death. Like you know something about it."

"Listen," she says, "I can tell the police I shot them in self-defense. Just leave the gun—" Amora's eyes then widen as her gaze shifts past him.

"*¡CUIDADO!*" she screams.

Matthias instantly dives, retreating into the nearby living room milliseconds before hearing booming gunfire behind him, the slugs crashing into the wall.

JoJo steps through the doorway into the apartment, gun in hand. He ignores the bodies in front of him and aims again at Matthias, who has scrambled behind the wall, out of sight. Then he catches Amora, aiming her gun at him.

Click. The gun is jammed.

"¡Mierda!" Amora exclaims, before retreating to the back of the apartment.

JoJo raises his gun, lining up a shot at her.

Matthias jumps from his cover for line of sight. He fires.

Bullets tear into JoJo's chest, causing him to collapse to the floor.

Matthias cringes from his jarring pains and walks over to JoJo, lifeless with Laquan and the other henchmen.

He turns to Amora, who peeks past the wall in the background. He steps further into the apartment, grabs her by the arm, and they step over the bodies toward the stairway.

"Stay behind me," Matthias instructs as he takes the lead down the stairs, alert for further threats. Once reaching street level, Matthias opens the door to the service area—where one more of Laquan's men awaits.

"You move, you're dead!" Matthias barks, getting the drop on Ox, gun aimed at his head.

Ox raises his hands in surrender. "Okay," he says. "You got it. Just let me go."

He twitches, finger on the trigger, still in target-kill mode. *What's one more body, after all?*

Matthias resists the temptation and lowers the weapon. A gunshot in the open air would echo louder than in the apartment, anyway. Instead, he delivers a body shot/uppercut combo, sending the large man tumbling before collapsing to the ground.

Matthias leads Amora out the service area and back onto West 85th Street and Columbus.

"What now?" Amora asks. "Where are we going?"

"Do you have your phone?"

"It's upstairs. I didn't have time to get it."

Matthias then hears a car horn blaring multiple times from across the street. It's his rental car.

"C'mon," he says, guiding Amora to the car. He opens the door for her to get in the backseat, then climbs in beside Nigel.

"You're the doorman in his building," Amora says to Nigel.

"He's the building manager," Matthias replies, then turns to Nigel. "How did you find me?"

"I followed you when they were putting you in the trunk," Nigel says. "Then I used the tracker to pinpoint your location."

"What tracker?"

"The key card I gave you. It has a GPS chip I can follow."

Matthias sneers. "You're still putting trackers on me?"

"I can make up the rules too," Nigel says. "Considering the circumstances, you should be glad I did."

"Whatever. Where's my phone?"

Nigel hands it to him. "How bad is the situation?"

"I killed five men, so the plan tonight had a few hiccups."

"The cops will be looking for me," Amora says. "How about you let me go and we can forget this whole thing? I can tell the police a story that won't have you involved."

"Murders in a swanky apartment won't be written off as a smash and dash." Matthias then says to Nigel, "Drive. Cross town to the highway and head to the pier."

As Nigel pulls into traffic, Matthias dials an international number. He lets it ring once, then hangs up.

The car flows through the night in silence. Moments later, Matthias' phone rings—from Unknown.

"What is your status?" Andreus says.

"I need a reservation to see the dolphins," Matthias says. "This is not a simulation. This is not an exercise."

"Projects do not get dolphin privileges," Andreus says. "What do you need to see them for?"

"I had an incident."

"Have you been compromised in your position?" Andreus then pauses, returning with a sterner tone. "Or are you acting on your own again?"

"I've told you this is urgent," Matthias demands. "I'm heading to the location now, so unless you want me throwing names around when I show up, you'll make me a fucking reservation."

There's a long silence from Andreus on the other end. Matthias notices both Nigel and Amora eyeing him.

"Your reservation will be ready in twenty minutes," Andreus says when he returns. "Expect a call from your mother shortly."

"And where are we going?" Nigel asks when Matthias hangs up.

"What do you know about the *Maison de Gaine?*"

Nigel turns to Matthias. "The *Maison de Gaine?* I heard stories about it when I worked at the insurance office. It's some kind of hotel."

"More like a safehouse," Matthias replies. "Because you can't stash defectors and political asylees in the Holiday Inn."

"And how do you know about this place?" Amora asks.

"My mother is one of its board of directors."

"Really?" she then says, slightly calculating. "Interesting."

"What's going to be interesting is what you tell me about his brother Damian, and Miguel Espinoza. And after what I've been through tonight, you owe me hazard pay."

CHAPTER 28

"This is unimpressive," Nigel says as he parks beneath an overpass along the city pier, down the street from a building that spans half a city block. "I somehow expected more."

"You haven't been inside," Matthias replies, pulling out the gun he's carrying and handing it to him. "Hold this and wait here. They'd know I have it once I pass the atrium."

"I can't go in? I can't have a look around?"

"We've already been through this, peeper. Stay in the car." He turns to Amora. "Let's go."

They step out and walk to the building with no signs to indicate its name or purpose. After passing through the double doors of the entrance and reaching the atrium—outfitted with an array of cameras and biometric scanners—they're met by two soldiers posted, each holding M4 carbine rifles.

"Please prepare to be scanned," one of them says.

They hold out their arms as one of them approaches, waving a handheld scanner across them. Matthias watches as the cameras and sensors light up and whirl to life, reading them with infrared, ultraviolet, and millimeter waves.

"You are clear for entry," the soldier says to Matthias and Amora. Passing a short hall, they enter the lobby.

Geometric murals adorn the enclosure, and the furniture ranges from modern sofas to vintage pedestals, displaying Murano glass art. And all underneath a chandelier hanging from the arched ceiling, illuminating a mosaic of dolphins leaping through shimmering waters.

"Welcome to the *Maison de Gaine,*" the concierge says with a French accent. "How may I help you, *monsieur?*"

"J'ai une réservation," Matthias replies. *"Pour refuge et havre de sécurité."*

"Quand votre réservation était-elle prévue ?" she asks.

"Dans la dernière heure."

The concierge checks her computer, and moments later hands Matthias a key card. *"Chambre 612, monsieur."*

"Merci," he says. They take the elevator to the sixth floor and walk through the halls lined with tapestries and plush carpet, to a modern suite overlooking the East River.

"Okay, *chica*," says Matthias, closing the door after they walk in. "We're out of danger. So now you can tell me what that was back there?"

"You're the one who stormed in my apartment," Amora says. "I told you to get information to make a case for me to use, not kill him."

"And how can you afford that place? Strippers don't make that much."

"Don't worry about my finances. Worry about the five dead bodies you made." Amora then changes her tone to be more mollifying. "Listen, right now no one knows what you did. If you leave now, you can get away. Or I can go and stall the police to give you time."

"Noone's leaving until you tell me everything," Matthias says. "Who is Miguel Espinoza? And what does Damian have to do with you?"

Amora's body language shows uneasiness, appearing cornered. "Is there a minibar here?"

"By the cabinets," he says. Then as he watches Amora retreat into the suite, his thoughts are usurped. *Fuck. The camera pendant. The one taken by Laquan's men. It's still at the apartment building.*

Amora returns with a glass in hand, and a flask of tequila in another. She downs the already half-filled glass.

"Stalled enough?" Matthias asks. "Who is Espinoza?"

"He owns Angelfish," she cringes from the liquor.

"Did he have Laquan's brother killed?"

"No. Some local gang took him out. They don't like it when New York guys flash money, so they caught him slipping."

"Then why was he gathering information about Miguel and sex-trafficking?"

"*¡Espera!*" Amora says. "Miguel isn't in that."

"He's looked at by the Feds for sex trafficking. Damian was working with them. That's why he approached him."

"You're wrong. Damian went to Miguel about getting some of Laquan's music playing there."

"I doubt anyone can go up to a club owner to get music played there unless there's a pipeline. Who hooked them together?"

"I did," Amora says. "I introduced them to each other."

"Were you and Damian fucking?"

Amora places her hand on her hip. "What is it to you if we did?"

"A girl taking the pipe makes her a good pipeline."

"So what are you saying? That he used me to get to Miguel?"

"Someone was using someone," Matthias replies.

Amora pauses for a moment, cracking open the flask of tequila, pouring it in the glass. She drinks from the glass in one shot, then clears her throat.

"We went out a little. That's why I was a little messed up when he was killed, so Miguel said I can work up here to get away from Miami for a while."

"Why were you trying to gather info on Damian through back channels?"

"What back channels?"

"The guy who mentioned me to you to hire."

"That fat fuck," she mutters, before turning to Matthias. "When Laquan found out I transferred here he kept hounding me for information. So, I wanted something to give to him, like a police update on who killed Damian. But when Pat wouldn't help me, I asked him if he knew someone that could. That's when I contacted you."

"So the story about him harassing you was just a story."

"Just so I can have something on him to leave me alone," she says. "He was harassing me, just not in the way I described it."

Matthias peers at her, drained in the face and with his pains coursing through him. Either she's lying—again—or he's too worn to read her tells. Getting battered and stuffed into a car trunk, and killing five people, can take a lot out a guy.

He then receives a call from Nigel. "Your mother called me, but I didn't answer. What should I do?"

"I'll be right down," Matthias says. He turns to Amora. "Stay here for the night. I'll come back with some things for you freshen to up with and have more details."

"I can't stay here. I need to move."

"Do yoga on the floor if you need to, but do not leave. Just order room service. The wagyu steak was rated five stars." Matthias then exits the suite.

CHAPTER 29

"You may have a concussion and a sternal fracture," says the examiner at the overnight clinic, hours later. "How did you get these injuries?"

"There was a stampede at the rodeo," Matthias says, then points to Nigel. "This guy beat up a Bengal tiger."

"He was in a bar fight," Nigel replies, looking at Matthias incredulously.

"You will need a thorough CAT scan," the examiner says, "to determine the extent of the injuries and to check for internal bleeding. You should've gone to the hospital."

"I don't have time. Just give me a bottle of Hydrocodone and 300 mg of Tylenol."

"You need a prescription and a hospital waiver for opioids. Federal rules."

Matthias then stretches out his hand to Nigel, who hands him an envelope retrieved from his office. "Listen, here's $2,000. You guys work overnights, barely make any real money, and deal with gangbangers getting shot and junkies faking for Oxy every night. Take the money and give me the drugs!"

"You ought to go easy with those," says Nigel, trailing behind Matthias, as an hour later they step into his office. "That's your third pill since we left the clinic."

"Thanks, Mum," chides Matthias, popping the Hydrocodone into his mouth. "Take several kicks and then tell me how to medicate."

Nigel reaches for his phone as it buzzes with a message. "Speaking of mothers, Ms. Gruber texted me again. I can't keep ignoring her."

Matthias walks over to one of his phones and sees several missed calls from Zurich. He presses to call back, waiting only a moment before it's answered.

"What in heaven's name have you done?" she asks irately. "Are you still using your bail enforcement cover while neglecting your project?"

"What makes you say that?"

"You will not be glib with me. You are very defiant when away from my guidance. And it's becoming clear that my dedication to you is often tested by your brazenness."

"The Swiss are not good with guilt trips, Mum," he replies.

"You've done something," she says suspiciously, as if wagging her finger at him through the phone. "Something egregious. That's why you needed a reservation at the *Maison de Gaine*. Andreus said you had an incident."

"He is mistaken."

"I do not believe he is. What did you do, Matthias?"

"If you must know, I wanted to go there because I had a date and I wanted to take her to a nice place to do my thing. He mistook urgency for horny."

"Are you going over my ear with this?" she says. "You did not bring a non-essential to the safehouse to have sex."

"Why don't you ask your logistics analyst to follow me? That's why you had him plant trackers in my clothes, and in the watch. To trail my every move."

"Those devices are to ensure you stay diligent to your project. Which, it seems, hasn't worked since you're still off the rails." She exhales heavily into the phone. "I will call an end to your project. You are to return to Zurich for further training."

"Fuck nein!" Matthias erupts. "No more training. Ever."

"You have tied my hands, Matthias," she says. "You are not ready—nor can you be trusted—to handle a mission. And considering the time and resources spent on your behalf over the many years, it's distressing."

"You know what's distressing? Being attacked by a fucking bear. Being tied to a chair with a suffocating bag over my head. Being stretched on a rack to grow because those eugenics-loving *Arschlöcher* thought I was too short at fourteen. Or how about when they injected me with enough steroids to fail the Olympics? You think that's fucking distressing?"

"You are being vulgar with me, Matthias," she warns, her voice low.

"Mir doch scheißegal," he hisses. "I'm not going back to Zurich. I'm finishing my project—and I don't need you or your Merchants of Perpetual Bullshit friends to tell me what to do or where to go. *Verstanden?"*

Silence on her end. Then, *click*—as she hangs up.

"What did she say?" Nigel asks when Matthias sets his phone down.

"What liars always say. Nothing." Matthias turns to him. "Now she's going to call you again. When she asks what you know about tonight, you'll tell her you tailed me and saw me pick up a girl at Angelfish. From there, we went to the *Maison de Gaine*. After that, you lost my trail. She'll ask why you didn't tell her sooner. You'll say you were embarrassed because I found your trackers and you couldn't monitor me remotely. She'll excuse the infraction, more convinced than ever that I'm just an asshole."

"She'll more likely describe it as gross impudence."

"Being impudent comes with the job. Welcome aboard. We have jackets."

"And what about your cargo at the hotel?" Nigel says.

"You mean *chica*? You can't call women cargo. That's sexist, you wonky wanker weirdo."

"I believe the pills you've taken are starting to kick in."

Maybe he's right. Matthias feels a wobbly sense of disillusion. His vision begins to double.

"Okay," says Nigel, catching Matthias before he hits the floor. "That's enough for you this evening. A night of murder and mayhem is bound to take down the best of us." Nigel then drags Matthias toward a sleeping bag and lowers him onto it.

"Leiden die Kinder," Matthias mumbles as he drifts into much-needed sleep.

"For yours is the Kingdom," Nigel replies. "Although after tonight, I'm sure you'll make a stop in purgatory first."

CHAPTER 30

The next day—his body still in pain but at least functional—Matthias drives to the *Maison de Gaine* with a duffle bag of items for Amora to freshen up with. He enters the safehouse and, after passing through security, steps into the lobby to find an extra layer of soldiers posted, rifles in hand. As he approaches the elevators, they tighten their grips on their weapons.

"Monsieur," calls out the concierge. "A word with you, please?"

As Matthias walks toward her, she speaks to him in hushed tones. "I've been informed your reservation has been rescinded."

"What? Why?"

"Management received an order from the board of directors to terminate your stay, and to alert the security staff in case you became problematic."

Shit. The tricky broad intervened. "But I have a guest here who requires safe harbor."

"Your guest has been informed that her stay is over, and she has left the premises."

"She left? Where did she go? Did she leave a message?"

"She left no message and didn't say where she was going."

He lets out a huff. He can't figure out his next move if she's an x-factor on the loose—whether the cops, or Laquan's men, are looking for her, or what she might tell whoever finds her first. Maybe she went back to Angelfish to lay low.

The concierge then leans in closer. "After you left, she arranged to have a suite booked for her within the safehouse."

Matthias looks at her, puzzled. Only authenticators can make a reservation.

"Apparently," she continues, "your guest knows a member of the board and was adamant that the night concierge contacts him so she could speak with him. She even mentioned his name loud enough for everyone to hear, which violates our policy of keeping identities confidential in public spaces. At that point, the night concierge felt compelled to contact the board member to prevent further exposure."

"And who is this board member?"

The concierge glances around, checking if any of the security detail are within earshot. "Sergio Espinoza," she says. "He then arranged the booking."

Matthias steps back from the desk. *Him? That sonuvabitch?*

"However," she adds, "staff are prohibited from contacting board members without management approval, so he wasn't pleased. He ordered management to dismiss the night concierge for the infraction."

"Is the guest still in the safehouse?"

"No, *monsieur*. She left early this morning. I tell you this because your mother is also on the board, and perhaps she could overturn the decision. The woman was a new hire, unfamiliar with procedures. She's a mother of two."

"Is there a problem?" asks one of the soldiers as he approaches the front desk, noticing the extended whispering between them. "You have been informed your stay has ended?"

"I'm going, I'm going," Matthias says, then turns to the concierge. *"Merci,"* he says, before leaving the safehouse.

Sergio Espinoza. The name makes Matthias sneer as he settles in his car, his mind boiling with vitriol. That bastard was the one who spiked the training for the apostolate program to a torturous degree—the cattle prods, the waterboarding, the stretch racks. And the sadistic idea of forcing children to fight wild animals. Like bears.

"Trainee is down," he flashes back to the forests of Romania, hearing Andreus yell into his two-way, the sound of footsteps sloshing through the marsh toward him. *"Emergency services needed now!"*

Matthias had looked up at the sky as sunlight filtered through the trees, his senses overwhelmed by agony. Lying on the ground, he glanced at his left side, where blood streamed from a gaping wound, with bones from his ribcage protruding through the gash. Turning his head, he saw the 500 lbs. animal not far off, squealing from the gunshots it's riddled with.

"Sergio!" Andreus yelled when he reached him, dropping the rifle that had stopped the bear and pulling out a medical kit. *"Help me dress his wounds!"*

"The helicopter will not get here in time," a man's voice said, his Spanish accent sharp and cold. *"It's best to put him out of his misery."*

"We can carry him to higher ground where the chopper can meet us."

"I carry no one," Sergio said. *"I am not here as a layman. I am here to judge."*

Andreus and Sergio then argued as blood began to pool in Matthias' mouth, choking him. That's when he first encountered those specters and demons, feeling them dance and writhe in the calamity in front of them.

Then he saw Sergio pull a gun to his head.

"It is glorious to die, child," he said with a chilling calm, *"for yours is the kingdom of Heaven."*

Sergio stood bathed in the light, his silhouette warping the beams into a Luciferian glow. Through the agony, choking, and dread, Matthias glanced past him to the trees, sure they would be the last thing he saw.

"And if you pull that trigger," replied Andreus, who in turn raised the rifle to Sergio, *"I'll be the one to punch your ticket to Hell."*

Neither man pulled their triggers, and Andreus on his own dragged Matthias to a clearance for the helicopter to arrive.

"You're a lucky boy," Sergio later said to Matthias, who was strapped in a trauma blanket and an oxygen mask before he was airlifted from the forest. *"It must be nice being the pet monkey."*

Matthias snaps from his recall and peers out the car window. *How is Sergio tied to this? Could it be part of the project?*

And how does Amora know him? And where is she now? So many questions—with no frame of mind to answer any of them, as his pain resurface through his chest and head. He pops a painkiller into his mouth before driving off.

CHAPTER 31

"This goose chase to find one guy is bullshit," says Burroughs, as he and Madison walks along downtown Manhattan. "All we're doing is following hearsay from office clerks with just a picture and a name. For all we know, he left the city."

"Then we'll follow him and track him down," replies Madison. "Everyone leaves a trail. We just have to find it."

"And what are we supposed to do once we find him? Tell him to turn his head and cough?"

"Bridges will relay his orders on what he wants when the decision presents itself."

"All he does is bark orders," bemoans Burroughs. "He should provide us more intel, instead of smoking cigars in his rocking chair, giving hand jobs to the Pentagon boys."

"You can quit if you're dissatisfied with the field," Madison says, turning to Burroughs as they approach One

Police Plaza. "Maybe go back to Border Patrol, and hopefully not get caught taking bribes again."

"I will," Burroughs replies, "if Bridges gets DHS to have my conviction expunged. Those gringos pay what they weigh to get their cocoa through."

Madison shakes his head as they enter the building and approach the officer at the main desk.

"I'm Special Agent Madison with the U.S. Defense Department. Earlier, I called to request access to the city's CrimeTrac system to inquire about a person of interest."

"Let me get you the desk sergeant." The officer disappears into the back office, returning moments later with another officer.

"Sgt. Giordano," he says, introducing himself. "How can I help you guys?"

Madison pulls out a folded picture of Matthias. "We would like to use your database to look for possible matches of this person of interest."

Sgt. Giordano looks at the picture and lets out a big scoff. "Ha! I remember this guy."

"You know him?" Burroughs asks.

"He's a bail enforcement agent who came here over a week ago, handing in a gang member. You're busting him for using those grenades in New Jersey?"

"It's under our investigation," Madison quickly lies. "Do you have the warrant file?"

"I told the guy he can't use pyros," says Sgt. Giordano as he types on his computer. "Yeah, here he is. Here is his address. I also have the address of the FFL dealer he purchased the pyros from."

As Madison goes to check on the target's address, Burroughs walks into a military surplus store and approaches a man behind the counter.

"I would like to speak to Jason Hodges," Burroughs says, showing his ID. "I'm Josh Burroughs, with the Defense Department."

"How can I help you?" Hodges replies warily.

"I'm here about one of your customers. Matthias Monroe. He's a bail enforcement agent."

"Uhhh," says Hodges, scratching his head. "I don't recall the name."

Burroughs instead reaches into his pocket and pulls out a picture of Matthias. "Take a good look. He would've come through here sometime in the past few weeks."

"I don't recall the guy," says Hodges after looking at the picture. "Most of my customers are veterans needing uniforms for ceremonies and parades, or campers wanting supplies."

"Or a bounty hunter needing equipment, since you have an FFL to import non-lethal gear. And there's an inquiry by the Camden Police Department of him using flashbangs to apprehend a fugitive. Some of it was traced back to this business."

"Well," says Hodges, "I can't control what people do with the stuff they buy. If a guy has the money and the credentials to buy left over stock, that's all I need."

Burroughs squints at Hodges. He's clearly lying. "Listen, I find it hard to believe you sold this guy pyros and don't remember him. I don't care if you're smuggling rocket launchers—just tell me what you know."

Hodges crosses his arms, his tone sharpening. "First off, any wrongful use of tactical devices falls under the ATF, not the DoD. So you have no jurisdiction to ask me any questions. And even if you did, I don't have to answer them unless I'm charged with a crime and have a lawyer present. So unless you're detaining me, you're wasting your time, buddy."

Burroughs huffs as he reaches into his pocket. Fine then.

"There aren't a lot of customers that come in here, are there?"

"What's it to you?" Hodges retorts.

Burroughs pulls out a set of brass knuckles, slipping them onto his fist. "Because I don't want any witnesses seeing what I'm about to do. Or how hard I'm going to be for it."

As he uses a rag to wipe the blood off his brass knuckles, his phone rings. It's Madison.

"So, did you find anything?"

"The suspect has been here a few times," Burroughs says. "He even tried to trade the store owner an expensive watch, but the guy said it had a GPS locator inside the casing. He said he broke the chip when he found out."

"See if he still has the watch and the chip," says Madison. "Bridges can analyze them."

"What about you? Did he show up yet?"

"I went to his office, but some nosy lady next door started asking questions, so I fell back. I'm staking out the building from across the street."

Burroughs turns his head as he hears a faint sound behind him—gurgling and gasping. "I should be done soon."

He hangs up and turns back to the storefront, taking in the chaos: smashed display cases, light fixtures ripped from the ceiling, and clothes scattered and ruined. His gaze shifts downward, following a trail of blood on the floor to Hodges, who struggles to recover from the beating inflicted on him.

"And where are you going?" Burroughs says. "You haven't finished answering my questions. Such as: where did you get this?" He holds up an assault rifle to Hodges. "I found this in your back office. An automatic AR-15 with a suppressor and a buttstock. Your FFL doesn't allow you to have this."

He then watches as Hodges continues crawling toward the front door, desperate to escape.

Burroughs spots a Bowie knife in one of the smashed display cases. He grabs it, unsheathes it, and returns to Hodges. Grabbing him by one of his legs, Burroughs menacingly slices into the flesh behind the knee.

Hodges screams, his cries echoing through the store, as the blade severs his popliteus tendon.

Burroughs then drops the leg and bends low, flipping Hodges onto his back. Pressing the knife to his jugular, he growls, "Where the fuck is that watch he gave you?"

For a few moments, Hodges' bloody face sputters air as the fresh pain makes him hyperventilate. "In the desk," he finally answers. "In the back."

Burroughs moves to the back office, already wrecked from his earlier rampage, having tossed the inventory and smashed the computer towers to disable the security cameras. At the desk, he yanks open the drawers, rifling through a litany of invoices and junk mail before spotting the black Patek Philippe. Examining its base, he sees the back of the timepiece has been pried open. Inside the drawer, next to where the watch lay, he finds a circular chip snapped in two.

He pockets the items and spots a box of roadside flares. He grabs one and leaves the office.

"Well," Burroughs says, "I guess I have what I need, so I'll be out of your way." He then picks back up the AR-15. "Oh, you don't mind if I take this, do you? I like to go skeet shooting."

He then strikes the flare and tosses it onto a pile of Army uniforms on the floor.

Flames smolder from the clothes, spreading embers from the tattered inventory toward the boxes and papers spread out on the floor.

"Thank you for your service, lieutenant," Burroughs says as he walks out of the store, hearing the flames build to consume everything inside. "Make sure you add a Purple Heart to your valor."

CHAPTER 32

Matthias tries to get onto his office's internet, to no avail. He switches laptops, readjusts the router—nothing. He tries other networks—nothing. He then checks the modem; its amber light steady, indicating no signal. Even his phones are sluggish on the cellular network. It's bad enough he isn't learning any details about Laquan's murder, but now he can't see if the police have any leads on him.

Then his phone rings. It's Fat Pat.

"You need to get to the hospital," he says, uncharacteristically panicked. "Something has happened to Hodges, and it involves you."

An hour later, Matthias enters the hospital and finds Fat Pat in the visitors' lounge. "How is he?"

"He's in surgery right now," Fat Pat replies uneasily. "The sonuvabitch beat him within an inch of his life. Then he set his store on fire. Luckily, the firemen found him in time."

"You said this involves me. How?"

"Because the guy who did this is looking for you. Hodges told me before they wheeled him to the operating room. His name is Josh Burroughs. He's some DoD agent."

"Why is the DoD looking for me?"

"Only you can answer that," Fat Pat says, "and why he got aggressive with Hodges to find you."

Matthias mulls over who this guy could be. *Maybe this is about the project. Or maybe he's assisting the police with the murders. No, it must be something else. He needs to find out more about this guy.*

"I'm going to need your computer," Matthias says to Fat Pat.

"You know this is illegal," Fat Pat says as he leads Matthias through the back office in his pawnshop. "Just because I can do federal searches doesn't mean I have clearance. Unauthorized access is a felony."

"You can say you're looking for a jumper," Matthias replies, "in case anyone inquires."

"Thanks for the lesson on how to skirt the law. I've only been in bail enforcement for over ten years." Fat Pat then plops into his chair at his desk and starts navigating on his computer.

"Here's the info on the prick," Fat Pat says. "Josh Burroughs, Interim Special Agent for the Department of Defense. He served with the Marines at Camp Pendleton, then spent seven years with the U.S. Border Patrol. He then got arrested for federal bribery and drug trafficking and was sentenced to three years." Fat Pat turns to Matthias. "When did the government start hiring ex-felons as agents?"

"They don't. He probably was hired by someone contracted with the DoD."

Fat Pat turns back to the computer screen. "It does say here that his director is some contractor, Robert Bridges."

"Robert Bridges?"

"You know him?"

"He's a friend of my father," Matthias says. "If you can call it that."

"Why is he looking for you?"

"I don't know."

"Well, your father's friend's friend just busted up my friend," Fat Pat says. "And for what it's worth, Hodges could've given you up to the ATF when they questioned him about the flashbangs from your New Jersey stunt. Or about buying an assault rifle with some watch that had a GPS tracker inside it."

"What do you know about that?"

"Hodges brought it to me to inspect. I'm the one who found the tracker. I told him to throw them away, but he said he wanted to keep the watch." Fat Pat then points at Matthias threateningly. "You need to track this guy down and fuck him up."

Matthias lets out a huff, making his chest and ribs ache. He needs a painkiller. "I'll track the guy down and see what he's searching me for."

"And fuck him up. Not to meet him for a champagne brunch. You! Better! Fuck! Him! Up!"

"I'll handle it. Now I need you to go back on your computer and find someone who committed a crime."

"Who are you looking for?"

"Me. Type my name."

Fat Pat types on his keyboard, pauses as the data loads, then swivels to Matthias. "Well, you've been a busy motherfucker."

Matthias walks over to Fat Pat and peers at the screen. Listed are the names of his victims: Laquan and his four henchmen. No eyewitnesses. No signs of a break-in. Objects of note: a hidden camera disguised as a pendant was recovered from one of the victims, along with two file links—one labeled as a JPEG, the other an audio file.

"Click on the JPEG," Matthias says.

Fat Pat opens the image to a grainy photo of Matthias, battered and bruised, taken in the bar. The police must have extracted it from the camera's metadata. Despite the poor quality, it's clear enough to identify him.

"Click on the audio file," Matthias then says, moments later hearing an emergency recording:

"9-1-1 Dispatch. How may I help you?"

"My name is Amora De la Cruz," goes the familiar voice. *"I want to report some people murdered yesterday."*

"What details do you have about the incident?"

"Five people were shot and killed in front of me."

"Can you tell me your location?"

"I can't. He said he would find me if he knew I told."

"Who is he?"

"Matthias Monroe. He's the one that killed them."

"How do you know this person?"

"Matthias was with Laquan. He was one of his employees or something."

"Who is Laquan?"

"Laquan Jackson. That was my boyfriend who he killed. Laquan and his crew came over to my apartment to hang out. This Matthias guy was with them. Then he just shot them. I don't know why. Then he said he would kill me if I told, and then he left."

"Can you provide a description of the person?"

"He's a big guy. A body builder type. And he has scars on his hands, like they were burnt. Very wound-up type of person."

"Ma'am, I would like to transfer your call to the detective in charge of this case. Please hold while I—"

[click]

Matthias squints as his face contorts. *Fine. Have it your way, chica.* "Do a federal search on the following names: Amora Navarro, Amora De la Cruz, Miguel Espinoza, and Sergio Espinoza."

"Is this connected to the guy that attacked Hodges?" Fat Pat says. "I'm not here to help you settle your vendettas."

"If you want me to take care of this Burroughs person, then do the search." Then as Fat Pat begins the inquiry, Matthias' phone buzzes with a direct message:

'You are declared *Ex-Delicto*. All financial accounts will be terminated. All passports will be flagged fraudulent. Any access in current use will be canceled. All privileges will no longer be at disposal. Do not reply. This is an auto-generated notification.'

CHAPTER 33

As Matthias drives along Manhattan's West Side Highway, he receives pings on his phone from his bank and credit card companies, informing him that his accounts have been frozen. He calls Mum. Disconnected. He calls Andreus. Disconnected. Then Nigel—the same. He tries email. His username has been deleted from its client domain.

"Fuck!" he yells, slamming the phone onto the passenger seat. He doesn't need this right now—between his chest injuries flaring, being hunted by some crazed DoD agent, and a femme fatale working with an authenticator. He turns off the highway and soon parks on the street behind the office building.

Matthias heads to the service alley gate and punches in the code on the keypad. Nothing. He tries again. Still nothing. Nigel must've changed the access code. He then looks up at the gate's barbed-wire crown and exhales a tired huff.

He returns to his car and takes out the driver's side floor mat. Back to the gate, he climbs halfway up and drapes the mat over the barbs to dull their edge. Bracing himself with a few sharp thrusts upward, he vaults over, rolling off the mat and crashing hard onto the alley floor.

Matthias groans as he rolls on the ground, pain lancing through his injured sternum. He forces himself upright, ignoring the deep ache in his chest and the fresh scrapes along his arms, and limps to the service elevator.

He steps out onto his floor, scans the hallway, then hustles to his office. The metal door bears scuff marks and dents—signs someone tried to force their way in. Matthias pulls out his key card, slides it through the slot, and punches in the code. Nothing. He tries again. Still nothing.

"Leiden die Kinder," he mutters, as exhaustion and pain begin dragging him down.

"Neighbor, neighbor," Matthias then hears, as Ms. Dereschuk steps from her office towards him in a hurried state. *"Kto-to byl zdes'. Nam nuzhno pogovorit."*

"How did you know I was here?" Matthias asks her.

"I have door camera, like you," she says, pointing to the camera mount perched on top of her door. "I made building manager put in keypad too. I pay rent here. I should have the same perks."

"Good for you. What is it that you want?"

Ms. Dereschuk then gesticulates with her hands as she speaks Russian rapidly, making Matthias put up his hands to her to slow her down. "English, Ms. Dereschuk," he says. "English."

"A man came for you," she says. "He bang on door, makes much noise. I first thought it was building manager when he was in office earlier, so I ask him what—"

"Nigel was in the office?"

"He said he was cleaning things. Then he left but then the other man came. When I ask him who he was, he come to me with questions about you."

"What did he say?"

"He asks how long you been there and is anyone with you. I then ask if he was police. He says he is government agent. He gave me card."

Ms. Dereschuk hands Matthias a business card. Brian Madison, Department of Defense. *Another one? Shit.*

"He then ask me about my immigration status," she says. "I told him none of his business. He said I am to call him when you show up or he will have me deported. I can't afford to leave and go back to Russia, but I said nothing, neighbor." she then looks over Matthias with concern.

"You look tired and beaten. And why you stand outside office?"

"It's been a rough few days. And my key card doesn't work so I can't get in."

"Hmm," Ms. Dereschuk murmurs. Before he can object, she takes the key card from his hand and steps to the office door. She swipes the card, taps a code into the keypad, then swipes again and enters another combination. The lock clicks. She pushes the door open.

"How did you do that?" Matthias asks.

"I had same problem," she says. "The building manager says to press five zeros, then to hold Enter button to reset and add new password."

God bless nosy neighbors. Matthias enters the office—many of the items have been cleared out: his phones and computers, the lockbox with petty cash and passports, the bulletproof vests and guns. He then spots a sheet of paper on the kitchenette counter. He picks it up. It's a note:

'I'm told to clear out the office when you leave. No hard feelings, I hope. By the way, I did not touch the safe.'

Analysts, Matthias reckons with an eye roll and a sneer. He then grabs an empty duffle bag off the floor and goes to the wall safe, opening it to $30,000 in cash, a flash drive with $25,000 in Bitcoin, one burner phone, his remaining

Glock 19, and a bottle of painkillers. He stuffs them into his duffle bag and leaves the office.

"You go now?" Ms. Dereschuk says, still waiting in the hallway as he closes the door behind him. "But what if that man comes back when you not here? He made threat to deport me."

"If he comes back, tell him you don't have to talk to him, and that you contacted the Inspector General and filed a complaint. That should back him off."

"I will do that," she says. "When will you be back?"

"I may not come back," Matthias says.

"Oh," she says disappointedly. "Where do you go?"

"I don't know. Maybe I'll be a cowboy and take up bull riding."

"Huh?" She scrunches her face. "What is bull riding?"

"Think of a Cossack on top of a buffalo," he says as he heads to the stairway. "See you around, Ms. Dereschuk."

CHAPTER 34

"Who is this?" McBride asks.

"It's me. Bridges."

"How did you find me?"

"The agents on your security detail are incompetent as shit. I could've followed you in a garbage truck and they wouldn't have noticed."

"But how did you get this number?"

"I could find an albino penguin in the Antarctic if I wanted to. I called to know how the briefing went?"

"It's more like a tribunal. These officials looked at me like I handed the launch codes to the Ayatollah."

"They're just assessing the national security implications and to find any policy gaps. They've all agreed not to bring charges against you for your testimony. Just tell them what you know about ARIES, and everything will be fine."

"The FBI separated me from my family and sequestered me in a hotel. They've got an agent at the door so I can't leave, and the only person I can talk to is my lawyer."

"That's their protocol. They do that for everyone."

"And my wife has been getting weird phone calls to the house."

"How do you know this?"

"My attorney told me. He has been checking on my family while I'm stuck here. They mostly hang up when she picks up, except one, who said, *yawm alhisab qadim la mahala'*.

"The day of reckoning is sure to come," Bridges translates from Arabic. "Tell Chambers your family is being harassed. It could help expedite the relocation process."

"Don't you tell me what to do," McBride snaps. "You've done enough to derail my life. All so you can run your shitty company like you're some Third World dictator."

"You should be grateful I'm even part of the investigation. Otherwise, you could be heading to Ft. Leavenworth instead of some resort in the Bahamas."

"You pulled every trick you could to make sure I was out of the way. Now you want thanks for it? How about this instead? Fuck you and burn in Hell!"

"Regardless of your sentiments," Bridges says, "I always look out for soldiers who risked their lives to protect this country. And you were a soldier. A stupid one—but a soldier, nonetheless. So take the life preserver you're given, but don't think you can piss on the sharks along the way."

Bridges hangs up the phone. *Ingrate. He would be better off if the military were just made of drones and bomb-sniffing dogs.*

He then feels a presence close by and turns to see Madison standing next to him.

"Why are you here? And you don't knock?"

"I did sir," Madison replies. "But you were too engrossed in your phone call to hear me."

"How did you get past the girls posted by the office door?"

"Charm, sir," says Madison dryly. "You said you wanted this analyzed, so I took the train to deliver it personally."

Madison reaches into his jacket and pulls out a clear plastic bag, containing the Patek Philippe watch and the broken GPS chip.

Bridges takes the bag from him. "You could've express-mailed the watch."

"I rather take the trip, sir."

"What's the matter, you don't like sharing the bathroom with your roommate?"

"He's undisciplined," Madison says. "He practically burned down a store the other day and nearly killed a guy for the watch. A veteran owner at that. Then he asked me to ask you scrub the video to eliminate the evidence from the police."

"Why are you telling this to me now?"

"I was only informed today, sir."

"I'll see what I can do. He's lucky I tolerate you enough to even consider doing this for him."

"I'll tell him of his good fortunes, sir," says Madison. "Now to update you on the mission—the target is some sort of bail enforcement agent."

"Is he alone?"

"As far as I know. Although I did see someone come out of his office and remove items while I was staking it out. When I described the person to the other tenants in the building, they said it sounded like the building manager. Apparently, he and the suspect were often seen together."

"Tell Burroughs to go to the building and look for information on the building manager. In the meantime, head to the forensics lab in Fairfax to trace the watch and GPS chip for its place of origin." Bridges then opens his desk drawer and pulls out a black SSD drive, the size of a smartphone, giving it to Madison. "And while you're there, take this to the senior encryptor there. I called him earlier, so he knows what it's for."

"If it all the same," Madison says, "I would like one of the girls outside the office to accompany me. The brunette, in particular."

"Rizzoli?" Bridges exclaims. "Oh, you must have a jones for her. Fine. Let it never be said I don't take care of my soldier's needs—despite what some people say. But if you get her pregnant, the child support is coming out of your paycheck."

CHAPTER 35

Two days later, Bridges receives a phone call from Chambers. "They're ready for your statement now."

"Now you call?" bemoans Bridges as he stands on the grounds of a golf club. "I'm on the fifth green. I'm not dressed for the briefing."

"Must be tough living your best life on a Monday. Be here in an hour."

Rather than argue over a rare day off, it's better to appease the puppetmasters and take a cab. Twenty minutes later, wearing a polo shirt and cargo shorts, he makes his way to the U.S. Capitol Building—and it's bureaucratic halls, ignoring the suited frowns provoked by his attire—to an unmarked room.

Something's happened, as he sees people frantically dart out of the room in all directions—including Chambers, who rushes past him.

"Aaron, what's wrong?" Bridges calls out. "Aaron. AARON! What happened?"

Chambers stops and turns to Bridges. "There was an incident at the hotel Quentin was staying. He's dead."

"Here we are, sir," Clarke says from behind the wheel, bringing the car to a stop across from the hotel. "And from the looks of it, all the bureaus are here—FBI, CIA, even the Secret Service. All of them for McBride?"

In the back seat, Bridges—now in a proper suit after a stop at his office—peers out the window. Barricades surround the hotel, with men in their agency jackets posted along the perimeter.

"The hotel is used to sequester witnesses," he explains. "A security breach forces them to relocate, which can be a nightmare to coordinate between agencies."

"Collaboration at its finest," Clarke mutters. "Should I drive around and find you an opening, sir?"

"No. I'll get out here. I'll call you when I'm finished."

Bridges hops out of the car and crosses to the barricades, where a police officer stands guard. After flashing his ID, the officer lets him through, and he walks into the hotel lobby, alive with irate agents, barking into their phones and at anyone within earshot. He weaves past the chaos and enters the elevator, riding it to the third floor.

There, the mood is more somber, as FBI agents and forensic techs work in hushed tones. Bridges continues past them until he spots Chambers with two agents outside a room sealed with a plastic sheet taped over the doorway. Pools of blood mark the carpet in front of its entrance.

Chambers turns, catches sight of Bridges, and steps from the doorway to meet him down the hall.

"What are you doing here?"

"I'm here to investigate what happened."

"You do not have the expertise to be here," Chambers replies. "You were not called for your input. This is outside the scope of your business."

"My CEO was killed, and you expect me to do nothing? And why is the FBI handling the crime scene when they are the ones that lost a witness?"

"Come with me," Chambers hisses at Bridges, leading him down the corridor until he finds a spot for privacy.

"These guys just lost a fellow agent. Don't be snarky around them. Furthermore, your presence risks the investigation being compromised."

"How so?"

Chambers folds his arms across his chest. "Why did you call Quentin two days ago?"

"I called him to find out how the briefing went. That's when he told me ARIES was threatening him."

"Yes," affirms Chambers. "That's what we picked up from the phone logs. His lawyer had a field day saying we violated the gag order as part of Quentin's relocation process."

"I didn't know he was under a gag order."

"You don't have to know everything we are doing. For all we know the call led to his location being leaked."

"You can't possibly think this is my fault," Bridges says,

"We're still gathering evidence, so right now nothing is off the table. And need I remind you that despite whatever security clearance you have, you're still a civilian involved in a federal investigation."

"So now I'm a civilian?"

"You're going to leave." Chambers then stares at him without wavering. "Or I will have you arrested for obstruction."

Bridges and Chambers then lock eyes, before he feels the weight of the decree. He walks away.

"And don't leave town," Chambers tosses.

As Bridges rides the elevator down, his thoughts map out how this could play. Not only will this throw the company into upheaval, but with him shut out from the details, he's unprepared for any fallout that may come. Furthermore, fallen soldiers deserve honor, so at least for him he'll have to get past the puppetmasters to find out what happened. Quentin may never had been his brand of vodka, but he didn't deserve this—whatever this was.

"The briefing is starting," he then hears above the clamor of the lobby as he weaves toward the exit. Moments later, the agents start to scurry to the mezzanine.

Bridges watches them funnel into a conference room in the upper tier. He heads to one of the lobby attendants.

"What's going on?" Bridges asks, flashing his ID.

"There's a briefing the FBI is having about today's events," the attendant replies. "And how to transfer some of the guests to other locations."

Bridges turns and follows the crowd, upstairs into the packed conference room. After a few minutes, a man steps to the front and approaches a podium.

"Good morning," the spokesperson begins. "These are the directives given by the FBI Director. For those agencies needing help with witness relocation for their cases, they can coordinate with the Witness Security Team for lodging and transportation."

"You can't secure your own guys," jeers from the agents. "What do we need you for?"

The spokesperson huffs to secure his decorum. "In return, we ask that your regional directors assign analysts to support our Evidence Team on the third floor. Those who agree should remain to receive the preliminary packet to pass along to them. Those who cannot are free to proceed with their own plans. Just be advised that we have authorization to commandeer the roads within the perimeter for the next twelve hours."

Bridges watches as some agents file out the conference room, grumbling under their breath from the terms. *Collaboration at its finest.*

"Here are the preliminaries," the spokesperson then says. "A suspect disguised as hotel staff with a cart approached the room where the FBI agent was posted. The suspect shot the agent with a silencer before the agent could respond. The suspect then barged into the room. Twenty seconds later, he reappeared on camera, dragged the agent in, shut the door, staged the cart in front of the room, and walked down the stairs."

"How old was the agent?" someone asks.

"He was twenty-six."

"You assigned a kid to guard a high-risk witness? You fucks are so dumb."

"Some respect, please," implores the spokesperson. "Anyway, about twenty minutes later, hotel security discovered the agent and the intended victim; a witness in a DHS investigation. No one else was harmed, and there's no indication of anyone else targeted."

"Did you get the car's license plate?"

"We're still going through the footage for an ID on the car. A composite of the suspect will be included in the packet, along with a picture of a ceramic figurine that was in the cart, we believed left by the suspect as some sort of marker."

"A figurine of what?" Bridges asks the spokesperson.

"We believe it's either a goat or a ram. It has words written on it in Arabic. We're analyzing it for DNA."

"What does it say?"

"We do not have an interpreter available at this time."

As the agents continue their questioning, Bridges leaves and exits the hotel. He's heard enough. Clarke can retrieve the packet while he waits in the car. Besides, from what he's gathered, he can guess what the writing on the ram says:

The day of reckoning is sure to come.

CHAPTER 36

"I found the subject's accomplice," Burroughs says into his phone. "His name is Nigel Laine."

"And who did you set on fire for the information?" Madison asks.

"No one, smartass. The number for the corporate office—Pierrepont Realty—was on the signage in the building's lobby. So I went there, said I had a meeting with the building manager about office space but lost his number, and the front desk gave me his profile. They even gave me his picture, so we know what he looks like."

"You may have some brain cells, after all," Madison says. "Forward me his info so Bridges can probe further."

"How's Fairfax?"

"The forensics lab is cross referencing the tracker's design. It's going to take a while."

"Then I'll call Bridges and forward the info myself," Burroughs replies snidely, "rather than have you relay it to him like you're my chaperone."

"It's a matter of protocol, Burroughs. But you can forward him the profile if you want."

"Why are you calling me?" Bridges asks into his phone, standing beneath the portico of the Pentagon.

"To deliver the status of the target," says Burroughs. "And since Madison is busy, I wanted to keep you informed of my progress."

"You haven't narrowed down his location? It's been over a week. Find the guy."

"I have his accomplice's information. He goes to Columbia University. I'm heading there now and should have the screws turned up on him by the end of the day."

"I'm sending Madison back to assist you. Don't do anything until he arrives." Bridges hangs up, tempted to ship the numb nut to Siberia—for forcing him to maneuver around any investigation he may have triggered.

"What do you mean it's a covert op?" the NYPD Chief of Patrol had asked hours earlier, after Bridges called in his request. *"A man's store was set on fire, and he's in the hospital."*

"He works for us," Bridges replied. *"It's part of a federal firearm license fraud operation. I guess the informant likes to play with matches."*

"The guy was beaten and stabbed in the back on the legs."

"Nonetheless, as this is a federal operation, the DoD will handle the investigation. On a side note, I have courtside seats to the Knicks game. Do you happen to know anyone who could use them?"

Bridges gets another call. It's Clarke.

"I think they're in recess, sir," she says. "His legal team is in the courtyard."

Bridges heads inside and makes his way through the Pentagon until he reaches the indoor courtyard on the main floor. He finds Clarke standing near one of the entranceways.

"They've been here for the past five minutes," she says as they walk along a pathway, moving among staff and visitors.

"You're sure those are his men?"

"As far as I could tell. I've seen them enter with the Deputy Secretary." Clarke stops and points to a table in the courtyard, where three men are seated together.

Bridges watches the men as they talk, before one of them gets up and leaves through one of the other exits.

"Stay here and keep an eye on the other two." Bridges trails behind the man as he exits the courtyard, through the halls, and into the men's room.

Bridges follows and steps up beside him.

"You're one of Benjamin McBride's men," he then says. "I can tell by your suit. Government employees don't dress that well. I mean, FBI agents do, but they're all Hollywood, and the guys at the DoJ—"

"Excuse me," says the man, looking at Bridges incredulously. "I'm busy here. Do I know you?"

"Your client has spent the day answering questions from agency directors about what he knows regarding his son, confirming details about him getting nuclear materials. Correct?"

"Listen," the man says. "I don't know who you are, but you don't approach people in the bathroom—"

"I've once stuck a terrorist's head in the toilet. I've done worse in a bathroom. Tell Benjamin that Robert Bridges needs ten minutes of his time. In exchange, I'll earmark Quentin's family a million dollars. And if that isn't enough incentive, tell him I said *Aziz al-Amin*. And since you were nice enough to not pee on my leg, I'll give you ten grand for relaying the message. He knows how to reach me."

Bridges then leaves the bathroom, hoping he didn't offer a bribe to a government official taking a leak.

CHAPTER 37

.

After spending a few days tucked away in a motel room and recover from his injuries and to plot his next move, Matthias stands at the pier along the East River. He checks his watch: 8:17 a.m. If he calculated correctly, she should be at the desk. If not, he might be confronted by the security team, as his name should be populated as a red flag from the *Ex-Delicto* by now. Only one way to find out.

He crosses the street to the plain-looking building, and after passing through the guarded atrium, approaches the front desk and to the familiar concierge.

"Welcome to the *Maison de Gaine*," she says before looking up to see who's in front of her. "How may I—"

Matthias puts a finger to his lips, signaling her to stay quiet. He then slips a few takeout menus onto the counter, before exiting the safehouse.

◇◇◇

Matthias sits in his car, parked along the side street by the safehouse. It's been nearly an hour since he slipped her the note, and she still hasn't responded. Maybe it was foolhardy to think her earlier request would have made her a viable asset. He'll give her another ten minutes before—

He then spots a woman in a full-length coat emerge from around the corner. She looks down the street timidly, before striding to his vehicle.

"Drive please," she says as she steps inside. "The safehouse has perimeter cameras."

Matthias pulls away, driving down the street.

"It was wise to place your letter between the takeout menus," she continues. "The front guard asked about you before I told him you were a delivery man dropping off leaflets."

"Do you have the transcripts?" Matthias asks.

The concierge reaches inside her coat and pulls out several folded sheets of paper, handing them to him. "Now will you be able to have the woman rehired?"

"Why is she so important to you?"

"She is my cousin," she says. "She came here from Paris. She needed a change of scenery, but she hasn't been able to get another position because management smeared her record. She is at risk of losing her work visa."

"Well, if these transcripts are legitimate, they might give me the leverage to force the board to reconsider."

The concierge then glances out the window. "You can let me out here, *monsieur*. It's best I'm not seen with you in case I've been surveilled."

Several blocks from the safehouse, Matthias pulls the car over to the curb to let her out.

"I trust the information suits you well," she says.

"Bonne journée," Matthias says as she exits, blending into the crowd before turning a corner and disappearing.

Matthias then goes through the transcripts, starting with the conversation between the desk phone and a Panamanian phone number:

+507 6999-0000 - *'How did you reach me at this number?'*

Desk Phone - *'Your target brought me to the safehouse.'*

+507 6999-0000 - *'He brought you there? Why'*

Desk Phone - *'Thinking I'm an asset to save. He just eliminated Miguel's problem. Now he'll be on the run, like you anticipated. However, your apartment is now compromised. It's where the murder happened.'*

+507 6999-0000 – *'He murdered them in my home?'* [silence] *'Come back to Miami. We will discuss this there.'*

Desk Phone – *'It's too late to catch a flight.'*

+507 6999-0000 – *'Stay there until morning. I will arrange a suite. Call me on the phone.'*

[end transmission]

Matthias flips to the second batch of transcripts, taken from the suite Amora switched to:

+507 6999-0000 – *'You will call 911 and point the police to him before you leave town. Do it on a spare phone. Not in safehouse. That should keep that changuito busy.'*

Guest – *'Between dodging the police and whatever that Ex-Delicto thing is, he should be out of your hair for good. And you and Miguel should be cleared to continue with the girls with Laquan out of the way. If I may ask, Sergio, what did he do to trouble you so much?'*

+507 6999-0000 – *'He has lived. His type should not exist.'*

Guest – *'And what type is that?'*

+507 6999-0000 – *'Defective.'*

[end transmission]

Matthias tightens as he reads the transcripts. *Had Espinoza set him up out of sheer spite? And how had he even found a way to get o him? Meeting Amora was random—she had just walked into his office when she was told of him by—*

"That fat bastard," Matthias mutters, as he peels the car towards uptown.

CHAPTER 38

After checking for signs that the police aren't on his tail, Matthias enters the pawnshop, where a group of men bang on the bulletproof casing and metal door, trying to break into the back office.

"Get out here, you sonuvabitch," one of them yells. "I know it was you who turned my boy in. You can't hide in there forever."

The gang of five continue to attempt prying into the fortress, not noticing Matthias behind them.

"Hey, guys," he calls out to them. "No need to make a ruckus. Let's see if we can be civilized and come to a resolution."

"What?" one of them barks, turning around. "Man, shut the fuck up and get the fuck out!"

"But I need to pay my ticket," Matthias replies. "I need to get my mama's ring."

"I'll make your mama cry over your casket," scolds another as he pulls a gun from his waistband. "Step out and act like you weren't here!"

Maybe it's the painkillers in him, but Matthias steps forward.

Stupid. Very, stupid.

Then again, life is stupid. Leiden die Kinder.

"It's my mama's ring," he says. "I have to have it."

"Motherfucker," the other man snarls, walking toward Matthias with his gun raised. "You got a death wish? I can make it come true—"

Matthias pivots low, fakes left, then darts right.

POW! POW! The gunman fires, just as Matthias pivots.

Before the man can readjust, Matthias drives a stunning kick into his face.

The man's eyes roll back as blood pours from his broken nose. He crumples to the floor.

The gang momentarily freezes, watching their comrade fall before turning to Matthias, now standing tall and holding their friend's gun.

"I just want my mama's ring," he says with a smirk.

"Kill this mother..." growls the big man, as he and another guy pull out their guns.

POW! POW! POW! POW! Matthias fires before they can get the drop.

The two men jerk back violently, bullets ripping into their shoulders and clavicles before they topple.

"DO NOT MOVE!" Matthias thunders, storming to the two. He aims the gun at them as they groan on the floor, kicking their weapons out of reach. He then whirls to the remaining two standing, pointing the gun in their direction. They immediately raise their hands in surrender.

"Turn around," he says. "Hands on the wall."

They nervously comply, and Matthias pats them down for weapons. Nothing. He then turns to one of them, who barely looks legal.

"How old are you?"

"Seventeen," the kid says.

"Get these fuckers out of here," he tells them.

The two move from the wall, help their friends to their feet, and shuffle toward the exit, peering back at Matthias as he trails behind them.

"And go to school, you fucks!" he yells, slamming and locking the front door behind them. Stepping over the pools of blood, he picks up the dropped guns and approaches the bulletproof window.

"Some soldier you are," he calls out. "The area's clear. Come from out the back."

Moments later, Fat Pat emerges from the back office, shotgun in hand.

"Look what they did to my place," he says from behind the partition. "The casings are cracked. There's blood on the floor. They punched holes in the sheetrock."

"I'm fine, by the way," Matthias says. "Thanks for asking."

"No, you're not," Fat Pat replies. "Your arm is bleeding."

Matthias glances down and sees an open wound along his left triceps—a bullet graze, bleeding steadily into his shirt. He figures he didn't zag enough. This will smart when the painkillers wear off.

"Do you know what you're doing?" Matthias asks as he sits in the back office, his arm stretched out across a table for suturing. "I don't want to get gangrene."

"Shut up, boy," Fat Pat replies as he works on the wound. "I was part of an Army medic battalion. I've patched up better guys than you on my worst day."

"What was that about, anyway?"

"Some clowns blamed me because their boy got rounded up by the Marshals. They think I snitched because he jumped bail a year ago."

"Did you?"

"I wish I did," he says. "That bum cost me five racks I'll never get back. I hope they examine his prostate with a taser."

Fat Pat finishes stitching Matthias up and tosses him a packet of gauze. "Wrap it tight. Change it every twelve hours."

Matthias opens the packet and starts wrapping his arm, wincing from the patchwork as the painkillers begin to wear off.

"You got any Ibuprofen?"

Fat Pat scoffs. "Suck it up, buttercup. There were soldiers who got shredded from an IED and still hopped on one foot to take down insurgents. You can handle a bee sting."

Matthias squints at him, then notices an open box of leaflets within the clutter of the back office. He walks over and picks up a familiar flyer: *Fat Pat the Bail Bondsman.*

"You give these out when you go over to Angelfish?"

"Yeah," Fat Pat says. "I hand them to some of the girls who might need the service or know someone who does. Why?"

Matthias scowls as the pieces fall into place. *Amora sent the leaflet to Espinoza, who sent it to the office, knowing he would need a bondsman for his cover, Then, once the seeds are planted, Amora feeds him a sob story and steer him to Laquan. Diabolical. Just like an authenticator.*

"You looked up the names I wanted you to pull?" Matthias then asks.

Fat Pat grabs two folders from his desk. "Here's what I could find. You could've made it easier by picking people on this continent."

Matthias takes the folders and starts with the one from the U.S. Attorney's Office. He scans the summary of the closed case.

'During his recruitment, confidential informant Damian Jackson reported that Miguel Espinoza and his brother, Sergio Espinoza—businessmen based in Panama City with ties to Miami—lured women from Central America into Mexico, then smuggled them across Eagle Pass, Texas. Once in the U.S., the women were coerced into sex work through strip clubs across the southern states.'

Matthias flips a page of the report. "Nothing came up on Amora?"

"Not a green card or a visa," Fat Pat replies. "Not even a picture ID."

Matthias scans the paperwork further, reading that the investigation was halted due to a lack of evidence following Jackson's death. *Well, Espinoza had no qualms putting children through the gauntlet, so eliminating a C.I. would be an easy day for him. But without evidence, the accusations would be no more than a cry in the dark. There needs to be more blood to make it stick.*

"I have to go," Matthias says, grabbing the folders. "Call the police if those guys come back."

"You didn't even ask how Hodges is doing," says Fat Pat.

"Well, I was a little preoccupied from getting shot and saving your ass. How is he?"

"The doctor says his hip's fractured, his kidneys are fucked up, and his lungs are a mess from all the smoke."

"Tell him the next time you see him that I'm on the case to find the guy. That should give him some fight."

Fat Pat points at Matthias. "And to fuck him up. You keep forgetting that part. You do what you have to do with Amora, but you'd better find this Burroughs guy and make him pay for what he did."

"Never figured you for the vengeful type."

"I hire people to catch bail jumpers. That's nothing but being vengeful. Besides, you don't fuck with the battalion.

So the next time I meet up with the squad, I want to say I made sure the asshole who did this got taken care of."

"I said I'll handle it," Matthias replies as he heads out. "In the meantime, channel that feeling into getting rid of that smell. You keep that dead mouse in here as if it pays you rent."

CHAPTER 39

Nigel leaves the computer lab deep in thought, brooding as he pushes through campus. There's so much to do in the next few days. He must tell the dorm manager he's breaking the lease, then inform the faculty he's dropping out. This, of course, will prompt them to ask why— something he'll need to come up with an answer for. Somehow, being summoned to the U.K. by a clandestine organization doesn't sound believable. Besides, there's still one question left to answer: where is he going? Because he has no intention of returning to London. Not if he wants to keep breathing with all his body parts intact.

Nigel enters his dormitory and approaches his flat, pulling out his key card. He swipes it through the slot and punches his code into the keypad. It doesn't work. He tries again. Nothing.

"Bloody rubbish," Nigel mutters, pulling out a set of keys to open the door manually. Once inside, he strolls into the studio-sized unit, frowning when he sees his telescope—usually perched in front of the windows—lying on the floor beside its tripod.

"How did this fall off?" he says to himself as he walks over to it. He then hears a faint creak from the hardwood floor behind him.

"Shame on you," a voice suddenly calls from behind, making him jolt. "Looking into people's windows. I have half a mind to call campus security."

He spins around to see Matthias stand at the front of the apartment.

Nigel backs further into the flat in a panic. *Oh God. He's going to kill me.* He looks for a way to escape. There is none—Matthias is by the front door. He then turns to the closet. If he could just reach inside and—

"If you're thinking about these..." Matthias says, pulling a duffle bag from behind him, "...I've taken them off your hands. The guns, the bullets, the grenades, the vests. Everything you stole from my office."

Nigel then turns to the windows. *It's only three flights down. He would survive the jump.*

"Nigel, relax," Matthias says. "I'm not going to hurt you. I'm having a bad day and killing you is not getting rid of this migraine."

Nigel looks relieved enough to speak. "I only did what Ms. Gruber told me. I don't know anything about how they arranged your removal."

"I know. This whole thing is bigger than both you and me. However, I may have a way around it, but first, I wanted to give you that."

Matthias points to Nigel's desk, where a folder lies—the other folder he retrieved from Fat Pat. Nigel goes and peers inside it, seeing paperwork with Interpol labeled on its letterhead.

"What is this?" Nigel asks.

"You wanted details on your sister, so there it is. Though you may not like what in it."

Nigel folds his arm across his chest; his emotions still tilted over the last few minutes. "How about you give me the laymen's terms, then?"

"Very well," Matthias says. "After boarding school, Keila joined the Finnish Army. She spent two years there, then served three more with NATO's Special Operations Forces. Going from the Finnish Army to NATO Special Ops isn't common. She was probably pulled in by someone at Pierrepont. Anyway, during a NATO summit, she went off the rails and killed a Bulgarian general. Maybe the general was someone Pierrepont had a problem with. Or maybe they had a problem with Bulgaria. In any case, after that she went AWOL, ended up on Interpol's Red Notice, and was charged with crimes by the ICC."

"What does that mean?"

"That means if she's caught, she's going to The Hague."

Nigel stands frozen for a moment before buckling slightly under the weight of the news. He pulls a chair from the desk to sit in, looking solemn as he continues to process the ordeal.

"Again, this is bigger than you," says Matthias. "She's an apostle, trained to follow Pierrepont's will. There's nothing you would have been able to do to stop it." He then walks closer to Nigel. "I'm telling you this not to upset you, but so you know who to go after. Who did this to your family."

"And how exactly am I supposed to do that?" Nigel asks, his voice tight. "I don't know a dozen ways to kill a man like you do. They've got the upper hand, and I've got no recourse but to swallow this pill and leave."

"What do you mean, leave?"

"Ms. Gruber dismissed me from the position. She said I might've been more effective in my tasks if I hadn't been so casual with you. I'm being sent back to London for retraining."

"But what about school?"

"Perhaps some other time," says Nigel with a somber calm.

"Nigel, usually analysts aren't retrained. They're retired, if you know what I mean."

"I gather. That is why I'm making plans to not return. To retreat to another country."

"Your passport would be flagged if it's to any destination other than England, so your chances of going somewhere else would be slim. But if you do what I ask, you could get cleared to go wherever you want."

Nigel scratches his head. "And what do you propose?"

"I need you to hack into a phone number, like you did with Russo."

"Whose?"

"An authenticator."

Nigel leans back in his chair. "I'm sure their mobiles would be encrypted. Firewalls, two-factor authentication, and even biometrics. It would be easier to break into a satellite."

"Where's the Nigel who had no issue placing trackers on me? Who told me about how his computer skills made him competent for the position?" Matthias then imitates Nigel mockingly. *"My investigation would be far more in-depth than someone mucking on a TOR browser."* He returns to his voice. "Now you can't do a lookup?"

Nigel narrows his eyes at Matthias. "I do not sound like that."

"Then prove to me you are as competent as you claim. Search the number for anything regarding sex trafficking."

"And if the lookup doesn't turn up anything?"

"Then we can be on the run together. We can hop trains like vagabonds." Matthias pulls out a slip of paper. "Here's the number, and the email address I set up to send me the info."

Nigel resigns with a huff as he takes the slip. "I can use the campus lab while I still have credentials. Speaking of campus, how did you get into the flat?"

Matthias pulls out his key card. "My card looks just like the ones used by the students, with the same keypads. So, I figured you used their locking mechanism for the office, so they might have the same default: resetting with five zeros."

"That would explain why my key card didn't work," Nigel says. "You changed the password."

"And Mum said I wasn't good at coding," he replies. "I should be back in a few days to go over what you find."

"Are you going somewhere?"

"To find *chica*." Mathias turns, picks up the duffle bag, and heads to the door.

"What happened to your arm? Why is it bandaged?"

"A fat kid bit me. He thought I was a turkey leg."

"College fucks," Burroughs mutters as he strides out of the university's administration building. He weaves through the student body toward the edge of campus, grumbling the whole way. He shouldn't have to issue threats just to get intel on this Nigel guy. He's the government—give him what he wants, instead of wasting his time with their self-righteous sermons about school policy and student privacy.

"We would need to see some type of warrant in order for us to give you his address," they told him.

Again, people and their need to see a warrant. "How about instead I get ICE over here to do a sweep? How do you think your enrollment numbers will look when half of them get deported? Give me the address."

Their resistance lasted only a few minutes before crumbling under his authority, and they handed over the address. Now, as Burroughs stands at the edge of campus, eyeing Nigel's dormitory across the street, he waits at the crosswalk. He then sees someone exit the building, heading in the opposite direction.

He squints to confirm what he's seeing. That's him. The suspect.

Burroughs pulls out his 9mm Beretta and breaks into a run to catch him, when a blaring horn from oncoming traffic forces him to dart back to the curb. He looks up the street as a steady flow of cars cuts off his pursuit. He then sees the suspect climb into a car and speed away, widening the distance between them.

"Okay, motherfucker," he snarls as he puts his gun back in the holster. "I'm through being nice."

CHAPTER 40

Fairfax, VA

Madison stirs from sleep as the morning light spills into his hotel room. Then he smells smoke—not electrical or wood-burning, but tobacco. Someone else is in the room. He shifts subtly, feigning a turn in his sleep, and slips a hand between the mattress for the 9mm Beretta he always stashes when he's on the road. His fingers find the grip, and in one swift motion, he whips around and aims at the intruder.

"I was here for forty-three seconds," Bridges says, standing by the entrance, cloaked in the room's darkness except for the amber glow of the cigar in his hand. "Fucking your coworker is making you slack, soldier."

"What time is it?" Madison says, lowering the gun.

"6:40. Which would be your time of death if I was the enemy. Now drop and give me fifty for your unpreparedness."

Madison pulls himself from the bed, and drops to the floor, launching into military-style pushups. Less than a minute later, he springs to his feet, squaring up to Bridges.

"Fifty-seven seconds," sneers Bridges, peering into his smartwatch. "Pitiful. You're fortunate I have a mission to run."

"How did you get in here?" Madison asks.

"Charm," he replies with a smirk. "That and Rizzoli giving me the spare key card to your room. I need her to come with me to Maryland, and for you to go back to New York to help your lunkhead partner."

"What about the forensics on the tracker? The lab is still breaking down the R&D."

"I have the results. I had to go there anyway for the SSD drive. The chip's architecture is proprietary. Since it's against FTC rules to use tech outside of the government's purview, it is imperative you track down this guy and figure out what his mission is."

"Can I say goodbye to Angela before I go?"

"There's no time for morning head," Bridges replies. "Tuck your hard-on back in your shorts and go to New York."

Potomac, MD.

Hours later, as chilly winds rustle along farmland stretching toward the horizon, Bridges leans against his car on a road beside it.

"It's 40°, sir," Rizzoli says as she gets out the car and approaches him. "Don't you want to wait in the car?"

"I once took out a KGB official while he was ice fishing in the Russian Arctic. If you can brave -20° in the Chukotka Mountains, you can handle a nippy breeze."

"Even so, we've been here for thirty minutes. Perhaps he's not showing up."

"He buried his son today. Give the guy some time."

About ten minutes later, a black sedan appears in the distance, heading their way. It slows to a stop beside them, and the man Bridges encountered at the Capitol steps out and walks over.

"Where's my money?" he demands.

"You might want to change your tone," Rizzoli says, resting her hand on the SIG Sauer M17 in her holster.

"That's fine, Rizzoli," Bridges says, pulling a check from his pocket and handing it to him.

The man glances at the check, then gestures for Bridges to follow.

Bridges turns to Rizzoli. "Wait here. I'll be right back."

He stops by his car to retrieve his briefcase, then follows the man to the back seat of the sedan, its door wide open. Bridges peers inside.

"Deputy Secretary," he says. "Let me say my condolences for your—"

"Get the fuck in the car," Benjamin McBride commands from the backseat.

Bridges steps in, and the door shuts behind him. He turns to the man beside him—about his age, though the weight of the world makes him look twenty years older. Benjamin, in turn, stares out as his man slips behind the wheel and drives away.

"These fields remind me of when I took Quentin to a pumpkin patch for Halloween," he says reflectively. "He dressed as a pirate. He was ten, then."

"Mr. Deputy Secretary, I know this time—"

"I've dealt with eight agencies over the past five days, on top of scheduling a funeral for my son. His mother, his wife, my grandchildren—all asking me why this happened. What makes you think I'm going to tell you something I didn't tell them?"

"Three reasons, Deputy Secretary. First, you know the agencies are only inquiring to see how they can fit Quentin into their narrative. He's the best kind of scapegoat: a dead one, and an alleged traitor."

Benjamin turns to Bridges. "My son is not a traitor. He was a U.S. Army soldier and engineer. You will speak of him with respect."

"I stand corrected, Deputy Secretary," Bridges says. "The second reason is money. The company takes out a million-dollar insurance policy on its executives, with it being the beneficiary."

"You insure your executives?"

"Someone should profit from us living in a dangerous world. But I don't have to wait to file the claim. I can wire the money to his family."

'Then do so," says Benjamin. "He did after all improve your company into a somewhat reputable organization."

"I could argue whether the company was already reputable, but instead, I'll give the payout to the family— just not the McBrides. Which brings us to the third reason, and why you were so interested in meeting with me."

Bridges opens his briefcase and pulls out a manila folder.

"While searching through his computer, I found emails to an *Aziz al-Amin*—the same name signed on the painting in his office and was used as his password. I've transferred the messages to an SSD drive and had my forensics team print the messages."

He hands Benjamin the folder, whose face and hands twitch as he thumbs through the pages inside.

"My forensics team tracked down the recipient emails," Bridges continues. "The geolocation came back to the National College of Art in Dublin. So, I contacted the school."

Benjamin peers at Bridges. "You did what?"

"I called the school's director under the pretense of notifying the girl about a death in the family. The director gave me the emergency contacts for her—her father and grandfather: Quentin and you. And if my math is right, she's seventeen. Which means Quentin had her before he turned stateside. Before he got married."

Benjamin turns back to the window, staring over the farmland as the sun begins to dip in the sky.

"Well," he then says. "Don't you get the super-sleuth award."

"Mr. Deputy Secretary, I have no interest in airing Quentin's laundry." He then reaches back into his briefcase and pulls out the SSD drive. "Before DHS confiscated his computer, I wiped the messages from the partition. This drive is the only proof that remains. You can do with it what you will."

"Am I supposed to trust you that this is the only copy?" Benjamin asks skeptically.

"Do you have a choice either way?"

Benjamin goes silent, then takes the SSD drive from Bridges.

"How did Quentin first got involved with ARIES?"

He clears his throat before he begins. "During the Gulf War, Taliban camps still controlled much of the Afghan infrastructure. Businessmen couldn't trade without going through checkpoints. So those who worked with Quentin in the past had him connect them with his commanding officers to broker a deal."

"What kind of deal?"

"The Corp would build a convoy route to the Gwadar port, where the businessmen would ship cargo to India. In exchange, they would give us intel on Taliban insurgents."

"That's too heavy of an endeavor to keep off the books," says Bridges. "Something that size would need approval from the State Department, which I'm sure as a senior diplomat of the Kubal province at that time, you had some influence on.”

“Even so,” Benjamin states, “an agreement was made with the goal of finding the insurgents’ locations, which was an obstacle the Armed Forces struggled to pinpoint.”

“And why the Corp had to stop their side hustle. It would’ve been an underlay to a government operation. Did this mission have an official name?”

“*Operation Roadside*,” Benjamin answers. “At first, everything went as agreed—we gave them maneuverability to trade; they gave us coordinates on the Taliban’s positions. But then friction began among the businessmen. Some didn’t want to be associated with the Americans and fed us false intel. And those who remained involved—well, there were reports their workers were shouting *yawm alkabsh* when the convoy reached the port. So, later when the U.S. evacuated Afghanistan, the Taliban executed anyone suspected of being an U.S. ally. One was a woman named Khalida. She had been an asset to the operation, so when she was killed, getting her family to safety became imperative.”

“Why? Because she had an *oops-baby* with Quentin?”

Benjamin’s face turns frigid. “Carl,” he says to his driver, “pull over and shoot this fuck in the head.”

"My apologies, Deputy Secretary. I'm told I lack a filter."

"No. You're just an obnoxious asshole."

"That too, sir."

Benjamin lets out an exhale before he continues. "Anyway, agreements had to be made to smuggle the family to where they would be granted asylum."

"Agreements with the same people who probably had her mother killed."

"You can't choose your devils," Benjamin replies. "And by then, Quentin was stateside and figured whatever deal he'd made would be moot."

"Until it wasn't. When did they contact Quentin again?"

"A year ago. They wanted blueprints for an RRD and for him to procure the materials so they could build a model."

"Is that why your department recommended him—so he'd have cover for his subterfuge?"

"He was already the CEO by then," Benjamin asserts. "Saving your God-forsaken company from the brink."

"He roped the company into acquiring radioactive materials. So that 'saving-the-company' line isn't going to land well with the Cabinet. Not to mention the President."

Benjamin turns his head and stares out the window once more. "Now I have three things for you. One, tomorrow Carl will go to your office with an account number for you to transfer the money. Two, whoever you have to disclose your investigation to, keep Quentin's name out of it. And three, get out of my car."

The sedan then slows to a stop as the farmland gives way to a strip of rustic shops on the edge of town, and Bridges grabs his briefcase and steps out, back into the cold. As he stands there, watching the car drive off, he pulls out his phone to call Rizzoli.

"Call the recon center to activate my phone's GPS and use the coordinates to pick me up."

"Look out onto the road, sir," she then says.

Bridges glances out, as moments later, his car appears from down the road and pulls up beside him.

"How did you know I was here?" Bridges asks as he gets in the back seat.

"I followed you," she says. "I didn't feel comfortable leaving you with them."

"Still, you disobeyed me. When we get back to Washington, you will drop and give me twenty."

CHAPTER 41

Miami, FL

Taking a flight isn't an option, even if he weren't on *Ex-Delicto*. He's not boarding a plane with a duffle bag full of guns and grenades. So, a road trip it is. Eighteen hours later, Matthias pulls into South Beach and stops across from a club—flanked by exotic cars and men with scantily clad women along its entrance.

Espinoza must really like fish, he concludes as he scans the terrain. *Angelfish in New York; this one, called Koi.* After surveying, he pops in a painkiller before he heads inside. The layout differs from the East Coast venue: the stage sits closer to the entrance and the VIP is on the same tier. Other than that, it's the same brand of lust and gluttony.

Matthias moves through the crowd to the bar, cluttered with patrons. A woman behind the counter walks over.

"What you're drinking?" she asks.

"Is Amora Navarro here?"

She eyes him with suspicion. "We don't have an Amora Navarro here. Perhaps you're thinking of someone from another club."

He reads her tells. She's holding back. Maybe the card will get her to open up.

"She also goes by De la Cruz, right? Amora De la Cruz." He then flashes the business card Amora gave him. "I met her in Angelfish. I manage some girls in Philly and they're looking to travel to other jawns down south. She said to check her out when I'm in town."

The bartender takes the card, pulls a phone from beneath the bar, and scans the QR code. Her expression then softens slightly before returning her attention to him.

"She was here yesterday," she says, "but she left. That's all I know."

"How about the owner Miguel Espinoza?"

"He's out of town, too."

"You have to have some way to reach them." Matthias reaches inside of his jacket and pulls out five one-hundred-dollar bills. "I didn't come all this way for nothing. Maybe you can find a number for her. Miguel's too. I would appreciate it." He then places the money on the counter.

For a moment her expression flickers, before she snatches the bills off the counter. Then she grabs a pen and a napkin to scribble on.

"You didn't get this from me," she says, sliding the napkin to him. "That's her emergency number."

Matthias looks at the number on the napkin. "She has a lot of responsibilities for a shift manager."

"She's not a shift manager," she says. "She runs all of the clubs."

He twists his mouth. *Of course, she'd lied about being a waitress and a shift manager. She's been lying to him from the start. Fucking numbskull.*

"You don't have Miguel's number?"

"We only have Amora's number," the bartender says. "Miguel doesn't even show up most times." She then points towards the crowd. "Ask the girl over there, in the pink and blue. She's one of his favorites. Maybe she has a way to reach him."

Matthias turns to see her, dressed in a pink and powder-blue teddy, the LED bracelet still on her wrist. She sits alone, looking like she'd rather be anywhere else.

He walks over and says into her ear, *"Me debes $100."*

Domencia looks ruffled as she sneers at him. *"¿Qué dijiste? ¿Te conozco de algo?"*

"From Angelfish," Matthias replies. "A few weeks ago."

"I meet lots of people. And I do not owe you money."

"I just said that to get your attention. So, are you working now?"

"I offer no service tonight," Domencia says defensively. "I have my woman time."

Matthias pulls an envelope from inside his jacket. "I can make it worth your while. But I need you for all night."

Matthias gives her a peek inside the envelope, stuffed with cash.

"I know you now," she then says, lighting up. "I remember you from your hands. Why you in Miami?"

"I came for business, but I'm glad you're here instead. I've been thinking about you since I met you. *Y quiero probar lo que he estado pensando.*"

Domencia looks again at the envelope, before grabbing her clutch bag beside her. "*Sígueme.*"

She takes Matthias by the hand and leads him out of the club. Past the crowd, they walk down Ocean Drive toward a pastoral-looking motel at the end of the block.

"You want me all night?" Domencia says, stroking the muscles along his arms as they step into the motel and to the front desk. "You pay for room. All night is $150."

He forks over the cash to the clerk, and Domencia leads Matthias down the hall to a rustic room, with stained walls and a nightstand, and a twin-size bed as its only furniture.

"Well, it's not the Four Seasons," he says as she closes the door behind them—before he hears a *click* near his ear.

"You put hands up," Domencia says, pressing the barrel of her gun to the back of his head. "Walk to bed."

Matthias grimaces as he raises his hands and walks to the front of the bed. *He knows better than to enter a room without checking the rear. These painkillers are making him stupid as shit.*

"You take money out and put on table," she says, "then turn around. You move crazy, I shoot you."

Matthias reaches for the envelope and toss it on the nightstand. He turns to see Domencia with a gun pointed at him.

"Take off clothes," she says. "Get undressed."

"Y'know, this is not how you do foreplay."

Domencia fires a warning shot at the floor, making him jolt. "*¡Ahora, cabrón!*"

"Okay, okay." He then strips to his underwear while Domencia eyes him.

"Turn around and put your hands on wall."

As Matthias does what he's told, she grabs the envelope and scoops his clothes off the floor.

"You're with Amora," she says. "That *puta* sent you to kill me."

"I'm not with Amora. I'm here to find out how she and Miguel are smuggling girls into the country. And how they ordered an informant to be killed."

"Damian?" Domencia says, slightly lowering the gun. "What you know about Damian?"

"He was working with the Feds to gather information on them. When he got too close, she had him taken out. Look, my ID is in my wallet, in my pants. I'm a bail enforcement agent and a private investigator. Go check."

Domencia reaches for his wallet and flips it open. "What are these words? Ball enforcer—"

"Bail enforcement. It means I find bad people. And there's this guy from Panama whose very bad, who has Amora and Miguel bring in women to work in the sex trade. Women like you. I trying to find this guy, but to get to him I need to know how he's operating. I just want to ask you some questions. And can I have my clothes back?"

Domencia squints at him skeptically before tossing his clothes back on the floor. "Put them on. Slowly."

Matthias gathers his clothes and gets dressed. "Tell me what you know, and you can leave and never see me again. You can keep the cash, too."

"I was keeping the money anyway."

"Fair enough. How do Amora and Miguel get girls into the country?"

Once again, Domencia lowers the gun. "We walked for miles to get to Panama, then we are put on a plane to Mexico. From there we're on a bus into Texas. Miguel and other men would then split us up to work to pay off debt. But Miguel is *El Diablo*. He lowers debt if you sleep with him. A lot."

"Is that what he does to you? Make you sleep with him?"

"I do not want to say," Domencia says quietly. "St. Mariana would see my sins." She then looks down to the floor. "Lily of Quito, may you cover my shame."

Really? A Catholic sex worker? What a world. "Why do you say Amora wants you dead?"

"She found out Damian and I were talking. He tried to get me to be witness. He said he was going to get me reloc...I don't know word for moving; the way he said it."

"Relocation," Matthias says. "He was trying to get you witness relocation to testify. But you're not being a citizen would've made it hard for the Feds to substantiate the evidence."

"Then after Amora and Miguel kill him, she says I was telling police. So she tried to set me up by giving me to Damian's brother, saying I was one to get him killed. But Miguel says no. He did not want me dead so he can continue doing things to me."

"Why don't you run away?"

Domencia then holds up her arm and points at the bracelet. "We wear this. It has tracker and we cannot take it off. Other than them changing it once a week I always have it on. Even now they know I'm in motel, thinking I do sex work."

"Let me see the bracelet," says Matthias. "I might be able to get it off."

"*¡Atrás!*" Domencia orders, pointing her gun at him. "You do not move."

"You have a gun on me, taken my cash, and told me your story with me half-naked. In some places that would make us married. You have to trust me, Domencia."

For a moment, she looks at Matthias, before she extends her arm towards him.

He walks over and examines the bracelet—less of an accessory and more like a shackle: a band of brass inset with LED lights, secured with a pin lock. He can't pry it off her wrist, and he doesn't have lockpicks to bypass the latch. Then, he glances at his hands.

"*¿Tiene algún limpiador de desagües?*" Matthias asks.

Domencia looks at him peculiarly. "*¿Que?*"

"Do you have any drain cleaner?"

CHAPTER 42

The motel clerk leads them to the basement, pointing out the shelf of cleaning products. There, at a table, Domencia sits and watches Matthias brew a pot of water on a stove, stirring a mug of blue liquid with a spoon.

"How do you know the clerk to let you have access to the basement?" Matthias asks as he pours hot water from the pot into another mug.

"He's Ecuadorian," she answers, "like me."

"He doesn't care about you shooting a gun in his room?"

"No one cares about gunshots here. It's Miami. So what does this do?"

"This," Matthias says, holding up the mug of drain cleaner, "is sodium hydroxide. When combined with hot water, it triggers a reaction that burns through metal—and skin. So this will hurt."

"How you know this?"

"That's how I got these," he replies, holding up his hands. "I'll try not to be quick. Now turn your hand palms up on the table."

Matthias sits at the table with the mugs while Domencia puts her shackled arm on it. He dips the spoon that stirred the drain cleaner into the hot water, causing it to bubble violently. Moving quickly, he stirs the drain cleaner again, then drizzles a spoonful of each liquid onto the bracelet. A sizzling sound begins as the chemicals start to corrode the brass.

"Hot," Domencia gripes. "But do more."

He repeats, watching the bracelet warp under the exothermic heat. The LED lights flicker and die. Tears well in her eyes as her wrist sizzles beneath the heat.

Bracing her arm, Matthias tugs at the bracelet with his free hand, his fingers now smoldering from the scorching metal. He twists the weakened brass—until Domencia's hand slips free.

"*¡Hijoputa!*" she moans, scrambling to the sink to douse her wrist and hand in cold water.

Matthias looks over the bracelet, still bubbling from the heat. Inside, he spots a small compartment and pries it open, revealing an alkaline battery. He pulls it out, then glances down at his hands, the scent of searing flesh rising from his palms and fingers.

Well, his dreams of being a hand model are kaput.

Changing into jeans and a T-shirt, and with her wrist and hand bandaged in gauze, Domencia steps out of the motel with Matthias behind her.

"They will start looking for me," she says. "They will wonder why the bracelet don't work."

Matthias follows as Domencia strides up the block opposite Koi, then turns the corner toward the beach.

"Where are you going?" he asks.

"I have cash now," she says, holding up her clutch bag, bulging with thousands stuffed inside. "Maybe I head back to Ecuador. This amount is good to move my family from mountains to better place. Oh—I give you this."

Domencia pulls a keychain from her pocket. "Damian gave me this. He told me to hold it for him. It has evidence on it. I don't read English well, so I don't know what it says."

She hands Matthias the keychain, which holds a small flash drive.

"I'll look into it," Matthias says, slipping it into his pocket.

"I go now. You do not follow." Domencia then leans in and kisses him, her unbandaged hand sliding across the back of his head like a lover.

She then pulls away and smirks, reading the dazed look in his eyes as he catches his breath.

"*Adios, guapo,*" Domencia says, before running off into the nighttime of South Beach.

CHAPTER 43

In the late-night hours of The District Diner, Bridges sits in his booth with a scowl, as local college students stream into the eatery after a night of partying. *Millennial waste*, he judges as he takes in their ramblings. *Maybe when World War III breaks out, they can invite the enemy for a round of beer pong.*

He looks up when a man enters, wearing a black T-shirt, camouflage shorts, and a bucket hat, carrying a plastic grocery bag. The man spots Bridges and walks to him.

"Nice outfit," Bridges says. "Did the homeless shelter have a fashion show?"

"Fuck off," the man replies, sliding into the booth across from him. "Do you have them?"

He reaches inside his jacket and pulls out an envelope, sliding it across the table. The man peeks inside. Satisfied, he takes the envelope and in turn slides the bag across the table.

Bridges goes in the bag and pulls out a report, stamped with the Department of State seal and titled *Operation Roadside.*

"Are we done here?" the man says.

"Yeah," Bridges says. "Enjoy the comp at Myrtle Beach. And if you walk on the golf course dressed like that, security will throw you in the lake."

The man leaves, and Bridges flips through the pages of the report. He recognizes some of the names it mentions— like the McBrides and the directors who sanctioned the mission—but it's the names he doesn't know that matter most. Bridges puts the report into his briefcase, along with the other reports he received tonight, from his moles in the DoD, FBI, SEC, and NSA. He can read these in the office.

"Hey, old man," a voice then calls out, snapping him from his thoughts. "Shouldn't you be in bed right now? You don't need that booth. Get up so we can sit down."

Bridges looks to see a large college kid hovering over his booth, wobbling from intoxication.

"Are you talking to me?"

"Your hearing aid ain't working? Come on and get up. The old folk's home is calling for 'ya."

"You're clearly drunk. How about you join the military where they'll make a man out of you?"

"I'm already a man." He flexes at Bridges. "Six-foot-two and 240 pounds of linebacker beef, motherfucker."

They make it so easy for him. "I thought I recognized you. You play for George Washington University. You guys suck."

The young man takes a moment to register the slight before his face twists into a frown. "You talking shit about my team?"

"Cheerleaders are a team. Marching band's a team. You guys are just trash. The only bowl game you're getting has a turd floating in it."

The young man growls and steps to Bridges, calling out to his teammates across the diner. "Hey guys, this fuck is talking shit about the team."

Bridges huffs and taps a button on his smartwatch, sending out a signal. They should be here in twenty seconds.

"You got a problem with how we play, geezer?" one of the football players says as they start closing in.

"Guy probably played when TVs were still black and white," another adds.

"How about we throw your ass out with your walker, bitch?"

A figure steps into the diner, moving toward the players. Then—*click.*

Clarke's arm is fully extended, holding an M17.

"Fuck around and find out," she says. "Then I'll smack your mother at the funeral for making you."

"DoD," Rizzoli announces as she storms through the entrance, her firearm already drawn as she flanks the crowd. "Give me a reason to shoot you assholes. Stand back!"

The football players retreat fast, while the rest of the diner freezes in place, eyes locked on the two-woman crew. Bridges checks his watch. Twelve seconds.

"It's been an adventure, boys," he then says as he calmly picks up his briefcase and stands from the booth. "Maybe we can do this again when you're potty trained."

"Come with me, sir," says Rizzoli, ushering him through the crowd.

"I'll see you again, old fuck," snarls the young man.

For a moment, Bridges considers grace—but they never taught that in sniper school. "Clarke, give this guy a souvenir." Then, as he steps out, a gunshot crackles through the diner.

"MY FOOT!!" the young man cries out. "YOU SHOT ME, YOU FUCKING BITCH!!"

To be fair, it wasn't as if he was getting drafted.

"Tell Bellinger that I need to see him today."

"It's 4 a.m.," Chambers says groggily over the phone. "Don't you sleep?"

"Sleep is for those who can't afford motivation. Schedule a meeting with Bellinger. I have what he's looking for."

"What's the point?" Chambers says. "Your involvement in this investigation is over. The briefing was halted, and Bellinger is taking what he has to The Cabinet for a unilateral decision on labeling ARIES a terrorist organization."

"All he has is Quentin acquiring nuclear materials and drafting blueprints for an RDD."

"He also collaborated with a rogue element."

"Tell him I want a meeting today. I have a solution to all his problems." Bridges then hangs up and, in his office, mentally plays out the impending conversation, refining his arguments. The company's reputation is on the line, and Quentin's—to avoid him being branded a double agent or a philandering gold smuggler whoring for the highest bidder.

There is a knock at the door. Rizzoli walks in, holding a package.

"Mr. Bridges," she says. "A courier dropped this off for you."

"Is Clarke with the police?" he asks as he takes the package from her.

"She's with that captain you told her to see," she answers. "He said he'd bury the incident at the diner—if we get him some Baltimore Raven's tickets. VIP seats."

Bridges opens the package and pulls out the contents: a purchase and sales agreement drafted by the Legal Department at his request. His board members will likely scream when they find out, cursing him for usurping their authority. *Fuck them. If this plays out right, they'll be well compensated. If not, they can write a tell-all when he's in prison.*

Bridges picks up the phone and dials an extension.

"Records Department," a voice answers. "Good early morning, Mr. Bridges. How may I help you?"

"Prepare the kill switch," he says.

"Uh... sir?"

"Prepare the kill switch," he repeats.

"Sir," she says, "that will require the unanimous approval from all of the board members."

"Checks and balances are for pussies. As president of the company, I'm issuing an executive order to override their approval. Prepare the kill switch and then wait for my command."

After a moment, she says, "It'll be ready in six hours."

Bridges hangs up and leans back in his chair, pulling a cigar from his desk drawer.

"Didn't the fire marshals tell you not to smoke in the office?" Rizzoli asks.

"If the flames don't burn us, the government will. Either way, I'm lighting the match."

CHAPTER 44

"I'm forwarding you pictures of a tracker and its circuitry," Matthias says into his phone from a Miami hotel room, standing in front of a table where tiny electrical parts— dissected from Domencia's bracelet—are spread out. "I need you to identify the source. I'm also sending you another number to look up."

"Well, I haven't had much luck with the number you gave me," Nigel replies. "I've only managed to pull a few call records and some metadata, but Sergio seems pretty good about swapping SIM cards and wiping the phone's logs."

"Then restart the search with the new number. And investigate the tracker. Judging by its design, I think you'll find it very familiar."

"*God ettermiddag.* Suisse Assurance and Securities. *Hvordan kan jeg dirigere anropet ditt?*"

"I'd like to leave a message for Delores Gruber."

"And who is calling?"

"Tell her it's Matthias Monroe. Tell her one of the authenticators is a defect. She'll know what it means."

"One moment, please," the receptionist says, putting him on hold for a few moments before returning. "The message has been relayed. She will respond at her earliest convenience."

"*Danke schön,*" Matthias hangs up and turns his attention to the computer in the hotel's lobby workstation, where after some sleep he's been poring over the flash drive Domencia gave him. About twenty minutes later, his phone rings. It's from Zurich.

"*Hallo, Ms. Gruber,*" he answers flatly with a German inflection.

"*Matthias,*" he hears instead, with a pronounced French accent. "*Il semble qu'on ne puisse pas se débarrasser de toi.* You're like a weed that can't be pulled out."

"*Et vous êtes ?*" Matthias asks.

"*C'est Raphael Benoît.*"

Matthias shifts within his seat. He remembers him sparingly—a high ranking general for the French military, and an authenticator.

"Where is she?" he asks Raphael.

"Madame Gruber is in a meeting," he says, "so she suggested that I intervene on your call."

"I left the message for her. Not for you."

"And yet I'm the one you're talking to. Furthermore, your message delivered has captured my interest. So tell me—what do you know about a defective authenticator?"

He doesn't like being brushed aside like child, but whatever. An authenticator is an authenticator. "I have evidence Sergio Espinoza is importing women into the U.S. for sex work. I have their names and the strip clubs they work in: Angelfish, Koi, and Neon Tetra. I have paperwork naming Sergio and his brother Miguel as the owners of these clubs. And I have a surveillance chip used to track these women. Funny how it looks like the chip she put in the watch she gave me."

Raphael's muteness roars like a bomb, before he speaks. "Am I to just believe your evidence at face value? And are not stories invented by someone desperate to save his own skin?"

"You can believe sharks swim with chickens for all I care. But in forty-eight hours, I want the *Ex-Delicto* lifted, my passport reinstated, and my bank accounts unfrozen with a million dollars deposited into them."

"Clearly you haven't the faintest what mercy means. Although you have been dismissed, Madame Gruber has gone through great measures to ensure we go easy on you."

"I'm flattered, really—that an organization that treats child abuse like a fender bender is concerned about my well-being."

"Be that as it may, if you continue down this path—this *plan tiré par les cheveux*—you will invoke the full effect of the *Ex-Delicto*. A clean-up unit will be dispatched to handle you. One could be sent over to you now. You are in Miami, are you not?"

Fuck. Matthias pulls out the flash drive from the computer and begins packing up from the workstation. *He's been tracked. He must leave. Now.*

"I believe I have your attention now," Raphael continues, almost whimsically. "I hear you scuffling on your end. Are you panicked from miscalculating our reach?"

Matthias leaves the hotel into the humid breeze of the Miami morning. "How about instead I hand everything over to the U.S. Attorney's Office. How much international scrutiny will you get if a board member of the Merchants of Pierrepont is arrested for sex crimes?"

"Do you really wish to test our resolve, Matthias?" Raphael asks. "No matter how stubborn the weed, it's eventually burned from the ground."

"Forty-eight hours, Raphael; or you'll witness Espinoza extradited to the U.S. in handcuffs." Matthias hangs up and throws away the phone, not stopping as it clanks into a storm drain.

CHAPTER 45

"I have identified seven individuals to be members of ARIES," Bridges says, sitting across from Bellinger and Deputy Bright in the Pentagon. "Each one has been convicted in their countries of government subversion and working with insurgent movements. And each has since fled to Lord knows where."

"And what corroborates your research?" Bellinger asks.

Bridges opens his briefcase and pulls out the reports he's gathered. "Three are board members of a railway company in Afghanistan, suspected of providing false intelligence to U.S. personnel. One was accused of attempting to embed trading algorithms on the Lisbon Stock Exchange. Two are affiliated with eco-terrorist groups targeting diamond mines in the DRC and Botswana. And the last two are Russian hackers who created a website called *Yesh'te Bogatykh*—which means 'Eat the Rich'—exposing government-sponsored cyberattacks, the locations of political prisoners, and the bank accounts of human rights violators."

"And how are these men linked?"

"They were all mentioned as businessmen opposed to *Operation Roadside*."

"Those look classified," Bright says, pointing to the reports. "How did you get them?"

"I'd prefer not to say," Bridges replies.

"I can't bring this to The Cabinet if the findings weren't obtained within the rule of law," Bellinger says.

"Everything was acquired legally. No money changed hands. I just didn't want to waste time with the bureaucracy."

"So how did you get them?"

"Through timeshares in Malibu, seats to Commanders games, weekend passes to the Myrtle Beach Classic, and tickets for someone named Taylor Swift."

Bellinger and Bright exchange a look before turning to Bridges. "We will confer with The Cabinet of your findings and then let you know the outcome."

"That's it? Even a dog gets a pat on the head when it retrieves a frisbee."

"You can return to your regular activities," Bright says. "But you may be called to testify in a classified hearing."

"And the whistleblower protection?"

"That will have to be determined by The Cabinet, pending any indictments."

Bridges turns to Bellinger. "But you said you were offering the protection."

"If this was solely a DHS investigation, we would. But since this will be a multi-agency investigation, we can only make the recommendation. The Cabinet will decide how it's applied."

"In other words, they might not pick up the investigation if you attach protections to the inquiry, so you rather keep it off so when they look at the company, we'll be left holding the bag."

"Like I said," Bellinger replies, "we'll recommend the protections as agreed."

"And what protections were you giving Quentin, other than the right to get his head blown off?"

"As unfortunate as that was," Bright says firmly, "McBride proliferated nuclear materials to a criminal threat. He had affiliations with this group for years, so full disclosure is imperative to understand the extent of their involvement."

Bridges then smirks at them. They had never intended to offer witness protection—only to use him to frame Quentin.

And what he prepared for.

"I don't like that idea," says Bridges. "And you shouldn't either."

"And why is that?" Bellinger asks.

"Because that's the kill switch, Kevin. The Cabinet will subpoena the company for full disclosure. And that is what we'll give them—full disclosure. Every assassination. Every puppet regime installed. Every coup d'état and false flag campaign. All of our dirty little secrets over the last thirty years."

"Any information not pertinent to the investigation will be deemed inadmissible," says Bellinger. "You know this."

"Inadmissible doesn't mean invisible," Bridges says. "And every agency has a mole—that's how I got these documents. When the other agencies find out, that's when the infighting will start."

"What infighting?" Bright asks with a slight squint.

"The kind that breaks out when the CIA learns the State Department sabotaged one of their black ops. Or when the FBI finds out DHS relocated one of their embedded assets. Or when Congress realizes the DoD redirected fuel convoys to manipulate foreign oil reserves in violation of military engagement treaties. And if other nations discover they were pawns, they might expel diplomats or restrict intelligence-sharing agreements. Some may even launch similar operations against the United States."

"You are threatening the United States with disclosure of classified information, anticipating retaliation?" Bellinger asks. "You do know the sentence for treason is life in prison."

"I'm not threatening the United States, Kevin. You are, if you subpoena the company. Fortunately, because I love this country so much. I have a solution."

Bridges opens his briefcase again, pulling out the legal document couriered to him, tossing it on the desk.

What is this?" asks Bellinger, picking up the document.

"A purchase and sales agreement. DHS will acquire the company's training centers, take over the building rights of our headquarters, and will consolidate our reconnaissance, cyber intelligence, and forensics centers into theirs. And I will step down as president of the company."

"You want to be bought out?"

"Everyone is saying that I'm too old for this game. Maybe everyone's right. Maybe instead I should be sipping

Mai Tai's on the Caribbean Sea, enticing young women to enjoy the yacht of a sugar daddy."

"Aside from that being disgusting," says Bright, "I'm sure the United States is not in the business of acquiring a paramilitary company past its prime."

"Don't tell me about being past its prime. You still use Dial-up for internet access." Bridges turns back to Bellinger. "I'll transfer all intellectual property over, parcel out the existing contracts, and issue severance packages for the operatives and clerical staff. From there, you can prop the company as a DHS front. That way, you can say Quentin was recruited as an operative to track nuclear materials, given he was a key figure in *Operation Roadside*. And all for the low rate of ten billion dollars."

Bellinger tosses the contract on the table. "You're out of your fucking mind."

"DHS has been allocated a hundred-billion-dollar budget this fiscal year. There are only so many proxy wars you can fund. And think of all the classified documents you'll gain access to. Thirty years of secrets buried by your counterparts. The blackmail you could expose. The quiet nudges and knowing winks you can exchange in Cabinet meetings. That kind of leverage can get a lot of requests moving through red tape."

Deputy Bright turns to Bellinger, taken aback when seeing his face mull over the idea.

"You can't possibly be contemplating this quack," she says.

"Going through committees for operation approval is a bitch," Bellinger replies.

"You take over the company, clear Quentin of any wrongdoing, and when you approach The Cabinet, it will be as an inquiry to a threat instead of dumping blood on a dead man's head." Bridges then grabs his briefcase and stands. "You two have plenty to discuss, so I'll leave you to your eye gouging. Deputy Bright, it's been a pleasure. Perhaps next time we meet, you'll learn that you shouldn't wear tweed. It makes you look like a rug."

CHAPTER 46

Nigel hunches over his laptop, with various decoding and surveillance peripherals connected to its hub, turning his desk into a bare bones satcom unit. He types into the terminal window of his hacking software, entering the number Matthias gave him. Then, after a few moments of debugging, he accesses the phone's file registry and clicks on the last folder of text messages:

Amora – *'We have a problem, sir. We have a runaway in Miami. The one I mentioned before, Domencia.'*

Sergio – *'Has the tracker been able to locate her?'*

Amora – *'No, sir. She must've disabled it.'*

Sergio – *'This is why we will implement the new trackers. In the meantime, you will send me information on her next of kin so they can be handled.'*

Nigel continues his search—scrolling through brief, useless messages—until another thread catches his eye.

Sergio — *'I have a new shipment of trackers that arrived. These will be inserted into the workers behind their ear.'*

Amora — *'Will the incision hurt?'*

Sergio — *'A surgeon will be with Miguel when the workers arrive. They will be anesthetized.'*

Amora — *'And if the girls refuse the tracker?'*

Sergio — *'Do I have to say what will happen to them?'*

Amora — *'No, sir.'*

Sergio — *'And what of Matthias?'*

Amora — *'As far as I know he is still in New York. He has not been apprehended by NYPD as of yet.'*

Sergio — *'He has been removed from my organization. That pequeño mono always thought his place in the world was bigger than what it is. He now learns how disposable he is.'*

Nigel copies the file and sends it to Matthias' email. That could be something he could use.

Then, there is a knock on the door. Maybe Matthias arrived early. Nigel gets up and looks through the peephole, to see two men standing on the other side.

"Mr. Laine," he hears as he opens the door. "I'm Special Agent Madison and this is Special Agent Burroughs, with the Defense Department. We would like to talk to you about a person of interest our agency has, one that you've been in contact with."

"Really? Who would that be?"

"A Matthias Monroe. He's a tenant of the office building you attend to."

"I do not recall the name," Nigel says. "I only attend matters there after classes."

"You sure about that?" Burroughs presses. "He was seen leaving this building a few days ago."

Nigel blinks, feigning surprise. "This building? You must be mistaken, sir. I don't interact with the tenants for them to know where I stay after hours."

"Interesting," replies Madison, sensing coyness in the answers. "Can we come in? We prefer to not discuss this in a public hallway."

"If it's all the same, I am rather exhausted. Perhaps you can leave me your card, and I will contact you tomorrow."

Madison rests his hand on the 9mm Beretta holstered on his side, for Nigel to see. "We really would like to pick your brain on where the subject is."

Nigel's eyes flick to his sidearm, then to Madison and Burroughs, who peer at him like hawks eyeing prey. With reluctant compliance, he steps aside and lets them in.

Burroughs enters, draws his sidearm, and begins sweeping the flat. He opens the closet door with his weapon raised, then moves into the kitchen with a soldier's glare.

"Is that necessary?" Nigel quibbles as Madison steps in.

"We're just checking to see if the subject is here," says Madison. "Stay where you are, and everything should be fine."

"Clear," then says Burroughs. "No one is here but him."

"I've could've told you that," Nigel says. "You didn't need to storm in like paratroopers."

"Your major is computer engineering, correct?" Madison then asks Nigel. "Mr. Monroe has been linked to surveillance materials that violate U.S. regulations. Perhaps you would know anything about where he got them?"

"I told you I haven't any idea of who you're looking for. I do not know this Monroe person."

"What is all this?" Burroughs asks, pointing to the table with the laptop and its peripherals. "It looks like you're trying to run a satellite or something."

"Do not touch that. It's a school project."

"Like the paper-mâché volcano in the 3rd grade? I like those. Let me see."

"All right now," says Nigel as he angles to the front door, "I'm going to ask you two to leave. I'm sure your lack of professionalism has violated several laws of some sort, and if you value your careers, you would be hasty to leave and not come back without proper authorization."

"I blame television for this," Madison smirks to Burroughs, who walks over from the table towards them. "It has people think they know the Constitution. Even illegal immigrants."

"I am on a student visa," says Nigel, "I am not an illeg—"

Nigel is then struck in the head, reeling as he crashes into the nearest wall.

Before he can regain his bearings, another blow slams into his face, dropping him to the floor.

A final punch collides onto his temple, knocking him out cold.

Burroughs rises from Nigel and turns to Madison, wiping blood from the brass knuckles on his fists. "And I blame you for entertaining this bitch for too long."

As Nigel lies on the floor, his hands zip-tied behind him, he's not awakened from the impact of his concussion, but from the searing pain of a needle piercing into his neck.

"Don't mind me," says Madison as he pulls the needle from his jugular. "It's just a shot of Haloperidol. Don't need you being a chatterbox while we search the place a little more."

"This guy has been sending the suspect messages," Burroughs then says, as he sits at the desk, looking over the laptop. "And it looks like he's tracing a phone number."

"Are you doing recon for our suspect?" Madison asks Nigel, whose eyes drift in a drugged haze from the sedative. "Don't worry, kid. I'll let you sleep for now. But when you wake up, you will be talking to us. A lot."

CHAPTER 47

Interstate 95. Northbound.

As the car speeds towards New York, Matthias gets a call—from Unknown.

"You are the bane of my existence," gripes Andreus over the phone. "I was enjoying my lunch on the balcony, looking onto the Mediterranean Sea, when I get a call to save your ass. Again."

"Please leave your number and I will get to you—"

"Hey Dipshit," Andreus barks. "You want a clean-up team to come and make you a pincushion? Then you'll listen and stop with the jokes."

"What makes you think I need your help? I'm fine on my own."

"Not if you're threatening Pierrepont with exposure tactics."

"If they want me to stay quiet on Espinoza, then they will reactivate the lifelines and deposit the monies I want. Or they will have to answer to why one of their board members is a sex trafficker."

"Or," Andreus interjects, "You will pick me up so we can address this personally."

"What do you mean, pick you up?"

"I'm heading to the jet now. It should land in six hours."

"You're heading back to the States?"

"Yes, because for some godforsaken reason, I have a visceral connection to your well-being. So be at the airport!"

Teterboro, NJ

In the early morning, Matthias waits in his car beside the private tarmac, as private charters take off and land. *What is Andreus here to do?* he wonders, *unless this is another authenticator trick. Then again, Andreus wouldn't really co-sign any involvement in that. Would he?*

He watches a Bombardier jet descend onto a secluded strip, and after a few minutes, its stairs unfold. A team of attendants rushes from the hangar to greet the plane, stepping briefly inside before reemerging with its lone passenger.

Matthias erases the thought of betrayal when he sees the man helped down the steps—still athletic, his frame solid, but now supported by a cane and a pair of glasses. He starts the car and drives onto the runway, stopping about ten feet away from the plane.

"I've seen people hug after long absences," Matthias says, as he walks toward the man who named him.

"Try it and I'll knee you in the nuts," Andreus replies. "Grab the bags from the attendants."

"You can pull in here," Andreus says, directing Matthias to a spot across from a building in Manhattan, enclosed by barricades and lined with black sedans along the curb.

"What is this building?" Matthias asks as he parks.

"It's where the person who's going to help you is," Andreus replies, then gets out of the car.

Matthias follows him as they walk to the building, passing the sedans and barricades to a security booth at the entrance, where two officers stand guard.

"We're here to see Ms. Vishwakarma," Andreus says.

One of the officer's step into the security booth. After a few moments on the phone, he motions to them. "You can proceed. She's on the 37th Floor."

Andreus and Matthias enter the building, pass through the lobby, and take the elevator to their destination: a lofty space, with white floors and black walls. LEDs glow along the baseboards and moldings, while cove lighting cycles through colors across the ceiling panels. The furniture is voguish, as if no one is allowed to use it. And the space is empty, filled only with an ambient hum.

"Did someone watch a Stanley Kubrick film before they designed this place?" Matthias quips. "Who's here that is getting me off *Ex-Delicto*?"

"That perhaps would be I," a voice is then heard, and they turn to see a woman of Indian descent come from the back of the office towards them. She immediately grins when close to Andreus, widening her arms. "Hello, my friend. It's been years."

Andreus steps to her and they hug, as they proceed to speak to one another in Bengali.

Oh, so now he takes hugs, Matthias reckons with a sneer.

"You two can get a room later," he then says, his words breaking their embrace. "Who are you?"

"He's rather petulant, isn't he?" She says to Andreus, before addressing Matthias. "I'm Daksha Vishwakarma. President of Pierrepont Realty U.S., and board member of the Merchants. So that would make me one of those 'mopheads' you like to insult. And as far as your *Ex-Delicto*, let's see how the evening goes."

Dak turns and grabs Andreus by the hand, leading him down the office. "I believe I have an idea that would be sufficient to everyone. If things go as plan, perhaps we can make it to Sotheby's afterwards."

"Sotheby's?" Matthias asks as he follows behind them. "For what?"

"Antiquing," she says before again turning to Andreus. "I would love to show you the Asian Art exhibit they're previewing for auction."

"What's the point in doing that?" Matthias asks.

"For you, none. You're not invited. I doubt you appreciate art. You must think Monet is what goes on a sandwich."

Dak detours into her office—decorated in a more modern style—and heads to her desk as Andreus and

Matthias enter. She motions for them to have a seat as she presses a button on her desk phone.

"Ladies and gentlemen of the board," she says into the speaker. "We have an update on a previous issue. Matthias Monroe is in my office, as well as his surrogate, Johnathan Monroe, also known as Thomas Andreus."

Silence from the other end at first, then small grumbles come through the speakerphone.

"Andreus," a familiar voice says. "Apparently bones on the Riviera don't whither as we thought."

"Hello to you too, Raphael," says Andreus.

"And Matthias, I was surveilling your travels up until you reached D.C. I take it you exited the interstate in Fredericksburg, Virginia to avoid the congestion, no?"

Matthias twists his mouth in response. *Fucking douchebag.*

"Dak," someone else says from the call, "This is unorthodox what you are doing. You are going against the traditions—"

"Ayton, I have argued in the past how certain treatments given to the trainees can escalate insubordination."

"Our training," Raphael replies, "it is modeled as any top-tier force would. If the trainees or operatives lose their way, do not blame the method—blame them."

"You threw me in a forest to fight bears," Matthias growls. "Now I'm the one clawing back on you *schlampen*."

"Matthias," goes another familiar voice from the call—Mum. "Perhaps if you calm down—"

"Anything happens to me and Espinoza will be delivered to the police. I want my passports reactivated and a million dollars transferred to my accounts. *Leiden die Kinder.*"

Dak and Andrus turn to him, as there's silence from the other end of the conference call. Matthias picks up their tells from their body language. *They're not frozen from the demands—they're already familiar with them. No, they appear curious.*

"Did he say *leiden die Kinder*?" someone says from the call. "Did he activate his German axiom?"

"It was made clear to me," Raphael says, "the trainees cannot trigger their axioms. A hypnotherapist must be present."

"Ayton," Andreus says. "You're the neuroscientist. Explain how a trainee can trigger their axioms unsupervised. Such a breech can lead to exposure of plans during interrogation."

More silence from the call, before Ayton says, "Clearly, this one is too dumb for advanced neurolinguistics."

"Fuck you!" snaps Matthias.

Dak presses a button to mute the call. "Settle down, tiger. I'll handle this." She returns to the conference call. "What he meant to say, is that he suffered physical—and apparently from his outbursts—psychological anguish, and that dedication will not come from mistreatment."

"His actions are clearly his own," says Ayton defensively. "He threatens us with extortion. He violated the safe space of the *Maison de Gaine*. He went over budget on his project, which remains incomplete. He also was a derelict of duty with his stunt in New Jersey. And earlier, when I checked the databases, his name came up as a suspect in the murder of five people. That would be seven kills in less than a month."

Again, Dak and Andreus turn to Matthias.

"I was undercover," he simply says.

"Dak," Ayton says, "just shoot the prick and be done with this. He's been trouble since he was born."

"You will not lay a hair on him," says Mum emphatically. "Perhaps we should reconsider our methods instead of just throwing the trainees in *Ex-Delicto* when they misbehave."

"Misbehave, you say? Your affections for this reprobate will be the death of you, Delores."

"Is that a threat, Ayton? Because that Tuscan villa you have may know the business end of a bazooka."

"Friends," Dak says as she takes over the call, "we can deal with the surety of our neurolinguistic methods, and Matthias' tantrums, another time. Right now, we have a presumed defect of high standing within our organization. That is of greater importance. Furthermore, if Espinoza has employed our tracking prototypes, it will raise significant concerns with the WTO." Dak then twirls a pen in her hand as she sits in her chair. "Let's find a compromise— one that won't burn the whole house down."

"What do you suggest?" Raphael asks.

Dak lets out a mischievous smile, as she continues to twirl her pen.

CHAPTER 48

An hour later, Dak, Andreus, and Matthias step out of the elevator and toward the exits.

"You must see this exhibit," Dak says to Andreus, her arm interlocked with his. "I'm eager to view the new pieces they've acquired for the Dalai Lama collection."

"You're going to Sotheby's now?" Matthias asks as he trails behind them. "It's 3 a.m."

"We'll go in the afternoon," Dak says as she turns to him. "You're rather dense for an operative. Read the room."

"Whatever, boss," Matthias says snidely.

"Is he always this mercurial?" she asks as they stroll out of the building toward a waiting limousine, its chauffeur holding the door open.

"Mercurial," Andreus repeats contemplatively. "That is more sophisticated than just calling him an asshole all the time."

"I'm neither mercurial nor an asshole," Matthias says. "I'm just looking for the fine print. Because every authenticator contract I've seen is written in invisible ink."

Dak stops short of the limo and turns to Matthias. "You have the terms you requested, do you not? Except for the one million dollars—because that would've been ridiculous. Your *Ex-Delicto* has been lifted, the punishment for your analyst has been rescinded, and even the concierge at the *Maison de Gaine* has been rehired."

"If I asked for a monkey in a tutu, you'd have given me that too. You don't give this much unless you're planning on hosing me."

"For one, I don't know what 'hosing' means—I don't speak in colloquialisms. And two, given the sensitivity of the mission, your demands were easy to accommodate."

"What then, a red herring? You drive off and these security officers gun me down?"

"If you still have trust issues," Dak says, "you're free to leave. You can live however you see fit. However, none of the things you requested will come to pass. The concierge will be deported, your analyst may meet an unfortunate fate, and you'll have to evade the law for those pesky murders you committed. Or... you can stay and play with the mopheads."

Dak smiles as Matthias sneers at his limited choices.

"I'll take your silence as an agreement," Dak says before ushering Andreus inside the limo. She steps in after him, and the chauffeur closes the door before hurrying to the driver's seat.

"Where are you staying?" Matthias asks Andreus.

"He'll be at the Baccarat Hotel," she answers. "You can pick him up there to take him to the airport after our meeting."

"You came all the way here to look at statues of Buddha?"

"I came here to broker your safety," Andreus replies. "Now I'm going to enjoy the rest of my stay. See if you can manage not to kill or destroy anything before taking me to the airport."

"The night is still young," Matthias says with a smirk. "Who knows what the winds will blow in."

"The world would be safer if you blew yourself." With that, the limousine drives off.

Matthias watches the limo pull away. At least his ledger is clear—though it means abandoning the project. Far be it from him to leave a vendetta unfinished, but payback for Russo will have to be put on ice. For now.

He crosses the street to his car and checks the phone he left on the seat, eyeing several missed calls. *Who is this? The number's from D.C. And there's a video message.*

"Matthias Monroe," a man says in a shadowy background. "This is Special Agent Burroughs with the Defense Department. And I have a message from your friend, Nigel Laine."

A gunshot cracks through the phone—followed by a scream that rips through the speakers.

The camera shifts, revealing Nigel on the ground in agony, blood streaming from a wound in his lower leg. The camera pans back to Burroughs.

"Every hour you do not call back," he says, "I will shoot higher. The quicker, the better."

The message ends. Matthias stares at the screen for a second, his jaw clenched in dread and wrath. Then he redials.

"You just made it," says Burroughs on the other end. "I was about to end any chance of this guy having kids."

"Who the fuck are you?"

"Someone who's been looking for you for the past few weeks, and I'm getting exhausted following your stink. So unless you want your friend in a box, you will meet me at this address."

CHAPTER 49

Long Island City, NY

Matthias drives through a blighted neighborhood where partially constructed high-rises blanket the waterfront. He parks in front of a warehouse, following the abductor's directions, and stops before a door with a piece of paper taped to it.

'Come here, bitch,' is scrawled in what looks like blood.

He gets out of the car, wearing his Kevlar vest, a Glock 19 in hand, and the other holstered and ready. He sweeps the street with his weapon, aiming at any potential threats. Then he rushes to the warehouse, staying close to its walls in case someone takes a shot from above. Reaching the door, he swings it open, gun raised into the darkness.

Clear. He steps inside.

Slivers of light stream through the windows as Matthias moves forward, passing through a narrow corridor into a wide, open space filled with storage racks.

"Follow the blood," he hears over a loudspeaker. It's Burroughs.

Matthias scans for anyone lurking in the rafters, then spots a crimson trail splattered across the floor. His eyes follow it to the end of an aisle, where someone is slumped in a chair, drenched in bruises. The person's right leg is bandaged, the gauze dark and soaked with blood.

"Nigel," Matthias says as he strides toward him.

"No!" Nigel sputters, seeing him. "Don't come—"

BAANNGG!!

The shot slams into his back, knocking the air from his lungs as the impact hits like a wave of sledgehammers. Matthias staggers, his knees buckling, and collapses to the ground.

For a moment, he's still, waiting for impeding perdition. Yet he still has his senses, and his arms and legs work.

"Oh, come on," a voice calls out as footsteps approach. "You can't take a .223 round while wearing a vest? What kind of pussy are you?"

Matthias checks his back. No blood, no wound—just the plates in his vest absorbing the brunt.

He crawls to his feet, locking eyes with the man from the video call—now standing twenty feet away, holding both of Matthias' Glock 19s.

Matthias checks his side holster. Empty. *Fuck. He must've dropped them both when he hit the ground.*

"You won't need these," Burroughs says, tossing the guns to the far end of the warehouse. They clatter against the concrete. "Matthias Monroe, on behalf of the Defense Department, you're under arrest for...well, a litany of shit, honestly."

"You're the asshole that's been tailing me," he huffs, his lungs still struggling to catch up. "The guy who messed up Hodges and burned his store down."

"The one who sold you illegal weapons? I haven't the faintest idea what you're talking about. Now, I was supposed to bring you in, but my fuckhead boss called earlier. He said the NYPD has you down as a suspect for some murders. Told me to pack it up. All that legwork to find you, and the cops get to make the collar? Fuck that."

Burroughs then pulls out his pair of brass knuckles and slips them on. "So here's the deal. I'll let you and your whiny British bitch there walk out and give you a head start—but you have to get past me first."

"So what, you want to fight me?"

"No one leaves my crosshairs. One way or another, you're gonna bleed."

Matthias exhales sharply, regaining his breath. "You should be focused on yourself. You've committed about ten crimes so far. Kidnapping and torture, false imprisonment, attempted murder. If this gets out, you'll be looking at twenty years in prison."

"That's the beauty of working for the Feds. We get away with shit. Besides, who do you think people will believe? A federal agent in pursuit of a suspect, or some black fuck who should've been aborted by his mother?"

Matthias growls as the insult hangs in the air. He's no longer winded—once more he breathes iron, as his blood boils.

"Matthias," Nigel mutters, his voice heavy. "This is what he wants. So give him what he wants. Do your '*leiden de Kinder*' shit."

He turns to Burroughs. "You already shot me once. How do I know you won't pull out a gun when I'm whipping your ass?"

"No gun, boy." Burroughs shrugs off his jacket and spreads out his arms, revealing no gun holstered. "So you can take that vest off."

Matthias unstraps the Kevlar and tosses it aside, along with his empty holster. As he steps forward, he sizes up his opponent: Six-foot-one, 220 lbs. Left-handed. He's in a Muay Thai stance—weight balanced forward, fists high. And with those brass knuckles, he'll hit like a wrecking ball.

Matthias bounces on his feet, raising his scarred fists, and settles into a boxer's stance.

"Leiden die Kinder, denn ihnen gehört das Himmelreich," he mutters as he charges. "See the sheep, kill the sheep."

CHAPTER 50

For a moment, they hold—each within the other's striking range. Then, Burroughs telegraphs a left hook.

Matthias ducks and counters with an uppercut to Burroughs' chin.

He takes the punch like it's nothing and fires back a right-left cross combo.

Matthias weaves under the combo and throws a front kick, forcing distance between them.

Matthias surges. He launches a left cross—miss. He follows with a flurry of rapid-fire strikes. Burroughs weaves out of their range.

Burroughs feints with quick left jabs as he reapproaches, dips low, and whips a spinning kick to the head.

Matthias leans back, the kick slicing past his face—but the dodge leaves his torso exposed.

Burroughs lands, pivots, and drives a back kick into Matthias's chest.

Matthias flails back, gasping as the impact crushes his lungs—pain searing through his sternum.

Burroughs charges, throwing a left jab.

Matthias slips right, then parries a strike from Burroughs, aimed at his stomach.

He pivots—turning to his side—and drives an elbow into Burroughs' eye socket, who recoils.

Matthias seizes the moment. He unloads an uppercut-cross combo. As Burroughs is reeling, he slips around him, locks into a bearhug, and launches him backwards.

Burroughs is tossed into the air, crashing on the concrete.

He stays motionless for a moment—then springs up, shaking it off, and reapproaches.

He telegraphs another right to Matthias, this time to bait him—who responds with a left hook.

Burroughs slips the hook and counters with a left jab.

Matthias reels from the impact—before Burroughs follows with a snap kick to the face.

With him sputtering, Burroughs grabs the back of his head and yanks him into a brutal knee into his chin.

Matthias crumples to the ground, the world spinning as blood spurts from his mouth.

Burroughs advances, ready to finish him—when one of his legs is suddenly grappled, locked in place.

He looks down to see Nigel—who crawled from his chair—clutching onto his foot.

"Get the FUCK OFF ME!" Burroughs snaps before using his free leg to stomp onto Nigel's head.

Nigel goes limp, blood pouring from the back of his head like a crushed tomato.

Burroughs then looks out into the shadows of the warehouse. "You didn't see him behind me?" he yells. "Why didn't you shoot him?"

A voice answers through the loudspeaker. "This is thoroughly entertaining. I wish I'd brought popcorn. Uhm...you should pay attention to your guy."

Burroughs turns—just as Matthias barrels into him, tackling him with full force. They crash deeper into the warehouse, smashing into the storage racks.

They hit the ground brawling—Matthias hammering body shots while Burroughs fires with punches to his jaw.

Then Burroughs twists inside the grapple, catches Matthias's left arm, and maneuvers on top, locking in a Kimura arm bar.

Matthias's eyes widen as his shoulder is wrenched at a brutal angle. He grits out strained grunts of pain.

Burroughs snarls, wrenching the arm back until—

CRACK!!

Matthias screams, the sound echoing through the warehouse, as the humerus is broken from his shoulder.

He thrashes like a wild bronco, bucking Burroughs off with raw, instinctive violence.

Then he lies on the ground, frozen in agony, when he's savagely kicked in the head. He's out.

Burroughs collapses to his knees, not far from the sprawled Matthias, panting in post-fight exhilaration as his chest heaves like a broken machine.

"Lightwork fuck," Burroughs says, before turning toward the darkness. "Thanks for your help. You can kill these two now."

As Matthias lays wrecked, his mind fractures:

Wolves. Andreus. Mum. Project. Sudan. Florianópolis. Bangkok. Angelfish. Romania. Zurich. Amora. Domencia. Espinoza.

It. Is. Glorious. To. Die.

Then—his mind finds what it is searching for:

"SOUFFREZ LES ENFANTS!" Nigel yells to him. *"CAR LE ROYAUME DES CIEUX EST À EUX."* Again. *"SOUFFREZ LES ENFANTS, CAR LE ROYAUME DES CIEUX EST À EUX."*

Suffer the children, for theirs is the kingdom of Heaven.

Matthias' consciousness reignites from the French axiom, as old lessons emerge:

Pain is subjective. Get up.

You have all of eternity to be dead. Get up.

Strength comes not from physical, but from the indomitable will. Get up.

The world breaks so that it can submit to who gets up from the broken.

Out of suffering is born the strong. Get up.

Matthias stirs—prompted from his recall to fight.

Burroughs watches with disgust as Matthias crawls to his feet.

With swollen eyes, a busted nose, and one arm hanging useless at his side, Matthias says, "That's all you got?"

Burroughs snarls and steps forward.

K1 E2 V3 A4...D1 K2...E1 L3 D3 H4 A2 is then relayed to Matthias from muscle memory. Fighting code—hardwired from years in the dojo, to make him move without thought.

Burroughs throws a right hook.

Matthias slips the punch, stepping in—front kick to the chest.

Burroughs stumbles and throws a counter kick. Miss.

Matthias advances. Palm strike to the chest.

Burroughs throws a cross-uppercut—Matthias dodges, steps away.

Burroughs huffs with rage, and charges, throwing a jab-cross-front kick. Miss. Miss.

Instinctively, Matthias throws up his broken arm to block the kick—and immediately recoils from the blinding pain. His guard drops.

Burroughs sees the opening and throws a finishing blow aimed at his chest.

Matthias dips and pivots—feeling the icy wind of the punch—then slams a low kick into his knee. Burroughs buckles.

A kick to the chest; and a high kick to the nose. Burroughs' face pours blood.

K3 V6 L5 V4 K3 A1 T3 relays to Matthias.

He follows his training with a neck strike to the trachea. Burroughs clutches his throat, gasping to breathe.

A punch to the liver—a strike to the spleen—Burroughs falls to his knees.

Matthias yanks Burroughs by the hair and drives his knee into the back of his head—where the skull meets the spine.

Burroughs whimpers as the impact scrambles his brainstem. He collapses flat to the ground.

Matthias stomps, unrelenting, on his neck and skull, hearing the crackle of bones as he feels the specters and demons inside him dance.

Kill him kill him kill him kill him. Wolves kill sheep.

Moments pass—how many, in this state he wouldn't know—before he stops and pulls from Burroughs.

"Don't ever talk about my mother again," Matthias says, as his victim froths a mix of blood and bile from his mouth.

"No," he then hears from Nigel—on his feet and hobbling towards him. "You can't stop now. Someone else—"

"Impressive," they hear from the darkness of the warehouse, as a man surfaces, pointing an AR-15 assault rifle at them—the one Hodges had procured for Matthias. "A little Muy Thai. A little Jujitsu and Krav Maga. And just straight brutality. I might have a boner." He walks towards them.

"So, what are you?" Matthias pants. "Round Three?"

"Kid," replies Madison, "with me there's never a Round Two." He then aims the assault rifle.

BAANNGG!! BAANNGG!!

Burroughs' body jerks from the blasts. His blood pools fast beneath him, coating the concrete.

Matthias and Nigel look at the lifeless Burroughs. They then turn to Madison.

"I think you would agree the guy was a complete asshole," he replies. "You're fortunate my boss is clearing the books, otherwise those shots would be for you." Madison then loops the machine gun over his shoulder. "Now I'm going to take a shit. If you're here when I come back, I'll clean up three bodies instead of one."

Madison takes several steps toward the darkness, when he stops and turns back to Matthias. "Oh, and my boss told me to relay a message to your father. One: Monaco is overrated. And two: He still is a piece of shit." Madison blends into the darkness.

The two are silent within the aftermath, before Nigel says, 'Let's get out of here."

"How did you know about the axiom?" Matthias asks.

"I read your dossier," Nigel says. "The languages you speak are listed in a particular order. After English and German, it's French, Spanish, and Russian. So I gathered your axiom is for each one of them. Just the deductive reasoning of a voyeur."

"Turns out analysts are good for more than spying in windows," says Matthias as he and Nigel limp out of the warehouse.

CHAPTER 51

The company has been acquired by the Department of Homeland Security.

All roles and duties of board members and personnel are terminated effective immediately.

All computers will be remotely locked, and all credentials and clearances will be revoked.

All active caseloads, contracts, and archives are now the property of DHS.

If you wish to continue your roles in whatever capacity is available, contact Aaron Chambers, Deputy Secretary of DHS.

In the meantime, severance packages of $1,000,000 per year of service will be allotted to all soldiers in the upcoming weeks. Trainees and clerical will receive $100,000. Board members will be allotted $500,000 per share.

Unless I never liked you. Then you get nothing.

Sincerely,

Robert Bridges.

Bridges is at his desk, when his phone rings. He rolls his eyes, hoping it's not another board member whining about their cut of the buyout. He glances at the caller ID, then answers.

"What's the status?" Bridges asks, hearing the hum of a vehicle in motion on the other end.

"The warehouse has been cleaned," Madison replies. "The garbage has been taken out. Only one bag."

"Well, aren't you benevolent. Letting the commoners see the light of day."

"The kid did well enough for Caesar to give him a thumbs up."

"Where are you now?"

"Heading home. I'll dump the garbage at a place I know for disposal." Madison then pauses before continuing. "If you knew where the kid's father was staying in Monaco, why didn't you have him eliminated?"

"Far-fetched for anyone to believe," he replies, "there are lines I don't cross. I don't kill soldiers indiscriminately. As long as he strolled along the beach and ate *linguine all'astice blu* in those fancy restaurants and kept out of my business—why do I care? Anyway, I'm finalizing the severance packages. I'll wire your payment soon. Stay on call in case I need you."

"Yes, sir," Madison says before he hangs up.

Bridges turns back to his computer, finishing sending out the mass email, when there's a knock on the door.

"Sir," says Clarke as she walks in, "Your car to the Pentagon has arrived."

Bridges stands, grabs an envelope on his desk, and walks over to Clarke. He hands her the envelope.

"What is this?" Clarke asks.

"A check for $100,000," he says. "Not bad for a few weeks' work. And you're fired."

"Mr. Bridges," she stammers. "Why? I haven't done anything—"

"I called the FBI Director and asked—well, more like insisted—him to reassign you back to Quantico. You'll be on probation with a conduct review, but as long as you don't have any more road rages, you should be fine."

Clarke's eyes widened in disbelief. "Mr. Bridges...I don't know how to—"

"You don't work for me anymore, so there's no need to be cordial. Have I told you the story about Robert and his Magic Beans?"

"Here's the corporate filings and dissolution papers," says Bridges to Chambers, as he hands him an SSD drive. "Also are the papers for the private shares being transferred, as well as all assets and intellectual properties, with all confidentiality papers signed by me and the board. I'll assume this will be kept in the dark to prevent an inquiry."

"It'll be treated as an under-the-hood purchase," says Chambers, taking the hard drive. "No need to be bothered with antitrust laws. Although I'm not happy babysitting your scraps to see what can be integrated into the agency."

"You should've gone into the private sector like me," says Bridges. "It pays better and lets you smoke cigars in the office. And speaking of payments, where's my check?"

Chambers goes inside his pocket, pulling out an envelope, handing it to Bridges.

Bridges pulls out a check from the envelope. He looks at it, then at Chambers. "What is this?"

"Your payment for the sale of your company."

"This isn't what was agreed."

"Even as part of the black budget, it would be hard to justify the acquisition to the President. To keep this from stirring, the amount would have to be low."

"How am I supposed to live off this?"

"You're kidding? It's 4.3 billion dollars."

"It was initially ten and then dropped to six. Where's Bellinger? Let me talk to him."

"He's in a Cabinet meeting," Chambers says. "But he did relay me to tell you that this is the final offer. Otherwise, it's no deal." Chambers then pulls out a computer tablet. "Sign here to officiate the acquisition. And I'm supposed to take your credentials."

Bridges sneers. *He's been a paramilitary powerhouse for decades, and this is how they treat him? But then, it's best to let the behemoth win at times. Still, only 4.3 billion dollars. What a gyp.*

"I'm nothing if not amenable," he then says, as he pockets the check, scribbles his signature on the tablet screen, and hands over his contractor's ID to Chambers. "You're up for lunch? Maybe the diner has something prissy for you to order."

"Can't," says Chambers. "I have to dispense a corporate forensics team to dismantle your company. And I was directed by Bellinger to do a scrub. Some company in the UK that is associates with one of the President's financial donors, contacted him to erase an arrest warrant and evidence of an incident in New York."

"Of what?"

"Of some guy who killed five gang members in some ambassador's apartment."

Bridges squints with recall. "By any chance his name is Matthias Monroe?"

Chambers stares at him. "How did you know that?"

Bridges laughs from the irony as Chambers looks at him incredulously.

"Aaron," he then says, stifling some of his chucking, "I know everything."

CHAPTER 52

"Have you settled in?" Matthias asks into the phone as he crosses the street toward the building, its barricades and black sedans less threatening in the daytime. He ignores the glances of pedestrians who pass by, sure they're wondering why his left arm is wrapped in a sling and his nose bandaged with a splint.

"It's a city I can barely communicate in," says Andreus on the other end. "It'll take me weeks to refamiliarize myself with Japanese. Plus, where I'm staying the kids in the suite next to mine blast that J-Pop music all day."

"You're staying in a five-star hotel," says Matthias. "Considering I was in the hospital for a week, you'd understand if I didn't bring out the sad clown for your problems."

"This is that bastard Bridges' fault," Andreus fumes. "I have no idea how he found out I stayed in Monaco."

"Maybe staying in the French Riviera wasn't the most inconspicuous thing to do. That's okay. People your age tend to slip up. Perhaps there's an attractive nurse in Osaka with boner pills for you."

Silence, before Andreus replies. "I could've given you to Hindu monks as a baby, y'know."

"Too late now. Adopt another kid and teach them the *moksha*. I'm approaching the building now."

"Call me when you finish."

"Don't you look like roadkill," Dak says as she sits behind her desk within her office. "I hope you didn't affront building security when you walked in resembling a cadaver."

"No one saw me come in," says Matthias. "Like you directed I took the freight elevator to the 27th floor, then walked up the remaining ten flights to your office. Not ideal treatment for an injured person, by the way."

"A small price for missing your initial appointment. I once made an operative walk the entire flight up the stairs, then made him retrieve my pen when I threw it out the window." Dak then opens one of her desk drawers and pulls out a folder. She hands it to Matthias. "Here is your mission with the commencement letter on top."

Matthias opens the folder and reads the top sheet. A $500,000 reward with a $125,000 budget. Mission: Removal. Target: WTO ambassador Sergio Espinoza.

"He's an ambassador?"

"So you see why this is a rather delicate situation."

"You want me to kill an ambassador?"

"We want him removed," replies Dak. "How that is accomplished is up to you." She reaches again into her desk and hands him a small duffle bag. "Here are your new passports and identification, and $125,000 in cash to prep."

Mathias looks through the bag, thumbing through the unmarked funds. He then pulls out an unmarked box. "What is this?"

"A gift from your mother. She made sure it was shipped here so you received it when you arrived."

He opens the box to show a black Audemars Piguet watch. Along with a card:

Perhaps in time we will be on better terms to talk again. Love, Mum.

He turns to Dak with a brusque tone. "Does this have a tracker in it too?"

"You complain a lot," Dak says. "Are you having a hormonal moment? Do you need some chamomile tea?"

Matthias decides not to respond, instead placing the box back in the duffle bag. Between riding with a broken nose, a separate shoulder, and multiple contusions with no painkillers, perhaps he's more testy than usual. He pulls out the passport to look over. "Matthew Vincent? Who's that?"

"That is your code name. Matthew for the apostle, and Vincent was a saint during the 16th century."

"That sounds like the guy bartending on a cruise ship. You don't have anything cooler than that?"

My apologies, but Secret Agent Mercurial Ass wasn't available." Dak then reaches out her hand. "Give me the folder."

Matthias does so and Dak places it on her desk. She flips through a few pages before she grabs a pen to scribble her signature.

"What are you doing?"

"I'm filling in the name of your analyst," she says. "Me."

"Say what now?"

"Running a corporate office was never to my taste," Dak says as she looks to Matthias. "A few years ago, a proposition was made between me and the other members. I would assist in getting the U.S. realty office established, and in turn I would go into semi-retirement, providing logistics from my beach house. And since this mission requires sensitive care, an experienced analyst will be needed. So guess who my first operative will be?"

Dak then walks to a small window within the office, opens it, and flicks the pen out into the high-rise air.

"Now retrieve the pen and come back to sign the letter," she says. "Hubris, hubris, Matthias with his hubris."

◇◇◇

"I'm still not clear on why you signed it," Nigel says as he walks on crutches gingerly, as he and Matthias enter his dorm building. "You were practically out of dealing with them altogether."

"Well, what can I tell you? They offer medical and have a good pension plan. In twenty years, I can retire in a camper."

"Did you arrange for me to get out of Pierrepont's sight? I do not want to be the reason you have to deal with their commands. I can find some other way to avoid their tentacles."

"Don't you worry about that. You have clear passage to focus on your rehab and finishing grad school so you can get your degree, in between peeping in people's windows."

"I am not a peeping..." Nigel starts when he enters the flat, stepping in to several potted plants throughout the floor.

"What are these?" Nigel asks.

"Ferns. Boston ferns. Asparagus ferns. And the ones with the colorful leaves are air plants. I figure your place could use a little sprucing up."

Nigel turns to him. "This is a wonderful gesture, Matthias."

"If you cry, I will stomp you on the foot." Matthias checks the time from the AP watch on his wrist. "Get settled in. I have to put the office back in order and deal with Ms. Dereschuk's stories about Russian soldiers making love while forcing the Germans from Leningrad. Then I'm heading out of town."

"Where are you going?"

"To finish what I started."

EPILOUGE

Six months later.

Ceará, Brazil.

A Jeep barrels down the countryside before swerving into the driveway of a beachfront estate. It charges another quarter mile into the property, roaring past plots of half-built homes before screeching to a stop outside a newly purchased house.

A man drunkenly stumbles out of the Jeep. As he wobbles forward, he takes a glance back at the car, knowing the estate's HOA will fine him for not parking in the garage. *Screw it. He's going to celebrate his win with shameless brothel-hopping and fuck it if they have a nutty about how he does it.*

Frank Russo steps inside his house and spots the blinking amber light from the alarm panel. The brownouts in the village must be screwing with the security system again. He resets it, then continues, into the kitchen, where he plops down at the table, in front of a letter mailed to him.

Good for you, bitch, as Russo rereads the divorce decree with post-marital glee. She only gets half the proceeds from the house sale in Rye, and none of his pension. And she thought she had him over a barrel—threatening to expose him for shaking down female immigrants. Fortunately, after a little pressure from the shadow squads he commanded at the NYPD, she was convinced otherwise. Besides, he was going to enjoy retirement no matter what, in a place where sexual assaults are hardly reported.

Russo perks up slightly, sensing a presence in the air. He thinks he hears footsteps behind him, before—

"AARRGH!" he screams, convulsing as electricity rips through his body. It hits again, slamming him to the kitchen floor. Another jolt rips through his side, then another strikes his head—everything goes black.

Russo finds himself in his backyard, sprawled out on the grass. With blurred vision and a lingering drunken haze, he sits up and puts his hand on top of his head. *He was just in*

the kitchen. How did he get out here? And where is that smoke coming from?

He then sees what's in front of him, as smoke rolls out the windows of the house and fire starts to spread through the interior.

"What the fuck?" Russo slurs, as his home burns.

"That's for Olufemi Noah," he hears nearby.

Russo turns to his side to see someone standing over him, holding a cattle prod and a gun.

"What?" Russo stammers. "Who? Who are you?"

"Someone who should kill you." Matthias kneels, pointing the gun to Russo's head. "You ruined a lot of people's lives to get your rocks off."

"I don't know what you're talking about," says Russo, scooting to get some distance from Matthias.

"Sucks being you then. But instead of taking you out, I'll treat you the way you treated your victims. Every now and then, I'm going to find you, and torture you. Like this."

POW!

Russo screams as blood gushes from his right side.

"Oh, stop your screaming," Matthias says. "I shot you in the hip. You'll live."

Russo grits his teeth and turns to Matthias with rage and pain. "Fucking asshole. You know who I am? You're fucking with—"

"Blah blah blah. We'll have time to chat—whenever I decide to come back and put my foot in your ass. *Leiden die Kinder.*"

Matthias walks off into the dark, leaving Russo writhing as the house becomes engulfed in flames.

ABOUT THE AUTHOR

Shawn Hicks is the C.E.O and President of Brok'n English Publications, with the goal of providing a medium for telling his literary works. He received an Associates Degree in Video Arts from the Borough of Manhattan Community College, and his Bachelor's Degree in Television & Radio from Brooklyn College. He currently lives in Brooklyn, New York.

His next novel, *Matthias: Interim* is forthcoming.